THE DUNGEONS OF LIDIR

'Over here, my little bird,' said the turnkey, 'we must fit you with your collar.'

'No . . .' cried Anya.

The turnkey suddenly stopped, a look of complete surprise on his face, as though Anya were actually a bird and now the bird had spoken. He held his finger up like a stick with which he would hit her if she annoyed him any further. 'My dear, perhaps I should have made things clearer. In the dungeons we do not permit *that word* from slaves in answer to a request . . .'

The Chronicles of Lidir

THE DUNGEONS OF LIDIR

A Saga of Erotic Domination

Aran Ashe

A Nexus Book
Published in 1991
by the Paperback Division of
WH Allen & Co Plc
26 Grand Union Centre
Ladbroke Grove, London W10 5AH

Typeset by Phoenix Photosetting, Chatham, Kent

ISBN 978-0-3523-4627-8

Slaves
  – of Love

The Random House Group Limited supports The Forest Stewardship
Council (FSC®), the leading international forest certification organisation.
Our books carrying the FSC label are printed on FSC® certified paper.
FSC is the only forest certification scheme endorsed by the leading
environmental organisations, including Greenpeace. Our
paper procurement policy can be found at
www.randomhouse.co.uk/environment

Printed and bound in Great Britain by Clays Ltd, St Ives PLC

[1]

Cat's Claw

On a night in spring, high up in the east wing of the Castle
of Lidir, a small, marauding black cat – the kitchen cat –
changed the course of Lidir's history. And, more significantly for the cat, perhaps, it gambled with its lives – all nine
of them, if folklore is to be believed – by padding softly and
inquisitively around a door that was so uncharacteristically
left ajar. For, on that night, a light burned in the bedroom of
those apartments.

The Taskmistress of Lidir was not herself, the Taskmistress was troubled. And though, to the cat, the night seemed
warm and perfumed with the fresh sweet scent of cherry
blossom on the air, to Ildren it was winter.

A long cold lonely loveless desolation struck deep into her
heart. Beneath her calm, detached exterior, her soft warm
heart was broken, and beneath the seething heap of furs
which, night by night, Ildren, had amassed upon her bed to
shield her from the seeping sadness, she would cry herself to
sleep. The Taskmistress of Lidir would cry just like a baby,
and with her fists and feet would pound her hapless mattress
into spent submission. For her lover had been wrenched
away and seduced by another's arms – even though those
other arms could never love that slave, nor understand her
needs, in quite the way that Ildren could. But the thought of
her lover in the Prince's bed each night, while Ildren lay
alone (or at any rate, bereft of that special slave against her
breast or tied to Ildren's bedframe) – the pain of it was
torture. And now the talk, everywhere – in the Bondslaves'
House and the kitchens – was of a royal wedding; that very
day, the Taskmistress had chanced to overhear it mooted
even in the Council of Lidir. These rumours hung like a

1

double-edged axe of execution over Ildren's head, just waiting there to chop her poor unwanted body into little pieces. For with that wedding, should it come to pass, not only would Ildren lose the Prince's ear, but Lidir would gain a Princess, and with the Princess of Lidir by statute designated Mistress of the Slaves, where would that leave Ildren?

That night Ildren had much time to dwell upon her situation, as sleep stood back from her to mock her in her torment, and she tossed and turned and wrestled with her furs and tried in vain to conjure up a formula to exorcise those haunting spectres from her mind.

At last, when cruel and fretful sleep had finally claimed her worn out body, and Ildren's furs, having lost the fight, were scattered all about her – on the bed or, half escaping, dangling limply down the side, or stretched out dead upon the floor – those ghostly fears drew sustenance from her poor defenceless dreaming state and terrorised that innocent creature, her childlike, sweet and inner self, across the landscape of her dreams, as she was held imprisoned by exhaustion in a thrall of hateful terror.

Yet against this backdrop of imperilment, and cautious though a cat purports to be, it seemed this particular small black pussy-cat either could not sense or possibly chose to ignore the tension in the air, the tight-coiled spring of viciousness and self-protection, the jack-in-the-box so loosely hasped, the pressurised, slowly bubbling Ildren-in-a-bottle, just waiting to explode and turn that careless cat into just another swatch of fur on Ildren's all-devouring bed.

The cat hesitated as he stepped across the threshold of the Taskmistress's sitting-room; he had indeed sensed something other than the lone bearskin left on the floor. He stretched his neck and closed his eyes and slowly sniffed the air, and as he did so, turned his head from side to side. It seemed there was some lingering fragrance there, perhaps a hint of something even more appealing than cherry blossom – to a cat, at least. Very softly, very carefully now, the cat advanced, then hesitated beneath a plush-piled couch to sniff once more, then smoothly slid across towards an unusual item of sitting-room furniture over by the window, a trestle with a padded horizontal beam. The scent came stronger now and wafted downwards from the beam above. The cat curled his slinky body round a trestle leg, rather in the manner of the fox fur which, at that very moment on Ildren's bed, lay curled round Ildren's ankle (although in Ildren's current dream, the fox fur had been transformed into a rope about her leg tethering her to an iron ring set in the wall. Ildren's dream had clearly taken a quite different turn, in which her fear was about to be laced with pleasure).

Back in the real world, the cat, in homing in upon that deliciously scented source, sat back at first, then stretched upwards along the angled wooden leg, then opened his mouth in a soft miaow, then sprang and landed squarely on the end of the padded beam to breathe at last the sweet intoxication of concentrated, human female musk infused into the padding.

That pussy-cat purred; he rubbed his fur along the beam and rolled onto his back; he drank the taste; he tried to clothe himself in those delectable distillations of female slavish heat. And Ildren, had she been awake to witness it, might well have empathised with those sentiments of feline joy and understood those urges fully. However, at that moment she was asleep and in a different world entirely – in the dungeons, being fastened by her lover to the wall. So when that sleek black cat – in his own sweet drunken state – snaked and rolled that little bit too far, forgetting he was several feet up in the air, and plummeted down to thump upon the floorboards, Ildren's body jerked, for her sub-conscious state took the very real thwack of cat on floor to be instead the imagined thrash of the strap against her back, and the plaintive feline cry to be the echo of her very own gasp of pleasure at that treatment.

Bouncing off the floor, the cat, pursued by ghosts of his own making, scuttled sideways into Ildren's bedroom where he flattened himself to the ground while he tried to take in his surroundings, which seemed to be dominated by a bed in which a mass of furry creatures nested.

3

The Taskmistress turned onto her back, then stretched her arms and smiled, for her dream had turned quite fully now to pleasure. And if the cat, instead of being stuck down to the floorboards, could somehow have defied gravity and floated up towards the ceiling (and the Taskmistress would, in due course, demonstrate that it could), then what might it have seen? Not a cringing, unattractive frightened creature, but a woman of great beauty, with high cheekbones, soft warm luscious lips, brown-black hair outspread upon the pillow and full firm breasts with unusually long and firmly pointed nipples; a woman whose hands reached back to grip the bedframe and keep that perfect body, the smoothly rounded belly and the tense slim thighs in motion. Slowly, rhythmically, Ildren's body moved as Ildren's dream progressed – to a dream in which her body could not move at all. The delicious vision unfolded now, before her tightly shut eyes, which in her dream were stinging from the sweat trickling off her forehead.

The woman she loved stood at her feet. Ildren lay stretched out on the rack, her hands tied back above her head, her body drawn out tautly. She could hear the crackle of the fire. The air was hot and musky. Soft sensual moans and subdued murmurs whispered all around her, echoes of nearby pleasures and denials. Ildren could not move her head enough to know precisely where they came from; she could only look straight ahead. The woman had long and flowing deep red hair and olive coloured eyes which calmly gazed at Ildren, whose own eyes were softly pleading now. The woman wore a long red velvet robe – Ildren's robe. But Ildren wore the golden chains of slavery about her waist and wrist and ankle. The women's roles had been reversed. In this deliciously twisted dream, the Taskmistress was the victim; she would know the double pleasure, for she would understand her lover's motives very fully even as she herself was forced to suffer, in submission, that cruel, prolonged and passionlessly administered torment of delight. Ildren shivered, even though her body burned. Her knotted muscles cramped and ached. She had lain there several hours. The air weighed hot and damp and heavily upon her, and now her skin was covered in a continuous film of sweat, as if it had been painted with

4

a thin oil, slicking down every skin hair and sealing her body in liquid heat. Rivulets of sweat ran warmly in between her breasts and curled round down the sides. Heavy droplets tickled down the joins at the tops of her thighs. A pool of concentrated salt sweat gathered in the hollow of her neck. Her hair was soaking in a thick and sticky heat. Her lips felt cracked; the sweat seeped from above her upper lip to burn into those cracks.

Looking at Ildren, her lover untied her robe and lifted her head up as she slowly parted the velvet across the soft white freckled breasts and the black and hardened buttons which Ildren yearned to touch and suck upon to make them harder yet. Ildren yearned to have her lover lean across and stroke her burning body with those stiffened fleshy tips and press them, point to point against her own. For Ildren had been denied that pleasure far too long. She wanted her lover just to kiss her even once and then she could do with Ildren's body as she wished.

Her lover had untied her feet; Ildren's heart was thumping.

'Keep your legs together,' her lover warned. Ildren was ecstatic.

The lover separated Ildren's toes, one by one, and with the tip of her little finger, tickled in between them.

'Look at me,' the lover commanded. 'Do not close your eyes.' The fingertip tickled that very tender skin, making Ildren almost want to pull her foot away. 'And do not move, unless I tell you. Now, press your thighs together. Squeeze very hard between your legs; keep looking at me.' The tickling still continued, moving over to the other foot, and working lightly on the stretched skin between the big toe and the next. 'Now, roll your hips. Do not stop. Keep rolling them – and squeezing – you shall make your fleshpot drip.' The tickling stopped. Ildren then relaxed. 'No! You shall squeeze until I instruct you to desist. Is that quite clear?' The woman took the tender flesh that she had only just been tickling and pinched it very hard.

'Yes, ma'am.' Ildren's belly quavered in her pain, and in the pleasure of her submission. Her lover seemed a mirror of Ildren's strictest, most unsparing self at her pinnacle of rugged domination.

'Good.' Her lover's slender fingers reached between Ildren's thighs and, searching out the deeply bedded lips of flesh within the bush of hair, she pinched them, then set her teeth and flattened them quite cruelly, not releasing till Ildren had cried out with the

pleasure of that pain. 'I told you, keep your thighs together tight; you shall squeeze that pot of lust until it is numb.' Ildren was quite numb enough already; her lips had gone quite dead, and yet her heart was beating in her throat for she found this kind of pleasure really so exciting.

Her lover stood beside her now. 'Turn your head and look at me.' Her lover had such strength of purpose. 'Tell me what I should do with you,' she said quite coldly.

'Please . . . kiss me, ma'am,' Ildren replied for this was what she needed most of all.

Her lover gave a short, sharp laugh. 'Put your head back. Open your mouth.' Ildren closed her eyes in sweet anticipation. Her lover's hands pressed into her, over Ildren's breasts, pushing downwards to the teats. Suddenly, the pressure was released. The breasts sprang back and, as they did, her lover slapped them very firmly. Three fingers slapped each nipple hard. Ildren found the slapping made her belly tighten. The procedure was repeated twice; Ildren felt the concentrated pressure, then the sweet rebound, followed very quickly by the stinging slap against that very sensitive, soft yet rapidly firming skin around her teats. 'Do not jerk, and do not close your mouth. Now keep very still.' This time, her lover squeezed her breasts as if to burst them, then smacked them that much harder.

Two fingers dipped into the welling pool of sweat at Ildren's neck and then the fiery liquid was smeared around her lips. The fingers, together with a thumb, were pushed into her mouth. They tasted sour and salted as they fastened round her tongue. Ildren felt she was gagging. Her lover licked the fingers of her other hand and traced the line of Ildren's eyebrows, then gathered Ildren's soaking hair and twisted it until her head was held rigidly between the twisted knot of hair and the fingers gripping round her tongue, and then her lover kissed her. Yet Ildren could not respond; she could not even move; her lover held her locked in that very cruel embrace while she bent and planted a single, soft and somehow very loving kiss, not on Ildren's lips, for they were otherwise occupied, closed round and sucking gently on the hand within her mouth, but on Ildren's burning forehead. Her belly melted at the sweetness of that kiss; her lover smiled as Ildren thanked her with her eyes. Then that smile faded very quickly, as if the kiss had meant nothing to the lover, as if it had been an accident or trick.

'Spread your thighs,' her lover murmured. 'I want to see you spread for me, in your submission.' Tiny tremors rippled through her lover's breasts as Ildren opened out her thighs, precipitating tiny reciprocal pleasure ripples deep in Ildren's belly. 'Bend your knees, my darling; lift those hips. I want that soft sweet pussy lifted up for me. Lift it off the table.' And Ildren quaked in delectation as she tensed her arms and raised her shaking hips and spread her thighs so very wide to offer up that moist and tender fleshpot, that slowly liquifying pussy which was burning for her lover to take it and do with it what she would . . .

And by coincidence, on a different plane entirely – a lower plane, below the bed – another pussy stirred, a blacker and more furry pussy who had sensed a movement up above him. The bed vibrated very slightly with the gentle undulations of Ildren's shaking hips; the doeskin, otter, the white fox and the sable – all the dangling, long-dead furry creatures spread about the bed were miraculously brought to life. The cat balanced, poised to strike, his eyes darting back and forth across that multitude of prey, the seething mass of furtive, nervous, stimulating twitchings. Then, in that moment of feline indecision, the disobliging creatures suddenly died again.

'Be still,' the dream lover commanded softly, as if she somehow understood the danger lurking near. 'Your body shall not stir one inch unless by my express instruction. Your pleasure must be withheld until I have taken mine, and my pleasure is to touch and tantalize you, to touch you till you pass out with pleasure, and then to waken you and pleasure you again. Would you like that, my beautiful one?' Ildren could not answer; her belly churned with love and deep desire. 'Good. Now I shall tie you with your ankles wide apart.'

Ildren was balanced with her knees above her head, her thighs spread wide and her ankles secured by leather ropes to the headframe of the rack; her hips were lifted and her weight was taken by her upper back and shoulders. Her body felt tight; she was gripped in the tightness of anticipation and uncertainty; she was aware of every muscle; her arms ached; the sweat was trickling down her body under the pressure of the humid heat. Her lover looked so cool and calm; her lover's cool slim fingers were touching Ildren's belly, feeling the drum-tight sweat-oiled skin stretched across those tense-drawn muscles, tracing every curve, dipping coolly into Ildren's burning navel, making her close her eyes.

A hand now closed around Ildren's left breast, pressing its substance down against her chest, yet leaving the nipple free for the fingers of the other hand to close around and pull it, gripping firmly at the base and stretching, drawing it out to quill-tip stiffness, while the first hand pressed harder and the stretching continued until the pleasure of the pulling turned to pain – first a prickling, then a sharp and cutting pain as the skin stretched to its limit and finally, even though she did not want that pulling pain to stop, Ildren cried out, for she could not help it . . .

Back on the floor, the cat crouched down and edged away; that cry had temporarily unnerved him. Was it bird or beast? And was the cry *attack*, or was it merely anguish?

'Ssh . . . my dear. You shall submit yourself to this pleasure without complaint. Your nipples are beautiful. They must be drawn out very fully from your breasts; they must stand up very stiffly, must they not?' Her lover had turned her attention to the right breast. Ildren closed her eyes again. 'Tell me why your nipples must be kept very long and pointed.'

'Because you so require them, ma'am.'

'Mmm . . .' And this time, Ildren felt her lover's fingernails digging into the base of her nipple before she pressed the breast and pulled, and pressed and pulled again until Ildren felt her flesh would snap.

'. . . There.' Her lover wet her fingers and worked those long hot tubular fluid filled nipples simultaneously; like small wet mouths, they sucked at them while her lover worked her warm wet tongue slowly and seductively in and out of Ildren's mouth, which wanted so to close about that tongue and suck it. Ildren was delirious at this treatment; she wanted her lover to touch her tongue against her, there between the legs, to taste her liquid flesh and slip that warm wet tongue into her body.

'I wish to touch you now – that special part of you, the part I like

8

*the best. May I do this to you – touch that loving part?' Ildren's
pulse pounded in her ears . . .*

The cat advanced again – very warily this time, keeping
very low. He circled round the bed, just waiting for those
furs to make another move. A powerful scent of musky
catnip billowed down around him.

*. . . Now, you must keep very still while I touch you,' her lover
said. Once again, she appeared to have sensed those feline vibrations from the corporeal plane.*

*Her lover, now behind Ildren's head, and looking down upon
her doubled-up body, reached over and touched her with a single
finger. It moved across the back of Ildren's right knee, stroking very
lightly in the hollow. And whilst the finger moved from side to
side, her lover watched Ildren – watching for the signal, the
movement of her lips and the arching back of Ildren's head, which
signified her lover had found that resonance which would very soon
travel down Ildren's tight-stretched inner thigh, across the surface
of the skin, across the crease and whisper so deliciously up into her
body, as if that fingertip were tickling, not the back of Ildren's
knee, but up against the inner wall of Ildren's willing sex. Her
lover knew just how to take her breath away. The finger was
moving downwards now, along that sensitized path, like a rabbit's
tail softly sweeping pleasure before it; a tumbling heap of pleasure-
tickles travelled downwards and spilled at last across the taut bridge
of flesh between Ildren's thighs, showering downy wisps of pure
delight on Ildren's gently throbbing sex and Ildren's very ticklish
bottom mouth. The pad of the finger pressed firmly into that bridge,
sending waves of pleasure down inside.*

*'Your body shall drip for me,' her lover murmured softly, as she
moved the pressing finger very slowly in a circle, so the bridge of
flesh moved with it. The finger felt as if it were circling round inside
her, searching for that deeper resonance, seeking out her lust,
making Ildren want to move against it. 'There, is that very nice?'
Her lover had closed her hand round Ildren's swollen sex.
'Mmm . . . You feel so hot. This part of you is so inviting.' The
hand squeezed gently, then relaxed. The squeeze had sent a pulse
of pleasure deep inside; it almost felt as if that hand had reached up*

*into her and squeezed around her heart. The squeezing continued
very slowly, rhythmically, until Ildren could not contain herself
and gasped out loud . . .*

That gasp was like another hand – an invisible hand which
dropped upon the cat's head and flattened it to the floor, but
left its tail stuck straight up in the air and its body bristling
fiercely.

*. . . Now Ildren's pulsing sex was released. Her lover teased apart
the burning lips of flesh and Ildren's upturned fleshpot dripped.
Her lover massaged the oily nectar into Ildren's belly. Suddenly,
her lover was gone. Ildren was left opened out, unable to move.*

*'Open your mouth very wide.' Ildren's eyes opened even wider,
for her lover held a chain of gold, and attached to it was a
pear-shaped golden weight. 'Wet it with your spittle.' Ildren tried
to wet it with her tongue, but her mouth was parched with fear, and
pleasure at having this particular degradation forced upon her.*

*Her lover suspended the pear above her sex, then lowered until
Ildren felt the cold weight of metal against her. 'Open, my sweet,
spread your flesh to take this golden fruit. Your body shall absorb it
very fully, and then I propose to pleasure you. Your flesh shall grip
it while I make you come.' Ildren's heartbeat surged at this promise
of deliverance to delight, by which she would be taken in so debased
a manner, with the pear embedded in her body, fastened to the
chain. Her lover pushed the pear and simultaneously pressed back
the joining of her flesh lips to expose the small pink pip of lust; she
gently stroked its liquid surface, making Ildren want to expand to
take the bulging fruit, yet at the same time, forcing her to contract
against the pleasure of the stroking. 'There, do you like that? Do
you like that stroking at your pip of lewdness?' Her lover moved
her finger in a circle round that knob of sweet delight, and pushed
the pear more firmly until Ildren felt she would split.*

*And now the pear had passed the point of no return, and slid
slowly, drawn by her contractions, up into her body, and her lover
released her nub to prevent the delicious precipitation at too prema-
ture a stage.*

*The chain stretched down from her lover's hand to disappear
between Ildren's thighs. 'Now grip very tight.' She contracted very*

firmly round the golden fruit. Her lover took the strain and pulled the chain and Ildren felt the delicious pulling deep inside her. 'Squeeze, and push that little pip out very hard. I wish to see it pulse with pleasure . . . There!' Her lover pushed back Ildren's fleshy hood and held it. Ildren was almost drowning in delight. 'Now I shall smack it.' Ildren shook. 'Would you like that? I shall smack it, and keep on smacking till you come.' Those words were waves of suggestive pleasure which surged down through Ildren's belly and out between her legs. The weight of lustful need was squeezing out her breath and making her dizzy with desire as her lover's hand was raised high above her, poised to strike – while the other hand pulled on the chain to keep her pip projecting – poised to slap that nub of pleasure, to smack and smack it till it burst and Ildren passed out with delight. Ildren tightened, tried to push to meet that slapping hand and shook her hips in pleasure.

And then – precisely at the moment that the hand of sweet chastisement dropped – the cat took off. The quaking on the bed, the furry stirrings triggered by those tremblings of pleasure, had struck a fundamental chord within the cat. Something in that cat had snapped – the cat was helpless against the deeper instinct which propelled him straight towards the focus of that nervous shuddering, that epicentre of delight, just as Ildren was quite powerless to stop the dream-hand, even as it fell to smack her sharply on the nubbin, transforming magically into a spinning spitting real-world ball of cat fur which scrabbled at her belly.

Ildren's loving dream had turned into a hateful waking nightmare in which she thought her furs had sprung to life and now were tearing at her innards. And though the cat had realised his error well before the Taskmistress had fully woken, he had no chance of escape, for Ildren's scream impaled him. It turned his supple furry body rigid. He was paralysed by the arrow of that scream. It pierced him between the eyes; it rent his eardrums, burrowed through his skull and down his backbone, fusing every vertebra solid, right down to his tail.

And then those eyes of Ildren's opened, striking beams of concentrated malice which nailed that pussy-cat down

11

while Ildren's hand, now formed into a claw, reached out to take the poor and relatively innocent creature by the neck to try to choke his little life away. Yet that cat – scared witless though he appeared to be, and frozen under Ildren's gaze – was surely telepathic. He could somehow sense some sinister intent in the claw-like posture of the hand which seemed to want to stroke so closely round his neck.

The cat shot back, but not quite quick enough. Ildren lunged and caught it on her foot and tried to kick it through the ceiling. It appeared to rise up in slow motion, emitting a curious wavering cry – accentuated by the spinning, probably – of feline disbelief as it flew across the room to land, after two full turns and one three-quarters, high up in the curtains, and very precariously facing downwards, where it had little option other than to watch the Taskmistress gather up her broom almost as if she might fly up in pursuit. Instead, she began beating the curtains without respite, trying to dislodge him, an action which, had she stopped to think about it, was certainly unwise. For a cornered, terrified cat is notoriously difficult to sweep up neatly with a broom, even when the cat is on the ground; but in this case, it was suspended near the ceiling, clinging for its life, with a naked Ildren down below it screaming for its blood and now using both hands to shake the curtains in giant waves of ill-advised displeasure.

The cat, to his credit, tried to miss her, as he flung himself out into the void, but Ildren, driven by her insane passion for revenge – a foible of her nature – jumped quickly back and caught him. Suddenly, the scene was transformed: two frozen creatures, two sets of eyes locked in mutual fear, two worst hopes realised. The cat impaled on Ildren's breasts stared up at Ildren in shock and disbelief, and Ildren just stared back. Perhaps he did not fully understand that those soft and fleshy mounds into which the curving needles on his toes were now bedded to the hilt were really part of Ildren – the same living, breathing, and now bleeding body which seemed to be staring through him, not at him any more. He knew those hands that closed around him were some kind of threat. He knew they would not let him go.

12

And as the hands tightened, so too did his claws tighten in sympathy until they were pumping at her breasts, pumping Ildren's life blood slowly out of her. However, Ildren was not looking at the cat any more, but was watching this blood, this fresh, red, almost sacrificial blood, well slowly out of her and dribble down her breasts, and Ildren's mind was working.

The cat, oblivious though he might have been to Ildren's train of thought, was quite aware that Ildren's mood had changed. She seemed no longer bent on murder. She was stroking the reluctant cat and smiling and looking out above his head, as if, in that letting of blood, all her anxieties had miraculously lifted from her mind.

Ildren kissed that cat while it dug its claws further in, then, when he had calmed a little, she unhooked him and fed him with a bowl of milk, and while he fed she worked vinegar into the lacerations in her breasts to keep them open, as a reminder of this night. She dubbed that cat 'Lucky', not because he was lucky to be alive, though that was surely true, but because he had proved a harbinger of good fortune. Thanks to him she had a plan, a plan that could not fail. She felt it in her belly, and in her deliciously stinging breasts from which the bright red droplets welled again.

[2]

Cruel Spring

Anya lay upon the Prince's great carved bed, asleep. Her long red hair shone like silken fire upon the pillow. The soft bright promise of a warm spring day drifted through the windows, lighting up the room, breathing life into the creatures framed upon the wall, the paintings of stags and hinds and birds of prey – hooded falcons, kestrels and an eagle on the wing – and horses, very many horses. Anya used to spend much time just looking at these horses, none of which was ever figured with a harness or a rider; the horses always seemed so full of life and powerful and free. She would imagine herself riding bareback, clinging to the mane of one of these noble creatures, racing on and on, never stopping, out across the landscape of Lidir. Anya's favourite picture hung opposite the bed. It was the largest painting of them all, a great white stallion, almost life-size, rearing up fearlessly above a nest of spitting vipers. She never tired of studying this picture. It used to reassure her to find it there whenever she awoke. She would ride a horse like that one day.

For once, the Prince's arms were not around her as she slept; the Prince was wide awake, not lying beside her now but sitting up, looking at her sleeping form, caressing her with his soft green eyes, which sparkled with the first sharp-sweet taste of liquid sadness – the realization that the time was drawing nigh. Two days from now, the two of them would part – not forever, it was true, but as the Prince felt now, it might just as well have been. The duties of state – a shapeless, feeble cloak of a term that now disguised the suffocating burden that the Council had laid upon him, the sticky web that bound him more surely than the slaves were bound, for the Prince's chains were duty while the slaves were bound to pleasure, the overwhelming tide of responsibility that only he could bear, would carry him away from the woman that he loved. At this moment, he would gladly have cast all of it aside, all the trappings of the court, all the privileges of princedom, and with his strong sword, cut those chains, and swept that woman up in his arms. Then, mounted on his fastest steed, they would have galloped off without a backward glance to begin again, to begin a new life, just the two of them, on that bright new day.

Anya gently stirred. Her soft full lips had murmured in her sleep; the coverlet had fallen away from her shoulders as she turned onto her back. She smiled at something in her dreams. The Prince smiled back. That image would remain with him throughout their parting – her softly smiling gently freckled face, those full and slightly parted lips which he pictured, brushing against his body once again, and her long silky copper-red curls which would, even in his memory, dangle down and tickle him while she kissed him. He wanted to press his cheek against the smooth curled coolness of those ringlets spread upon the pillow, but he did not want to waken her. He wanted to absorb this picture very fully, this picture of a slave who had overpowered him with her beauty. Her tender eyes had reached out to his heart to enfold it in a gentle loving warmth; her body had burned him with her strength of passion and desire. And when the Prince returned, the slave would be his Princess. That was the only thing that was driving him onwards to complete this unasked-for mission to that far-off corner of Lidir – the certainty of his return, and the sureness that nothing then would be allowed to keep the two of them apart.

Her eyelids flickered and opened, and she smiled at him, as if she had expected him to be there, watching over her as she slept. Her olive eyes expanded to liquid blackness. She loved him. She loved that face; she loved the single earring which would tickle her tongue each time she sucked his earlobe; and she loved the way she could read his feelings in his eyes – the pleasure as he looked upon her, and the sadness behind the joy. She could read that too. She knew why he was sad and that knowledge gave her strength; it held at bay her apprehension at the prospect that she would very soon be left alone without him. At times, over the last few days, often when she least expected it, the fear had surged from deep inside to try to choke her. But always, the Prince's loving look, or tender touch or soft sweet kiss, or his broad hand spread so reassuringly across her belly as he cuddled up behind her – those little messages of love, sometimes just a finger touched against hers, tip to tip – had been enough to push that apprehension back again.

Anya's worst foreboding – the gravest dread of all – was that when the Prince was gone the tide of loneliness and bleak despair might swell to overwhelm her. Her throat tightened at the thought of that; she kept her eyes fixed on his, hoping this might help her fight against the tears of sadness that were welling now, against her will, in cool and giant drops which made her vision swim. The longer she looked upon his face, his strong and gentle face that soon would have to leave her, the worse she felt, until her lips were trembling and finally she had to look away to hide her weakness and her sorrow.

'Anya? Do not turn away . . .' That voice, that soft deep voice which always sent such deep round resonances through to Anya's belly, had this time faltered, forcing her to throw herself so hard against him that she almost knocked him backwards. She flung her arms around him as if she'd never let him go. The cool, sad tears had turned to fiery rivulets of unabated passion burning through his chest.

'Take me with you,' she sobbed and then, forestalling the reply she did not want to hear, 'Why do you need to go?'

The Prince's heart was heavy. 'I wish I did not have to, my darling. If there were any way . . .' He trailed off. He seemed deep in thought. Anya held her breath. He curled her hair around his finger and softly stroked her brow. But now her hopes were dashed. 'It will not be for long,' he said.

'But you could be away for weeks – a week at least, ten days more like, to get there . . . and then the journey back, and then the talks – all that talking, meetings, probably for

16

days. Why do you not send someone from the Council? One of their lordships? Some old windbag?' Anya had attended several meetings of the Council, and she knew its workings well. The Prince smiled, for he would be taking with him certain lords of this very specification, to help to blanket the debate, should it turn sour or even dangerous.

'Anya, it isn't quite like that. These are delicate negotiations. My presence is required as a mark of respect to the peoples of the outlying provinces. We shall need to tread carefully . . .'

Anya read between the lines. 'You will be in danger?' She held him that much tighter; the Prince could feel her heartbeat and those delectable breasts which Anya pressed so firmly up against him.

'No . . . I go to negotiate a treaty, not to fight a war,' and yet he said that last word with just that little bit too much emphasis for this reassurance to sound as persuasive as he wanted it to be.

'I will come with you – to protect you.' She looked defiantly into his eyes, as if daring him to deny she had the strength. The Prince did not blink as he replied.

'I know you would . . . if I could, if it could be done, I would have you by my side – believe me – but this parting is something that we *both* must bear.' Then his voice turned softer. 'I love you. Every day I am not with you will be a knife-wound in my heart . . .'

Anya pressed her lips to his chest, as if to heal that wounded heart. 'I am afraid, my Prince,' she said. 'I am afraid of what might happen to me when you are away.'

'No . . .' He held her head against his breast and gently rocked her. 'You will be quite safe here. No harm can come to you here in the castle.'

'But the Taskmistress. . . ?'

'No my love. Do not fear. While I am gone, you are safe – you will be under the protection of the Council. I have issued the directive in advance, so that all may be aware. No one can harm you.'

She laid her head upon his shoulder, and he intertwined the fingers of one hand with hers. He hesitated, then he said:

'When I return . . .' then more softly, 'when I return, you shall be my Princess – if you will have me as your Prince,' he added in a whisper.

Anya looked up into his eyes; she could not answer; instead she offered up her trembling lips for him to kiss, softly.

'On Thursday – tomorrow – the Council of Lidir will give its consent,' he said.

'What if it should be refused?' Anya did not fully trust their lordships.

'No. That will not happen. It is but a formality . . .' Then he held her by the shoulders and he beamed. 'Besides, how could anybody refuse someone so beautiful as you?'

She looked away, from shyness, and then looked back again, smiling. 'Love me, my Prince,' she said. 'Love me with your body. Touch me. Let me feel your strength against me . . . Drown me in delight.' Anya lay on the pillow with her hands spread back against it, her underarms exposed. Her cheeks glowed; her lips seemed so inviting.

The Prince loved to look at her when she was in this mood, when her body seemed to overflow with sensuality, seemed to ripple with desire. He loved to smell her, too, to drink in her perfume; but most of all he loved to taste her, to brush her body as he tasted, to caress the hairs upon her skin, to delve within those secret places so his tongue could sense the delicious range of textures, warmth and moistness as it tickled her and tasted Anya's loving heat.

This time, the Prince began by turning the coverlet down to her waist and then he turned her on her side. Her breasts lay, full and heavy, balanced uncertainly, one above the other, with their weight directed forwards. The nipples swelled like acorns sheathed in soft black velvet. The lower nipple pressed into the soft pile of the bedsheet; the upper one rolled slightly up and to the side.

Anya liked the Prince at first to lie alongside her, facing her, just looking into her eyes. Frequently, the two of them would lie like this, immobile, for quite a while. The Prince would feel the cool brush of Anya's breath across his cheek. Anya would watch the Prince's eyes dilate. The Prince would be hypnotised by the depth of blackness in her eyes; the faint scent of jasmine in her hair would gradually envelop him. Anya's breasts would feel sensitized from the way that she was poised; their weighted softness would be concentrated towards the tips and they would very gently roll against each other or against the bedsheet with each breath she took, so she was aware now of her breathing becoming uneven as perhaps she hesitated momentarily, and that in turn would send a minute shudder through her breasts to make the flesh around her nipples gather. Her belly, held pushed towards him though not touching his, would feel so tight and heavy as she curved her back to push it out the more and have those thick curls of his – even in imagination – touch her. She would think about them brushing softly against her smoothly stretched skin until even the idea of that brushing sent delicious tickles through her navel, down inside her, somehow tickling from within. And yet still the two of them would not have touched – but Anya would be liquifying.

And now that she was ready, Anya would trigger him. She would do this by some very tiny, very indirect action: she might make her eyelids appear very slightly heavy, or move her head a little back to expose the smooth curve of her neck, or more palpably might edge towards him till her nipples, almost as if by accident, stroked across his chest – or of course she might in reality push her belly forwards till it brushed him. On this occasion, Anya merely parted her lips a fraction as she looked at him, and she felt that warm firm silk-skinned rod of flesh twitch across her thigh and very quickly stiffen up. She eased her body up against him softly, so they touched together at breast and belly and thighs, with the Prince's cock nudging smoothly in between her legs, not touching her sex as yet, but tickling itself against her fiery bush.

Anya liked to feel this urgency of tension in the Prince – this burgeoning arousal that her body mirrored too, though in an all-pervading way, more diffuse than his perhaps, but no less exciting in the way her cheeks suffused with warmth, and her upper lip felt swollen, and soft prickles seemed to tease her nipples outwards; in the way her belly felt so tight, with that feeling deep inside, low down, as if a ball of pleasure were expanding, slowly distending her between the legs, as if invisible hands were stroking her inner thighs in soft upstrokes, lifting up the skin hairs, coaxing her body, concentrating diffuse pleasure there, causing her tiny bud of flesh to push against the swelling leaves that moulded tightly round it, making her body drip. Anya felt she was melting in the slow pulse of anticipation, the gentle waves which lapped so warmly round her belly and kissed her with those promises of long-drawn-out delight.

The Prince pushed out his tongue and Anya slowly sucked it. He loved the way she did this to him; that suck was so seductive. He closed his eyes. Anya's soft moist lips imprisoned him; the feeling seemed to draw down through his body. It was as though her soft sweet lips had closed around his cockstem. The Prince could feel her breathing more strongly now against his face, as she breathed out through her nose; and with each breath, her belly swelled and her curls brushed and sprang and tickled against his tight filled cock, and her nipples dabbed his chest. Throughout this sucking and brushing, this breathing and dabbing, the tip of Anya's tongue slid up the groove below his tongue, then circled round the tip, then traced neatly down again, back and forth, while Anya's lips kept squeezing his tongue around its middle and then releasing, pumping it, until the Prince could feel the deep down ball of swelling pleasure too. It came so strongly that he had to fight against the urge to take her then and there, to thrust his cock between her legs and deep inside her body and, not drawing back at all, to thrust forwards, deeper, ever harder till he came.

Anya now released his tongue, so he could taste her flesh and stroke her body with it. She took the Prince's head within her palm and gently pulled him to her breast. 'Lick me,' she said. 'Suck me. Taste my breasts.' And the Prince's face was pressed against her, with his nose between those softly rounded, weighted, warm smooth instruments of delight, and the velvet-coated, hardened acorns were tantalizing him, brushing along the side of his nose and pressing warmth against his cheeks. Filling his nostrils was the delicious scent of Anya's skin, the scent of almond oil and butter. Anya shivered as he licked that skin and tasted Anya's butter, licking underneath her breasts, moving back and forth between them, stirring them, lifting them on his tongue, keeping pleasure rippling through them, watching how her black-brown nipples moved and swelled from velvet soft to polished smoothness. Then, moistening his lips, he fitted them to each rounded underbelly, pulling upon the nipples from below to make them poke out stiffer than before, then closing his lips at last around each burning bubble of delight, he tickled it with his tongue-tip as he sucked. Whilst this slow, wet pleasuring of Anya's breasts continued, the Prince's fingertips explored her, seeking out the sensitive places of taut-stretched ticklish skin and lightly stroking – kissing, almost, the fingertip coolness against the warmth of the skin – in the hollow of her armpit, whispering in the curls, brushing slowly upwards against the soft pile of Anya's hair upon her tightened belly, circling the little fingertip just inside her navel, not venturing downwards yet, but allowing his fingertips to float across her skin to trace the smooth incurve of her side, above her hips, then to stroke a slow seductive circle through the haze of downy hairs in the small of her back until Anya was trapped between the spiralling tickling low down in her back and the intermittent soft sucking through each nipple. And now she was burning to be touched between the legs. She wanted him to lick her there and drink her honeydew, this nectar that her body made for him.

The Prince removed the cover completely from her body. He took Anya's upper leg and lifted it, then made her bend it and place the foot flat upon her outstretched lower thigh, so the upper leg formed a tight triangle balanced on the lower, and Anya's thighs were separated. The Prince could now look upon her while she squeezed for him, while she allowed her sex to tighten and relax. He loved to watch her do this; he loved to imagine her sex around his cockstem when it happened. He loved the way the lips about her sex were full and firm on these occasions; he liked to think of them as swollen up with pleasure. But most of all, he loved their deep dark colour, which stood out starkly against the paleness of her skin. Their blackness was unique. It was as if a paintbrush charged with powdered burnt sienna had drawn down across those lips when they were pursed and swollen, in this state, in a single stroke which split the brush about them, and then the brush had been recharged and the swath of colour, richer, deeper now, had drawn down underneath, within the groove, to a swirl of black – a final flourish of artistic satisfaction – around the well of Anya's bottom.

No other living woman in Lidir showed such markings. Every time he looked upon her they filled the Prince with awe, but now that awe was spiced with a dully burning ache of wanting deep within his belly – from the way those waves of movement kept rippling through her flesh. He knew his lover performed that squeezing just for him, to make her body liquify.

Now, he made her keep her leg angled in that way while he gently rolled her over, onto her front, so her breasts pressed into the surface of the mattress, and her leg now angled to the side. He took the other leg and carefully bent it like the first one, which brought her feet together across the surface of bed until they touched. Her thighs were therefore opened out very fully and the sharp upcurve of her bottom formed two quite separate mounds. A delicious shiver rippled through this part of her, for she thought she knew what he meant to do. But he waited before he made his move, not only to keep her guessing, but to gaze at her in this outspread state, to savour her, to watch the way her body rose and fell with her breathing, to wait until those tight round bottom cheeks shivered yet again. And then he touched her with his little finger, or rather, the skin upon the pad of his little finger came so close to the sensitive out-turned surface of the mouth of Anya's bottom that she could feel it, not by touch, but by the coolness of its imminence against the burning beacon that just waited to be touched; her tender mouth could sense it by the tiny breath of turbulence as it wavered just above her; the feeling sent a fine cool jet of pleasure down inside her, as if her bottom had been opened and her lover's mouth had blown a narrow stream of air against her and the stream had spilled inside to tickle her. Then the finger really touched her, skin to skin.

The pleasure made her gasp. It struck down into her belly as if a heavy weight had dropped against her from inside and pinned her belly to the bed. Yet the finger was not pressing; it was trembling very slightly, for the Prince understood the intensity of her feelings from the way her breathing was now uneven, with Anya taking small snatches of breath only when she remembered that she needed them to live, if only to have the feelings continue and progress. The fingertip swept gently; it hesitated frequently; then it was lifted up completely. Then the pleasuring was repeated, pressing lightly, brushing back and to across the pushed out mouth, stroking in the velvet, making Anya almost pass out with the pleasure, for in her mind she was picturing her lover buttering her bottom, dipping his finger in the bowl until an oily film had melted round it, then sweeping across her tender flesh, smearing that oiliness onto her until a pool of melted butter had gathered in the well. And now her lover wet his finger with his spittle, and the liquid, oily feeling there was turned into reality.

The Prince gently but definitely closed his hand about Anya's feet, which lay pressed together on the bed. That feeling, as his strong hand captured her feet, sent a peculiar sensation through her; even though the pressure was not great, it felt as if her feet were tied together so she could not move to close her thighs. Although her posture had not changed, the feeling of being held that way, exposed and subject to his loving will, made her belly overturn as though a living thing had moved inside her. The fingertip was wetted again and smoothed against that spot. The Prince's hand closed around her feet a little tighter and pushed them fractionally up the bed, bending her knees more, increasing the tension in her thighs to an echo of an ache and spreading those cheeks wider, so the finger, wetted now to dripping

23

point and moving not from side to side but downwards – in one direction only, starting at a point within the groove and sliding wetly down – slipped across then slapped against and briefly slipped into her bottom and out again before the wetting and the downward slide of pleasure was repeated. The Prince worked methodically in this delicious treatment, not rushing it but persisting until he felt she was ready. Anya was dissolving; her sex was weeping honeydew; her liquid seepage formed a patch upon the bed.

His hand released her feet, but squeezed them tightly first. She took it to be a signal that she should keep them pressed together. His hand was free now, free to reach beneath her and form a shield which closed around her sex, encompassing it but not touching it directly, forming a pressure line around it so, as the pressure was increased, Anya's sex swelled up with pleasure as the blood pumped in. She could feel her pulse against the tight constriction of his hand. She knew that she was dripping on his palm. She could not help it; she did not care. Her heartbeat throbbed between her legs. And now, with her sex held captive in one hand, the little finger of the other hand entered her – that long thin little finger, wetted fully with his spittle, slid very slowly but permitting no refusal, against her slippery tightness and up into her bottom as Anya drew a long slow gasp of breath that swelled her lungs to bursting. The finger curled around inside towards the wall and, precisely as it touched, the hand was softly squeezed about her sex. Anya thought she would burst with pleasure. Now the finger was withdrawn; the hand released her sex, which felt bathed in a gently pulsing warmth. She wanted him to penetrate her belly now, with her in this position, with his weight upon her and with her feet held together firmly by his knees, so she could push and that pushing would open out her thighs more fully, to let him in more deeply. She wanted that cockstem thrust into her to the hilt so the pressure of his swelling would split her leaves and push her nubbin outwards till it burrowed into the soft pile of the bedsheet. And then as he thrust, her nubbin would massage itself against the soft seductive moistened pile until she gasped out loud in pleasure.

The Prince made Anya turn over while he lay beside her and looked upon her intimate person. He had her lie upon her back, with her hands behind her head, and first of all he brushed his lips upwards through the softened curls beneath her arms. When he did this, his lips were parted and his nostrils flared for he was drinking in her delicate musky scent. She lay with her knees bent, with one leg on its side and the other angled upwards. In this position, her hips were slightly turned; her thighs lay open. The Prince could rest his head upon the leg that lay upon the bed; her thigh formed a pillow of warmth. He liked to look upon her like this, so closely that he could almost feel her heat. He loved the way her curls burned bright red as her breathing stirred them and they caught the morning light, the way in which her belly curved away in smoothness and in roundness with, in the distance now, those delectable creamy mounds capped with pearls of blackness. He loved the tension in her body; those swollen leaves of flesh would burn his tongue with the pressure of their heat, and that heavy musk – that delicious warm musk of Anya's body that rolled across to drug him – was filling his lungs and soaking into his blood in a softly burning fire that made his cockstem throb.

Anya closed her eyes and waited for the Prince to lay her body open with his tongue; he would cut her yearning flesh and make her nectar leak across her thigh. She pushed her belly out to meet him, spreading till she ached, bearing down to make herself tighter there, to make it swell, to make the cut of pleasure sweeter. The Prince could feel the depth of wanting in that woman. He placed his palm behind her, low down against her back, and gently pulled her to him. Anya found the pressure in that spot, pushing her defenceless swollen fleshpot forwards, curving her body even tighter, was deliciously exquisite and when he licked her once, then split her with his tongue – not pushed inside but pressed against her so her lips just burst apart and his tongue-tip kissed her nubbin – she almost passed out with delight. The Prince lay like that for quite some time – he could have lain like that forever, savouring the loving tension in her body, and the dew of sweat that filmed her back, savouring her sensuality, while her nectar spilled against the pressure of his tongue upon her flesh and gently welled into his mouth to permeate his being with that soft and special intoxication, the rapture of desire.

But Anya wanted him inside her now; she wanted him to fill her up to bursting point before her pleasure came. She wanted him behind her, cuddled up very tight while she pushed back against him; she wanted his arms to enfold her – after he had lifted up her hair and pressed his lips against her neck – with his hand about her belly and his cockstem curved underneath, pushed inside and swollen very hard, to distend her and to push her nubbin outwards when she squeezed.

Now she could feel his strength against her; the warm thick stem of flesh passed between her legs and entered her. She tried to seal her sex around it. She would not let him move inside her. She wanted just to squeeze until their flesh became as one. The Prince murmured softly against her neck, a faint protest against the tender cruelty of that pressure. She raised her leg and placed her hand around the base of his cockstem, moulding her fingers to his firmness, pressing against the tube, then gathering up his bag of bumps and pushing her fingertips beneath them, maintaining his tension all the while with intermittent squeezes, but refusing his body leave to thrust against her or even to gently pump.

Anya massaged his cockstem with her body oil, coating him in liquid, coating herself, then pressing the hand to his face, so he could smell her, so his cock would swell up harder, as she knew it would, to distend her yet more fully, then oiling her fingers again and reaching underneath, laying them along the bridge between his cockstem and his bottom, pressing there in that sensitive spot, dipping a fingertip into him and turning her head round to meet him so she could kiss him while she probed him, pushing her tongue into his mouth, forcing him onwards even though he tried to hold back, forcing him to tighten round her finger, dictating the progress of his pleasure, moving him up to that plateau of postponement. She took his hand and pushed his middle finger in her mouth, then folded her tongue around it and she sucked it. And as she sucked, her fleshpot milked his cock. Her other hand still lay against him, in between her legs; her fingertips tickled him just below the stem. He almost came. She could sense his tautness, the imminence of his pleasure; she could sense everything about him. The coolness of his breath against her neck had turned to heat; his breathing caught; she could feel the tightness in his chest; his heartbeat pounded through her back; though he did not move, his body was drenched in sweat; he held his belly back as if afraid to press against her. She moved her hips very gently against him to torture him, then lifted her hand away and softly closed her thighs around him to keep his curving cockstem captive. She gently squeezed again, and sucked upon his finger, to make him moan with pleasure; she wanted to keep bestowing these messages of love and lust upon him till he could not bear the burden of pleasure any more.

She did not want him to forget her when he was away.

And she wanted to take her own pleasure by his hand. She took that middle finger that had lain within her mouth and, with her other hand pressed against her belly in place of his, lifting, pulling back, keeping her belly very tight, she circled that moistened pad around her nubbin, closing her eyes, throwing back her head and breathing deeply through her mouth until she nearly cried out with delight. Then she held her breath and pushed the fingertip very hard against the bud, pushing it back into her body, then kept it there and turned her head and said, 'Kiss me.' And the Prince could feel the trembling need in those sweetly moistened lips and in the tongue that pushed its liquid softness in his mouth. He could feel her body turning to a ball of tight desire. She moved his finger once again, forcing tiny tremors through her belly, making her murmur soft protestations even though it was she who guided his finger all along, and finally she pulled his hand away and held her breath again. The Prince felt her body spasm round his fleshy plum in little tiny jerks, before she swallowed, took breath again and reapplied the finger in that fashion – the circling, then the

27

pressing of his fingerpad against the hard slippery pip, and then the easing, followed by the trembling wave of tightness through her sex, threatening to burst him in delicious pleasure, until at last it made him bite into her neck. But he loved her in this state of abandonment to pleasure, in the way she delivered her luscious body so delectably, by slow degrees of provocation, to the fullness of delight.

He loved the way she was transformed by pleasure, the way nothing else mattered to her now but that this pleasuring should continue. Her hips were moving in a slow dance of seduction; her body was filmed in perspiration; she was wet between the legs. The Prince could feel her wetness seeping down his thighs; he could smell her liquid heat. When he brushed his hand across her breasts, they felt smooth and round and oiled and tight – the nipples sprang in hardened pips between his fingers. Now the massaging of her nubbin was more systematic; she did not pause as she slid his finger back and forth across her oily button, and as she stroked she kept contracting round his cockstem, moving him onwards once again, even as she moved herself, and only when the Prince tensed and moaned out loud did those sweet contractions ease. And still she buttered his finger across that burning nubbin until she too gasped and swung her lower leg back beneath him, turning and lifting him so she lay face down with him on top. She spread her legs out wide across the bed but kept the hand trapped there beneath her so she could grind her nubbin up and down his stretched out finger while he pushed up and through her slippery heat until his plum had burst so hard he felt as if a hand had closed around him deep inside to force his miltings out. And as he spurted, Anya contracted round his cock so tightly that the liquid squirted back and when the thickness wet his finger, she cried out loud and came.

Then afterwards, the Prince wiped her sweat-soaked breasts, her back, her liquid-coated thighs and belly dry with a large soft fragrant towel. He covered her up, and lay beside her, and Anya fell asleep.

'Anya?' A smell like warm sweet milk enveloped her. 'It is almost noon, my darling.'

She stared up into a chubby, pink-cheeked face with small bright eyes.

'Marella?'

The woman smiled. Anya wondered where she was, and then she suddenly felt afraid. The Prince was not beside her, though she was in his bed. She did not understand; she was frightened by what it might mean. 'Is it . . . is it Friday?' she asked in disbelief. 'Surely, it cannot be?'

'Why, no my dear,' Marella was looking at her strangely, 'it's only Wednesday.' Then she bit her lip and looked away and Anya knew it must be true. She could feel the teardrops welling:

'Is he? He is gone?' She looked up at Marella, hoping that she would deny it.

Marella only sat beside her on the bed and put her arm about her.

It was true, then. But why?

'Why did he leave without telling me? Why did he pretend?' Anya felt so cheated. If she had known, she could have planned, she could have adjusted to it. She could have said goodbye . . . The tears rolled down her cheeks. 'He is gone and I will never see him again.'

'There, there my darling. Don't say such things. Don't even think them.'

'I know it, Marella.' This was Anya's fear, that their parting might be final. She had never said it to the Prince. Those two days lost were now like two years plucked from her life.

'No. He will be back, and sooner than you think, I'm sure,' Marella said, but she did not sound sure. 'Here, look – he left this for you. You see, he would never let you down . . .'

Marella handed her a folded sheet of vellum. It bore the Prince's seal, the Sword of Lidir. Anya turned it over. On it was a cipher of her name. She recognised it; the Prince had drawn it for her many times. But now that name was turning into just a blur of tears. She broke the seal and unfolded the sheet. Four rows of smoothly sweeping ciphers were spread across it, and Anya looked at it while the teardrops splashed upon the page. She was picturing that soft sweet face, and the earlobe with the ring . . . She would never see that face again.

'Read it to me, Marella. Please?' she said at length. Marella took her hand from around Anya's shoulder then, taking the note, held it at arm's length. She had to use two hands. Her hands were shaking.

Marella read in a slow unsteady whisper. '*My darling, when this message reaches you I will be long gone.*' Marella sniffed. '*Spring has come quickly – the Great River is moving into spate early. We must make haste if we are to cross at all.*' Marella paused; when she spoke again her voice was choked with sadness. '*I could not hurt you for the world, but I could not say goodbye.*'

Marella held the letter loosely. Anya was looking straight ahead. She got up off the bed and walked to the window. Marella followed. Looking out into that beautiful day, Anya said, 'Which way is the Great River? How far is it?' Marella hesitated. She did not know.

Then Anya raised her arm towards the sunlit scene. Her face was grim. Her hand was clenched into a fist, making Marella stand back from her.

'Cruel spring!' she cried out. Her voice echoed out across the rooftops. 'Why must you take my lover from me?'

A pair of ravens took flight from the furthermost tower and circled, calling back as if to mock her. Then Anya bowed her head and whispered, 'Why do you not permit me even two more days. . . ?'

Marella's eyes were blinded with tears as Anya turned and put her arms around her. 'I am so afraid, Marella,' she said.

[3]

The Round Table

The Taskmistress stood on her balcony. Far below her, the cherry orchard lay transformed into a gently swelling sea of green with rolling pink-white spindrifts scintillating in the morning sun. Today, Ildren was feeling lyrical. Spring was really here at last, and spring had never smelled so sweet. And this particular spring day would be presenting Ildren with a rare treasure in the person of a very special spring-fresh creature, a slave whom Ildren had not even met and yet, paradoxically, a slave who was now pivotal to Ildren's calculations. She closed her eyes and stood there, drinking in the perfumed air, soaking up the morning sun. Life seemed so exhilarating. All the blackness and the pain had dissolved away; her confidence was back. But now, she thought, to business: a Taskmistress has her duties, be it spring or be it winter; the Taskmistress must prepare for this very special, very close investigation . . .

She selected from her wardrobe a freshly laundered deep red robe and a matching pair of slippers; she would not wear her boots today. But what about her jewellery? She settled for a pendant, a gold clasp fastened round a polished, large and heavy black stone. This pendant, on a suitable chain, could be worn around the neck so it dangled down between the breasts to provide some weighted stimulation to a wearer so inclined. Ildren liked the way the rounded weight rolled back and forth across her belly and caused the chain to swing across and on occasion catch upon her nipples. For underwear, she chose something very simple – a well-oiled, very thin and very long piece of leather cord, knotted closely round her waist at one end, with the excess length left dangling very casually; she liked the feel of the cool

31

supple cord just brushing against her inner thighs in unpredictable tickles manifesting themselves at inappropriate times.

And now – what equipment would she need for the inspection? She would need to think about it; she would need to browse. Strictly speaking, it wasn't essential that the new slaves be examined in detail. A single glance would normally suffice. She had only to look at a slave to know approximately how he or she would respond to training. True, there were exceptions, the unpredictable ones that Ildren found so delightfully interesting, and the intractable ones, as their impatient lordships liked to put it, that provided the challenge. Yet even without these minor fascinations and tricky little problems, Ildren loved these inspections; the innocent, beautiful creatures filled her with delight, especially when the examination was both meticulous and prolonged – which was where the equipment was required. The nature of the instrument did not seem to matter. Ildren had found that what counted was its presence rather than its specification. Inanimate as it might – in most cases – be, it nevertheless constituted a third party at the examination, an implied threat, to be introduced at any point where a bondslave might be feeling vulnerable.

So, as Ildren opened drawers and rummaged through the cupboards of her storeroom, she wasn't searching for anything in particular. She would use whatever provided inspiration when it came to hand. For example, the item she had just picked up held for her a curious fascination. It had a basic quality of roundness yet it wasn't round in detail. It was made of wood, a dense black wood, ebony perhaps, and was very smoothly carved and polished. It was large, too large for one hand really, and yet the palm seemed to fit so naturally around it, with the middle finger fitted along the smooth and shallow groove beneath. It was a sculpture of a man's part – a very large pair of ballocks with a small retracted cock. This was what made it so unusual – most of Ildren's sculptured pieces were fiercely erect. As it stood, it wasn't any use – no part of it could be conveniently applied or easily inserted – but then neither was it ornament, for she kept it in the drawer. Ildren could never understand the secret of its fascination, and yet, even as her eyes roamed around for something a little more practical, she found herself moulding her palm around it and absent-mindedly pulling at the end.

Then she spotted, in the same drawer, the very things she needed – a broad-bladed spatula of wood and a wooden drumstick with a bulbous end. Two finds in one go – this was so auspicious. She slipped them quickly into the pocket of her robe and set off straight away, with the leather cord tickling so deliciously up against her person, out into the corridor, down the stairs, beaming at the guards and servants as she passed them and wishing them 'good day'. And now, she surprised herself by deciding on impulse to take a detour through the stables. It would be an opportunity to see how the preparations for the Prince's departure were progressing. She liked to see the grooms and stable-hands busying about their work; perhaps one of their lord-ships might be entertaining a slave or two in one of the stalls, in which case Ildren might be able to offer some advice or even casual assistance.

But as she crossed the courtyard, she realised something was amiss. There seemed to be hardly anyone about and no activity at all. Ildren challenged the only person she could find, a stable-boy sitting kicking his heels, on a barrel by the door.

'Boy!' The lad fell off the barrel. 'Think yourself lucky it wasn't the Prince that caught you idling.'

The boy rubbed his elbow and looked about him uneasily before replying in a very uncertain tone, as if he didn't want to contradict. 'But Taskmistress – the Prince is gone . . .'

Ildren was taken aback. Her mind was working quickly. 'Gone . . . But are you sure of this, my child?' Her voice was softer now, more encouraging, for this could be good news, even better than she could have hoped for – much better than her wildest dreams.

'Yes. Two hours since.' The boy was gaining confidence now. 'They had to leave two days early on account of the river.' The Taskmistress's eyes widened. 'Soon it will be in flood,' he pronounced with authority, as though he himself had sat upon the bank, looking askance at the other side, with the water lapping around his toes and working up towards his ankles.

Now Ildren was dizzy with exhilaration; she knew that fate was on her side. She wanted to pick that urchin up and kiss him like she'd kissed the cat, but the timid creature only backed against the stable wall. She had to content herself with blowing him a kiss before continuing on her quest. The boy looked mystified and then a little worried.

Ildren leisurely climbed the broad stairs to the Great Hall, thinking. With the Prince gone, how could she possibly fail? She turned into the west wing, along the corridor and through into the Bondslaves' House, smiling at the house-guards and resisting the sudden temptation to peek beneath their loincloths. Unless directed, they never seemed to move a well-oiled muscle, Ildren mused; they seemed a different breed entirely from the castle guards. She had once witnessed one of these hulking creatures carrying four bondslaves, two under each arm, from here to her apartments, and even then, even at a brisk trot, Ildren had scarcely been able to keep up with him.

The conversation died as the Taskmistress swept through the sea of beautiful women in golden chains and purple cloaks, leaving a trail of bowed heads in her wake. Today, with three new slaves requiring close investigation, she did not really have the time or even the inclination to dally with the others. Marella was waiting for her over at the far side. That woman really ought to lose some weight; she never stopped wheezing these days.

'Good morning, Taskmistress. The slaves are ready.'

'Good. Bring them in. No . . . take them straight into the examination room. I think we shall need some privacy. Wait!' Marella had something in her hand. 'What's that?'

'A note, Taskmistress . . . just an errand for one of their lordships; I am supposed to deliver it before noon . . .' Marella slipped the folded piece of vellum into her pocket. 'But what with one thing and another, and having to wait so long for your arrival . . . well, it's almost noon now, Taskmistress.' She started wheezing.

Ildren frowned. She did not like the servants being cheeky. But today, she would let it pass, and though she always liked to maintain an interest in their lordships' little schemes, other matters were much more pressing. 'Then you had better take it now, Marella.' Marella turned to go. 'But first of all, bring me the slaves if you please – as I requested some while ago.'

The examination room was set out according Ildren's speci-fication. It had a soft, deep carpet, two chairs, a low uphol-stered bench and stool, a wooden bar supported at waist height – very convenient for quick examinations – and, in the middle, a circular table closely covered in soft leather and of a height such that the Taskmistress could if necessary reach the centre without having to resort to acrobatics. She would use this table today, when the pace would be more leisurely. While she waited, Ildren lifted her robe and sat upon the table, running her fingers over the softness of the leather, spreading her thighs, feeling the softness kissing her person, reliving past pleasures, daydreaming . . .

'The slaves, ma'am.' Ildren got up quickly and adjusted her dress.

'Thank you Marella. That will be all.'

The Taskmistress closed her eyes for a moment or two to clear her mind completely. Then she looked upon the slaves – the sweet fresh nubile bodies, with their eyes downcast in innocence, their hands held limply at their sides, and those breasts so softly trembling – those full and nervous breasts with tender fleshy nipples – and then the feeling came, that delicious feeling, the heavy weight that blocked her throat at first then sank so slowly down to swell her breast and press against her heart, then slid again to drop into her belly, making Ildren catch her breath and spread her thighs to let the weight bed itself lower. For there, on the right, was the very girl she needed for her plan. There, looking even more dejected than she could have dared to hope, more soft, more pliable, more pink and fresh and so much more delicious, was innocence personified. She could tell it straight away; she would not even need to check.

Now Ildren was drowning in the waves of honeyed wanting. The weight inside moved again; she wanted it to sink and sink between her thighs to swell her so she could not close her legs. Ildren felt so drugged with desire that she could not move. She could not speak. She could hardly even breathe. All she could do was caress that innocent body with her eyes. At last, she forced herself to drag her eyes away.

The other two girls looked as if they might be sisters, one a little taller, with dark hair, the other with even darker, curlier hair and slightly fuller breasts. But both were from the same basic mould and both of them quite delectable, with those sensuous lips that were always so attractive in a slave. Neither one would disgrace the Prince's bechamber, and very soon now, given that innocent body which was the centrepiece of Ildren's melodrama, there was sure to be a vacancy in the royal bed. Their training to that end would bring Ildren much joy and satisfaction. She could tell it at a glance. She would probably wish to train the two of them together.

'Introduce yourselves, my darlings,' Ildren murmured in her most seductive voice. No one spoke at first; then the taller one answered in a whisper:

'Lianna, ma'am.'

'Lisarn,' the darker one chipped in quickly, then added, 'ma'am,' and curtsied.

So, Ildren had been right; they were sisters. But both of these beauties were eclipsed by the soft sweet treasure standing so forlornly beside them, on the point of tears. She was too afraid to speak. Her long pale golden hair was swept round over her left shoulder so it draped across her breast, where it broke into glass-like open curls which danced across the surface then curled around to frame the nipple, which shook very gently with the tremors of her breathing. Her breasts, though not large, seemed so full for so young a body, as if her tightly gloving skin had not expanded fast enough to keep pace with her burgeoning womanhood; the pressure of their substance filled them to the tips. The caps

36

had inturned ends, as if the centres of her nipples were attached inside by threads which held them back against their growth and needed to be cut. Her belly formed a rounded oval, with faintly softened curls below, and her hips were already full; she had the narrow waist, but the perfectly proportioned fullness for her size, and the warm softness that Ildren knew men desired. And not only men . . . This girl was perfect, like a soft bronzed-pink peach – her upper arms, her belly and thighs, her whole body, seemed to be covered in a fine golden haze, an aura almost, a soft, soft down which Ildren would take such delight in brushing with her fingertips and tongue. Yes, this girl was the one. And this examination would be so sweet a pleasure for the Taskmistress, behind the mask of sternness which Ildren must now draw down to conceal the fire of lust that burned right through her belly.

'You! On the end – yes. No! Keep your eyes down!' The blonde girl cringed back as Ildren took a step towards her. Her eyes had flashed deep blue.

'What is your name?' Ildren snapped.

'F . . . Fawn, ma'am, if . . . if it should please you.'

It surely did. The Taskmistress felt queasy. The oily thong was tickling her between the legs, just when she needed it least – no, most. 'On the table, Fawn.' The girl tried to look around the room whilst keeping her eyes downcast. The other two slaves looked very frightened. They would have their turn. 'Quickly!' Ildren could see the tears begin to well as Fawn took nervously shuffling steps towards the large round table. Then of course she did not know what to do, or how the Taskmistress wanted her positioned on the table. In the end she stood beside it, half facing Ildren, the tears rolling silently down her face, with the edge of the table pressing against the back of her upper thigh, lifting one cheek of that perfect bottom, pushing it out and making Ildren almost pass out there and then. 'Turn round; bend over the table,' she said suddenly. She had to touch that bottom *now*. Otherwise she would die. 'Lie flat. Move back. Press those breasts flatter to the table.' She wanted the bottom curved up stronger, tighter. 'Stand on tiptoes. Oooh yes.' Ildren could not stop the exclamation of desire. She brushed her palm shakily over the curve, down one side then, allowing her fingertips to kiss the softened inner surface, brushed upwards over the other. The skin felt tight and yet so soft and downy. The bondslave quietly whimpered. 'Up . . . higher on your toes.' Ildren's voice had nearly failed her. She brushed again; it felt so heavenly. 'On your back . . .' Ildren's knees were buckling, from suppressed desire, and the cool cord tickling her precisely *there*. 'Head in the middle, feet over the edge. Do not look at me. Look straight up.' Fawn suddenly looked terrified; Ildren smiled. 'Hands by your side. Keep your head still. Thighs together tight. Tighter! Now do not move a muscle.'

Ildren had no idea how she had managed all those words; the weight inside was moving up again to choke her. The girl was trembling, as was Ildren beneath her velvet robe. Her nipples were stiff – deliciously stiff, she could not help it and she would not have it otherwise. She wanted to kneel down beside the table and have Fawn's soft feet, those delicate toes, slip beneath her robe and up her belly and tickle her nipples tenderly, brush the soft young toepads back and forth across her stiffly poking tips; but regrettably, she could not permit herself such self-indulgence while she was on duty. This was Ildren's rule.

The Taskmistress now positioned the other two girls – or had them position themselves – with care and precision. She knew that little details such as this were so important at this early stage; with a suitably intensive course of training, the first twenty-four hours could condition a slave for life. This was why Ildren was so certain she would be able to bring her wayward lover – the Prince's harlot – very soon, and very firmly, back again to heel.

All three girls were evenly spaced on their backs around the table. They formed a perfectly symmetrical pattern, touching each other only at the head, so they were aware of each other's presence, and could hear each other's breathing, but because their eyes were directed straight towards the ceiling, at the painting (again to Ildren's specification, it was of a slave in chains, on a table just like this one seen from above, with her thighs held wide apart whilst the long red tongue of a smooth green snake licked out to taste her fleshpot), they could not see each other and therefore could not know what was taking place beside them, other than on the basis of the sounds – usually soft ambiguous moistened sounds or sighs or tender womanly moans – which might, under Ildren's orchestrations, drift across at intervals.

In fact, Ildren was very pleased indeed with this room layout; it was most effective when, as now, there were several slaves available for examination. Three, she had found, was the ideal number since, with this spacing, both access and awareness were enhanced. The impassioned resonances with three slaves under simultaneous stimulation were always very deep and moving. Nobody felt left out – least of all, Ildren.

She began with Lianna, the taller of the dark-haired girls, by merely standing in front of the girl with her velvet robe just brushing Lianna's knees. The girl, in looking directly upwards at the lewd scene above her head, couldn't see Ildren at all; she could merely feel the tickling. She might well have been imagining the worst – that Ildren actually had a snake concealed about her person. On this occasion, of course, the Taskmistress did not, for she wanted the girl to remain on the table throughout the examination. She waited until Lianna's eyelids flickered and her pupils momentarily darted from side to side; this was the signal for Ildren to proceed.

'Part your thighs, my dear.' This utterance to a new slave would always make Ildren's belly quiver. Lianna spread a little, revealing a dark brown bush and, peeping so invitingly, a pair of soft pink prominent lips. 'Wider!' Ildren's sudden shout made all three women jump and the blonde begin to whimper once again. 'Get those legs apart. Your Taskmistress requires good extent.' And now Lianna was straining to keep her legs held very wide indeed. Ildren could see the muscles standing tense upon her inner thigh. She stroked those firm smooth muscles tenderly, very softly, and very near the top, to counterpoise the straining tension in that skin, using the tips of the fingers of both hands, while she watched the velvet lips expand. 'Bear down, my sweet, tighten your belly, make those lips swell for me . . .' Ildren gently brushed the curls away from them but did not touch the flesh; it was much too soon for that. 'Good,' she said. 'Now, keep bearing down. Do not stop.' Lianna held her breath and pushed while Ildren's belly overturned to witness the rippling and the tightness – that wantonness spread so lusciously before her – and the polished, blood filled lips. 'And keep those legs apart.' And now the Taskmistress was impaled upon a sudden urge – an urge to wet her fingers and to smack them very hard against Lianna's swollen lips while that slave was made to keep very tight and open to the smacking – but once again she denied herself yet another delight and somehow managed to unhook her squirming belly from the pleasure of that urge. Instead, she quickly dipped a fingertip into the gently rolling navel atop the tense round surface – she just could not resist that at least – before moving to the sister and instructing her as follows:

'Turn over, Lisarn; turn on your belly.' Lisarn looked stunned. 'Quickly now. Your Taskmistress must examine you very fully,' Ildren explained, although this didn't seem to help the girl relax. 'Turn your head – lie on your cheek. Good. Now – what must a girl do next? Hmm?' Ildren watched the soft pale cheek suddenly flood with pink. Ildren was ecstatic – Lisarn must know precisely what was needed. The girl hesitated, then very slowly, very self-consciously edged apart her thighs. Ildren's head was swimming beneath the luscious waves of pleasure as she watched the sweet creature spreading so slowly and so delectably, exposing just for her the tightly swirling flesh within the secret groove and the full soft furry peach of love below it.

'Very good, my darling. Very, very good,' she managed in a deep and husky voice, for this slave clearly now was full of promise. She could tell this from the way Lisarn had spread so very wide, without having to be told, and from the way she had closed her eyes – not tightly, out of shame, but with the heavy-lidded expectancy of pleasure; her lips had parted very slightly, and most significantly of all, perhaps, the girl was trying to arch her back to lift and push that sweet peach back – to offer it to Ildren. This creature possessed a quality of lewdness which Ildren needed to encourage. Therefore, she brought across a cushion and, from behind and between Lisarn's legs, pushed it underneath the girl, not lifting her belly first, but merely pushing firmly, applying her weight to slide it underneath her. This action was important, for by this means the cushion was compressed and would press very firmly against that belly, stretching the skin back from the mound, thereby imposing a tightness round the peach which would stir the girl's desire. Ildren placed her fingertip low down on the flat part of Lisarn's back and drew it round and round. Lisarn arched her neck and moved against the cushion. Ildren reached very carefully in between the girl's legs and, taking great care not to touch her anywhere else, not even to brush against her curls, very precisely fitted her longest fingernail beneath the hood of flesh and nervously – very ticklishly – lifted it back to make the hard little nub poke out and, in touching briefly against the back of Ildren's fingernail, deposit a dab of stickiness there. Lisarn emitted a low murmur of half-pleasure.

'Good, my child,' Ildren said, touching the nub once more only, then sucking her fingertip. 'Now keep this delicious nubbin pushed out very firmly. Your Taskmistress loves to see a woman's nubbin at attention.' But Ildren was careful not to touch that nubbin again even though she dearly would have loved to, for a slave's pleasure must be administered very slowly, in precisely measured doses, sometimes, as with this very promising one, over several days. She tenderly stroked Lisarn's back again, then spread her bottom cheeks, and the delicious creature's belly shook. How Ildren loved this lewd little bondslave. She wanted to take the oily thong that dangled from her waist and push the end very firmly up into that whirlpool of temptation whilst she worried the syrupy nubbin to distraction . . . But according to her rule, such a thing was not allowed.

When the Taskmistress moved round the table to where Fawn lay, her mask of duty almost dissolved away; her belly nearly melted. Her loving heart reached out to that soft sweet thing with liquid lines of sadness drawn across her cheeks, and though she should never have done it, she no longer cared about the rule, for even Ildren's rules were not totally inflexible. That would be too cruel. Ildren reached across and kissed the teardrops, then brushed her moistened lips against the girl's, which felt hot; her lips were burning, making Ildren want to take her there and then. She had to wrench herself away to deny herself that pleasure which, she supposed in retrospect, only served to emphasize the purpose of the rule.

'Look into my eyes,' she said. Fawn's deep blue eyes seemed full of fear and longing. Ildren must hone the fear to a keener edge, must make the longing deeper and make the slave's pleasure, when it finally came, that much more profound. For the Taskmistress had decided that, of all the three, Fawn would be the only one to be permitted her deliverance that day.

She knelt above the girl, produced the spatula, held it up and watched her eyes widen first to uncertainty, turning very quickly into terror as Ildren waved it with a flourish. Ildren then held up the drumstick. Fawn's eyes darted from side to side, then looked imploringly at Ildren. Ildren's very breath was taken by her soft blue liquid gaze, and the slow wave of anticipation that disturbed the smoothness of her belly. She very lovingly ran her palm over that tight and frightened belly, then brushed it with her fingers, then quietly climbed off the table and returned to Lianna, whose thighs were still spread very wide and whose belly was pushed out so temptingly but whose eyes were still directed straight upwards, so she could only try to guess by feel alone the nature of the cruel device now being applied between her legs.

It was, of course, the spatula – what else could it have been against those luscious lips? The Taskmistress was using it to *develop* them, as she put it, vibrating it from side to side, slowly at first then faster, trying to find the critical vibration – there! The girl had suddenly gasped. Ildren knew these resonances from Lianna's thickened fleshy lips would be drilling up inside her; her nipples were stiffening up. Ildren decided to kneel beside her, so she could pull and stretch her nipples while she worked her to the brink. When Lianna gasped again, a much stronger gasp, Ildren changed the pattern of stimulation by pressing the spatula to one side of Lianna's lips, then very suddenly flicking it, so the lips shook, then applying it to the other side, very firmly, and flicking once again, and doing this pressing and flicking until the girl's hips jerked upwards from the table.

'Is your pleasure very near?' Ildren asked her very sweetly. Lianna murmured indistinctly; the meaning nonetheless was clear.

'May your Taskmistress split you now? Examine that pip of love?' Lianna shuddered as if the hand of pleasure, instead of flicking at her lips of lust, had closed inside her belly. Ildren pressed two fingers just above the hooded flesh, then placed the edge of the spatula along the line of join and carefully twisted it from side to side, as if the flesh were a pink and tight-lipped oyster. Against the murmurs, against the shudders, the lips split smoothly open. The hood was carefully teased back, exposing the burning pearl of lust, while Ildren drew the edge of the spatula very lightly, very cruelly and as slowly as she possibly could across the polished nubbin. She could feel the belly beginning to squirm beneath her palm. It was clearly time for her to move on to the sister. But first, she planted a single kiss upon that deliciously squirming belly as she drew the spatula down again before delicately spreading apart the lips (which had now gone very much softer, like leaves of moistened dough) to keep the fleshpot fully open, like those widespread thighs, and instructed Lianna to keep bearing down to maintain her tiny point of loving pleasure very firm – and very full of wanting.

Moving round then to the promising one, as Ildren tended to think of Lisarn, who still lay belly-down, the Taskmistress found that she could not look upon the split and tightly rounded bottom, with that fleshy peach beneath it and the lustful pip still peeping out, without a feeling of light-headedness, and now, as she reached out to touch it, a slamming breathlessness against her breast which threatened to stop her heart completely. Ildren laid her right palm against the left cheek of Lisarn's bottom in such a way that the side of her little finger lay snugly in the crease and, though the firm resilient cheek felt cool against the palm, her little finger could very definitely taste the woman's heat. Ildren drew it lightly downwards in the groove, then kissed its pad against the hot little mouth of very silken twisted skin. Lisarn's breathing sounded clear and very carefully controlled, as if she did not trust her body to breathe correctly without her instigation. Ildren loved to hear that sign of tense pleasure in a woman's body; it was the first step on the slow ascent to delirium. She fitted the palm now to the other cheek and this time brushed her thumbpad very softly back and forth across the tightened rim. 'Do you like that, my sweet?' she whispered, touching repeatedly in that spot. 'Does it stir those naughty feelings? Does it make this delectable bottom mouth feel very, very lewd? Would it like a cock pushed up it?'

It was necessary for the Taskmistress to use rude phrases such as this; her duties required her to excite the slaves to the point of wild abandon. Even at this stage, so early in their training, she needed to nurture that inner quality of lickerishness which their lordships prized so highly. She might have done it anyway, however, simply because it gave her pleasure. She loved it; she loved the effect it had. And now, she was very pleased to see the tried and trusted combination of suggestiveness and stroking of the slavish bottom mouth was working – making the slave's peach of love pulsate.

It was time to produce the drumstick; she would beat the tiny little drumskin to distraction. Ildren spread the cheeks to make the drumskin tight and, holding the stick quite lightly, swung it down to tap precisely in the centre. Lisarn jerked in pleasure; the mouth contracted and then pushed out more strongly then before as if reaching to kiss the instrument of punishment. 'Now, I want you to hold these cheeks apart for me . . . would you do that my darling? Hmmm?' Ildren tapped again; the bondslave caught her breath so sweetly. 'Now stretch very tight and hold still.' Ildren reached underneath, into the soaking peach, and closed her fingertips round the pip; she held it, gently rotating now and then, as the mood took her, but keeping the flesh lips at all times open while she tapped upon the drum, until Lisarn began to move her hips slowly in a circle, then more urgently back and forth, attempting to push down, to spread herself more fully and to slip her nubbin between Ildren's very lightly touching fingers rather more positively than Ildren cared to sanction at this juncture.

Ildren had other plans; she needed to see how that little mouth might close around and suck upon the drumstick bulb. 'Open, my sweet,' she said, carefully rotating the end against the tightened whirlpool, 'let this instrument of pleasure twirl round inside your body.' Ildren encouraged her by once again working her fleshy tip, which now felt dangerously hard between her softly sucking fingers. Therefore, when the bondslave drew breath very sharply, she paused – partly to wet the bulb and reapply it. Ildren knew that time was on her side; eventually, yet curiously just at the point when Lisarn's body went tense, the bulbil slipped in smoothly. So now, as Ildren milked upon the nubbin and the Lisarn's breath came in nervous little jerks and random tremors shook her body, Ildren could test the gripping of that mouth, not pushed out now so much as pulled, as she twirled the stick until the girl gave out a long low grunt – a growl almost – and her body went rigid.

'Very good, my darling,' Ildren coaxed her. 'Do not move. Hold back that pleasure . . .' And yet Ildren could not resist one final little squeeze of love upon the slippery nubbin before she laid her palm across the bottom, with her fingers to each side of the stick, and very slowly drew out the stub – and she too felt a delicious shiver as the lifted rim of rubbery flesh very briefly touched against her fingers. But before moving on, the Taskmistress gently cupped one hand between those outspread thighs and held her slave, whispering words of tender reassurance, while Lisarn's tight little body leaked slowly through her fingers and onto the table top.

As a direct consequence of these prolonged but as yet inconclusive investigations into these young women's bodily needs, the Taskmistress was quite drunk with desire, even before she slid open the slim broad drawer beneath the table, folded back the soft yellow cloth and removed the set of gold chains. Fawn, the blonde young creature watching her (illicitly but not unnoticed), was not, as might have been suspected, paralysed with fear. Her fear was real enough and certainly well-founded, and yet by now the fear had been tempered by so many soft sweet moans, so many sounds of moistness and of pleasure, and by the all-pervasive heat of female wanting which enveloped her in a cloud of heavy-scented seduction, a sea of lust in which the young girl's innocence was slowly drowning. Her deep blue eyes were being swallowed up by blackness as Ildren lay beside her, washing her body with her eyes, caressing her softness, wanting to brush her lips across the smoothness of Fawn's thin-skinned tight-filled breasts, wanting to suck upon the nipples till the tiny retractions yielded to her tongue. She lifted the bondslave's left hand, kissed the inside of her wrist and fastened the chain around it, then made her raise her right leg whilst Ildren likewise kissed the ankle – again on the inside, merely brushing her lips against it – and slipped the chain around, then kissed her belly, with a soft kiss like baby's breath across the misted skin. Ildren's heart was thumping when that tender belly arched to allow her to slip the chain beneath it and to fasten it around.

'Open your thighs, my darling. Lift your knees. Submit your body to my caress.' And Fawn was balanced so invitingly with legs uplifted, open, gently angled above her while Ildren's hand cradled her head and Ildren's robe was parted. The Taskmistress took her own long and fleshy nipple and brushed it back and forth across the full warm lips and watched the searching pools of eyes and waited, brushing all the time, until the full lips parted and the long deep violet tube slipped in to suckle while Ildren's fingertips whispered downwards over the belly, between the balanced thighs, through the pale golden silken curls to touch at last the small lips, flushed hot now with desire, and very gently to part them – to open out their tenderness and feel the burning heat, the soft wall of moistness and the tight constriction that could barely kiss the tip of Ildren's little finger and, moving up, the hard and wanton pip of lewdness which belied that innocence.

'Rock, my sweet . . .' As the bondslave took her suck, her delicately balanced open thighs, one higher than the other, gently swayed in rhythm with the delicious drawing down through Ildren's nipple, and in sympathy with the soft, liquid pulling of three wet tips-of-fingertips which formed a tiny sucking mouth around the little nubbin. And when at last the belly tightened to a hard little knot and rippled with waves of wanton girlish shudders and the tongue around her nipple tried to burrow underneath it to nip it from her bosom altogether, Ildren held the young girl's head very tightly to her breast while the length of silken hair cascaded down across her belly and she whispered, as the shudders came again to make those hot tight lips contract so strongly round her fingertips: 'Let your pleasure overflow, my precious; have no fear; your Taskmistress will keep you safe.'

Which was surely very true, for the Taskmistress would be taking very great care to keep her special bondslave very safe and very fresh indeed . . . until the morrow.

[4]

A Consent to Degradation

Despite the plush-looking upholstered seat and armrests and
the elaborate carvings which made it look so imposing, the
large high-backed polished wooden chair that Anya sat upon
was uncomfortable. It would not yield; it might have been
worked from stone. Anya was convinced these chairs were
designed that way – like everything else in this hard and hollow rectangular ante-room, with its smoothly polished
marble floor and featureless pale grey walls, and that black
and long thin table – simply to unnerve people as they waited
to go before the Council. It was just the kind of thing their
lordships would want to do. The end of the armrest was a
square knob with three grooves cut into it, so when Anya
gripped it, her fingers had to bend sharply round the hard
edge and her little finger, having nowhere to slot, was left
dangling unsatisfactorily in the air. Every little sound in the
room was magnified as it echoed from one end to the other –
every uncertain shuffle that Marella made and every little
wheeze. Anya began fiddling again with the hem of her pale
blue cloak, pulling at a thread. This waiting was driving her
to distraction. Why was it taking so long? The thread
unwound; the hem came undone; she suddenly smacked her
hand very hard against the stupid armrest. Marella jumped.
The sound was as piercing as if the wood had cracked.

Then Anya was on her feet again, pacing up and down.
Her boots clicked down the length of the room, the echoes
multiplying to an army of clicks pursuing her and simultaneously marching back towards her across the ceiling.
Marella stood in one corner, looking alternately concerned
and reproachful; in the other corner sat Axine, looking
totally unruffled.

Axine was Anya's friend – her close friend. She was almost like a sister to her, though she didn't resemble Anya in the least. She had blue eyes and very short matt black hair and an almost boyish figure. Axine had taught Anya many things about the castle and its ways; she had helped her many times; she had even rescued her once; but now, like Anya, she could do nothing but wait.

Anya felt so nervous. She wanted all of this waiting to be over.

'Marella – why is the Council taking all this time? What are they doing in there?' She put her ear against the great panelled door, but she could hear nothing. No sound at all came through; surely the door was not that thick? She wasn't sure she believed any more that anyone was actually in there. How could it be so quiet if the whole Council of Lidir was in session behind the door?

'Anya – no!' Marella rushed towards her. 'You must not open that door!' She put her hand round Anya's and gently but firmly pulled it from the handle. 'We must wait until we are summoned – my dear,' she said more softly, now that she could see the torment in her face. Axine stood up and began pacing up and down in place of Anya.

'But Marella,' said Anya, 'I cannot bear this any more. Why did I agree to it? Why did you make me do it?'

Marella sounded almost stern. 'Now Anya, you know that isn't so. You did not have to be present. You are a ward of the Council – the proclamation of consent can be made in your absence. You could be taking a nap, or a walk in the orchard, or doing some sewing,' she said, looking at the hem of Anya's cloak, 'instead of us having to wait here.' Her voice had carried a mild reproach.

'But I do not trust them, Marella. I had to be here. The Prince would expect it of me.' Now her eyes began to shine. Marella could see she was on the point of tears. She put her arm around her. 'Things might be said about me, behind my back, to try to turn the Council against me . . .'

'Now, my darling . . . who would want to do such a thing to you?' Marella said. 'Except for your impatience?'

'I am serious, Marella. The Taskmistress – I know she hates me.'

'No, no, that is not true, Anya. She is just a little stern. That is just her nature. She is like that with everyone, almost.' Marella was recalling her abruptness yesterday.

'She wants to drive a wedge between us – between the Prince and me.'

'Now Anya, why would she want to do that? Why, only this morning she was asking about you. I think she likes you, Anya.'

'What?'

'She likes you.'

'No – what was she asking?' Anya was concerned.

'Just – how were you taking the Prince's departure. And would you be present for the declaration of consent.'

Axine stopped; she folded her arms across her purple cloak and listened.

Anya was shaking her head.

'You didn't tell her, Marella, did you?'

Marella looked put out. 'It isn't any secret, Anya. The Taskmistress was interested, that's all. The whole castle is interested. Everybody's looking forward to it. That's why.' Now she sounded hurt.

Anya put her ear to the door again.

'Is she in there, Marella? Turning them against me? Oh, I wish I could hear what was going on . . .'

Marella put her hand on Anya's shoulder, trying to calm her. She knew that Anya was getting all worked up for nothing; she had that hunted look – the look she had had that first night, all those months ago . . . It was understandable then, but there was nothing for her to fear now. But how could she calm her down?

The woman took Anya's hand, made her turn around and then she looked into her soft and frightened eyes. 'You must not fear,' she said. 'The Prince rules this land, not the Council, not anybody else. You know the Prince would never let you down. And neither would I, my darling.' And Marella kissed the turquoise ring which Anya still wore on her middle finger, the birthday ring which Marella had given her all that time ago, and Anya understood the meaning of that kiss and she put her arms around Marella and hugged her, bending down and pressing her cheek to Marella's soft warm neck. She wished she had taken Marella's advice in the first place and stayed away. She felt too upset to go before the Council now.

The door opened soundlessly beside her. The realization that the time had come at last – yet now had come so suddenly – struck into Anya like a freezing hand that knotted in her belly. The man, dressed in black, bowed slightly.

'Your presence is required, my lady,' he said, and stretched his hand towards a second door separated from the outer one by a short length of corridor. That was why she had heard nothing earlier. Marella made a move to follow, but his other hand quickly swung round to bar her progress. Anya's heart sank.

'Good luck!' Axine's voice had sounded for the first time. Anya smiled weakly. Marella barely had time to squeeze her hand again, very tightly, before the door was closed between them.

Anya was led through the second door; suddenly she was submerged in a sea of sound and jostling colour and was standing in the centre of the long chamber. She had never seen the room so full, with rank upon rank of nobles; no two lords appeared to wear robes of exactly the same style or colour; their lordships were talking animatedly amongst themselves, arguing or laughing, but as they noticed her, each fell silent; a wave of silence slowly swept across the room. Anya felt the weight of that silence, and of all those iron faces turned towards her; she could even feel the chilling gazes bearing into the back of her neck. Now she was self-conscious, aware of every stride she had to take, and more aware still of the way it made her cloak fall open. And it did not matter how many times the Prince had tried to reassure her, she still felt this way – so embarrassed by her nudity in anyone else's presence but his. Then her embarrassment was very quickly turned to deepest shame, for there, sitting at the end of the chamber, in the centre of a

51

dais, with an empty chair to either side of him, was a figure she recalled vividly. There, clad in a robe of deep old gold, sat Lord Aldrid.

'Come, sit up here beside me, my child. There is nothing to fear from us.' And yet, even as he said it, even as she ascended the wooden steps and looked into those sparkling grey eyes and that old and craggy face, then looked away again, her feet began to turn to lead and her cheeks began to colour at the memories – the way this man had taken her on that first night and tortured her body with unremitting cruel pleasures while the pearl of love gripped round the burning point of flesh between her thighs. And that recollection forced a gentle throb of desire there now, as if the pearl were still pressing there, holding Anya's nub a prisoner against the honeyed swell of wanton stimulation.

Anya kept her head bowed at first as she sat upon the chair to Aldrid's right; she could not bear all the staring faces. But she could not resist an occasional glance about the room. At the far end hung a familiar painting of an eagle balanced on the hilt of the Great Sword of Lidir. However, Anya was looking for something else, or rather someone – the Taskmistress. But the Taskmistress did not appear to be there. Anya could not understand it; she could not believe the woman would be far away.

Lord Aldrid raised his voice and spoke to the assembly. 'My lords, after long and heated argument this day, the business now moves on to an item which, I think we all agree, will be a cause for joy and celebration, and not only within these walls but throughout this land.' Murmurs of approval blossomed round the dry and crusty roomful, and now all the faces were smiling. Anya felt relieved; the weight had lifted from her shoulders. She sat back in the chair and looked up at the high arched ceiling above the main body of the chamber. The plasterwork was painted a pale and glowing orange and the beams were balanced on columns surmounted by sculptures of giants whose bowed shoulders appeared to strain against the weight of the enormous roof. A pair of sparrows were perched upon the eyebrows of the nearest colossus; suddenly they flew off, chasing each other through the rafters, chirping very loudly, oblivious of the illustrious convocation gathered down below. 'It is my pleasure now to welcome, on behalf of your lordships, a very special person – a light unto our darkness, no less – a woman whose beauty is nothing short of legendary . . .' He was interrupted by enthusiastic clapping; then he raised his hand for silence. 'This woman, as many of you are aware, has been chosen by our Prince as his royal helpmate.' Aldrid sighed, and smiled, and looked at Anya. 'At long, long last, Lidir is to have a Princess . . .'

The room was now in an uproar of cheering. Anya was overwhelmed; her throat felt tight. She had never expected this reaction from these lords, most of whom she had never met, and even those she had had always seemed so aloof and indifferent. Yet now they accepted her with open-handed warmth and generosity. '. . . And now, my lords, according to statute, I must ask the Council for its consent to this betrothal – although I feel from your kind response that it must surely be a mere formality . . .'

'My lord. . . ?' Now all the eyes turned round to look upon that single voice of discord. Anya was immediately apprehensive, for here was yet another noble that she knew and had come to fear even after a single encounter – at the banquet. This lord, clad in emerald green, was not smiling as the others were; his face was set and stern, with that same hard look he had had then, when he had scolded her in front of everyone for something that was an accident – and he had known it.

'Lord Sardroc?' Lord Aldrid was unsettled by this interruption.

The lord in green stood up. His voice was strong and sure; it seemed to carry authority; everyone paid close attention. 'My lords, I too wish to extend my welcome to our Princess-to-be . . .' Aldrid relaxed a little, but Anya was well aware this person did not mean it. 'But I do not feel that such a welcome should necessarily extend to a devaluation of the purpose of this Council.' These words sent a wave of consternation round the room. 'This is yet another case of a major item being taken on the nod. Soon we shall not need a Council at all; the Prince will do precisely as he pleases . . .'

He was interrupted by a very loud whisper to his left. 'And then we shall at least have some time to attend to the affairs of our own estates . . .'

Lord Sardroc ignored the remark, but waited till the laughter died away.

'No my lords. We must show this woman due respect, as a possible future Princess, but the Prince, for his part, must respect the Council.' He looked around theatrically and held out his arms. 'His Highness is not even present . . .'

'But he has been called away on business of great urgency and profound import – as well you know, Lord Sardroc.'

'That may be so – '

'It is so.' Lord Aldrid sounded quite impatient. 'So, what would you have us do, my lord? Have this woman jump through hoops, perhaps, before we give consent?' The laughter echoed in the roof-beams. 'This is the woman chosen by the Prince, not by you or I. No woman is more beautiful or more appropriate – so who are we to gainsay that decision?' Anya could tell from the way their lordships would scowl at Sardroc and then would look at her and smile, that the Council was fully behind Lord Aldrid.

Lord Sardroc now changed his direction of attack. 'Your lordship misunderstands. The point I make – and I feel the Council at least can see it, even if you yourself choose not to – is that this is not a marriage of simple folk, an everyday occurrence. We are talking about the forging of a special link, a timeless link which will influence the royal lineage of Lidir for ever more. Is it too much to ask the status of this woman's background? Perhaps your lordship could enlighten us?' Anya's heart sank amid the surge of murmurs of agreement. How could the feeling of the Council change so quickly? Lord Aldrid looked shaken; he was unprepared for this, though Anya ought to have guessed it might be raised. But even she could not have helped with this, of all questions.

'But – the markings? Her body bears the legendary markings of the long lost Princess of Lidir.' Now all the faces turned to Sardroc as if daring him to deny that incontrovertible fact.

'Markings – yes. But are those markings proof of royal blood, or just the whim of nature?' And then that tongue turned vicious. 'For nature, as your lordships are well aware, is fickle. Even the lowest mongrel bitch may display unusual markings – which may provide some temporary amusement or diversion – but in time, perhaps too late, her mongrel status will out,' he had to shout against the growing cries of dissent, '. . . when her litter has been tainted!'

Anya cried out, 'No!' then buried her face in her hands; she could not hold back the tears. Those words, however evil and uncalled for, had stirred a deep disquiet, for she did not know her pedigree either, and she had always felt stigmatized by those markings, as if they were indeed a living taint upon her flesh.

The assembly was thrown into turmoil now, with Sardroc being threatened, people jumping up and down, everybody trying to talk at once and a grey-faced Aldrid trying to calm them. 'My lords, I beg of you, be seated . . .' He finally got them settled, then turned to Sardroc, who stood there confidently, almost smiling, satisfied with the progress of his evil efforts. 'Lord Sardroc. Ignoring for the moment the vicious nature of this attack upon so innocent a person . . .' Anya's face remained hidden, despite the murmurs of encouragement. '. . . I would say simply this. Is it not clear to you, regardless of any markings, regardless of any weight we might attach to the Prince's judgment, that this woman has that nobleness of spirit?' Anya forced herself to hold her head up high.

'And would you, Lord Aldrid, say that she is experienced, or even familiar with this castle and its customs?'

That made Lord Aldrid frown; his answer this time was guarded. 'Not fully conversant with every detail, perhaps, but that is not required. She has never been found wanting, and that is what counts. She has always stood the test,' he declared with confidence.

'And yet, as Princess she will have to stand many tests – tests of courage, my lord, not tests of lickerishness under your direction,' he added with a sly smile, which generated many nods and knowing winks amongst the assembled throng and made Anya flush bright red. Lord Aldrid was unsettled. He coughed, then, seeming to gather all his strength, he banged his fist down on the chair.

'I repeat,' he shouted, then spread his arms out wide as if to encompass all the fickle, uncertain faces, 'this woman can withstand any test. She will fulfil all her royal duties without shirking.'

A smile spread over Lord Sardroc's face; he had led the old grey wolf at last into the trap. 'Then let her take the test.' The room fell silent, with all eyes directed towards Sardroc. Anya felt a slow chill creeping up her spine.

'What test is that, my lord?' Aldrid was forced to ask.

Sardroc was playing games with him. 'It should not matter, you said she can withstand any; but perhaps a simple test of duty. Let us see . . .' Sardroc pursed his lips and stroked his chin. Anya knew that all of this was a sham; she knew this diatribe to be full of sinister intent. 'How about – the preparation of a slave?'

'But the Taskmistress normally performs that duty, should your lordships require a formal preparation.'

'But only in the absence of the Princess. Lord Aldrid, for one so advanced in years, you appear to have little knowledge of protocol, or history. The Princess, as Mistress of the Slaves, has a duty to see the slaves are prepared in all respects. Although that duty may be delegated in part, it is her responsibility nonetheless!'

Lord Aldrid looked unsure; he turned to Anya and whispered, 'What do you think, my dear? Could you do that if called upon to do so? I fear he will try to steer the Council in that direction, and it is better that we cut the ground from under him.'

Anya knew what was involved; she knew at first hand about the ceremonial washing, and the grooming, and how embarrassing it was. She would if called upon be very careful, very gentle with their tenderness; she would take great care not to frighten them. Yes, she could, if needs be, do that preparation. She nodded to Lord Aldrid, who took her hand and squeezed it. 'You are very brave my child. My lords,' he declared with satisfaction, amid general approval, 'Anya will take the test!'

Sardroc seemed taken aback, then recovered. 'Ah, but when and where, my lord?'

'At any time or place you care to designate.'

'What about here and now?'

'Certainly.' But Anya was concerned; she hadn't expected this, having to do it in front of everyone. And it would be worse still for the slave. She did not like those looks upon their lordships' faces; she did not really wish to go ahead in public, but now it was too late. 'Have the Taskmistress select an appropriate slave.' Now Anya was even more worried – the Taskmistress would be making her appearance after all. She did not want to meet that evil woman face to face again. All of this was very disturbing.

An icy wave descended over her when she saw the red robe, the dark hair tied back so neatly and then that calm expression which even from this distance, she knew, disguised such calculating malice. And now her heart went out to that poor innocent creature, filled with fear, that Ildren led into the centre of the room then, as if to compound her degradation, forced to lie across the table in front of everyone. Ildren spread the girl's blonde hair out on the cloth before disappearing, then reappearing with a bowl, which she carefully placed on the table, and a white towel, which she positioned beneath the girl's hips.

'My lords, the slave is ready. She awaits your pleasure.' Ildren stood back and clasped her hands together, bowed her head and waited. Then Anya realised that all the eyes had turned upon herself. Lord Aldrid nodded to her. 'But. . . ?' She did not know what to do.

He whispered, 'Go on, my child. The Taskmistress will assist you.' Again, that chill came.

Anya steeled herself and descended the steps towards the evil creature and the nervous, frightened slave. Her heart overflowed with sadness; she placed her hand upon the hand that lay so limply on the table, whispering, 'Do not be afraid, my darling,' then reached into the bowl – and jumped. Her hand had touched something unexpected; the bowl contained not water and a cloth but something solid, something hard – a wooden stick. She ought to have guessed it would be some deceit.

She turned upon the Taskmistress. 'What trick is this?'

Ildren looked hurt. 'Trick? But I do not understand, ma'am.' She took the thing from the bowl, 'Here . . .' and forced it into Anya's palm. The stick was a carving of a man's excited part. Anya was bewildered. All around were murmurs. It was some kind of trick. 'I do not want this . . . where is the water?'

'But the request was for a slave requiring preparation. This is such a slave.' Then she raised her voice, and spoke slowly and clearly, as if explaining to someone to whom the tongue was foreign: 'The slave's innocence awaits your penetration, ma'am. Hence the cockstem . . .' Then, when Anya only looked stunned, Ildren turned her head to one side at first and appeared perplexed, then widened her eyes as if the realisation had finally dawned: 'Ah, I see . . . Milady prefers to use her bare hands?'

'No!' Anya dropped the cockstem to the floor, causing shock and consternation all around the room. She knew the trap was sprung, but trap or no, she could never be a party to this public display of cruelty. She kicked the cockstem underneath the table. Ildren's face remained impassive as Anya's cheeks burned bright. But still she did not care; she pulled the bondslave off the table. 'Go,' she said, 'go quickly. Go from here!' The girl looked from the Taskmistress to Anya and back again, but would not move until Ildren nodded. The slave left quickly, with one last glance at Anya, and bowed low as she passed Ildren, as if afraid of being beaten. But Ildren was not concerned with that one; she was looking at Anya with quiet satisfaction. The room was now in uproar.

Eventually Lord Sardroc's clear hard voice cut through the rabble:

'Any test, I think you said, my lord? And shall the Council now proceed with the *formalities* of consent?'

Aldrid collapsed into his chair, as if struck a mortal blow.

The chamber fell silent. Anya hung her head; she had let him down; she had let the Council down – she had let the Prince down. The burden of that responsibility weighed upon her and yet in her heart she knew she was right to take a stand against such cruelty.

'My lords. Lord Aldrid?' That softened voice cut into Anya like a knife. It was an effort for Lord Aldrid even to wave his hand. His face was weary.

'Yes, Taskmistress?'

'My lords, it is not my place to speak at all at so noble a gathering . . .' Anya hated this ingratiatingly evil creature whose voice was crawling like a snake across the floor.

'Please proceed.'

'My lords, it seems – although I have not been a party to the debate and cannot therefore appreciate all the nuances . . .' Ildren glanced uncertainly from Aldrid to Sardroc and back again, but Anya knew all of this was pretence. Why couldn't the Council see through her? 'From what I am able to gather, it seems to me that *both* of the cases put are quite correct.' And now, Ildren had the attention of the entire assembly. They were hanging on every word. Anya detested this calculating crawling poison-minded vixen that she was being forced to listen to. 'Lord Aldrid has spoken warmly for Milady. I would go further – I found her to be unique. This is no ordinary woman.' Lord Aldrid smiled with satisfaction; Sardroc scowled, then just as quickly nodded his head in agreement. 'And yet, Lord Sardroc is quite right to point out the deficiencies – which are in fact of training, not of character, for her training was prematurely cut short.' Ildren waited for the words to sink in. 'His Highness recognised immediately the qualities of this slave,' Anya was well aware that Ildren had been systematically degrading her status as the devious monologue progressed; she would be calling her a harlot next. 'I would even venture that, had the training of the Prince's . . . concubine been fuller from the start, then today would indeed have been a cause for joy instead of acrimony.' And then she paused, before casting out the crucial line. 'But of course, all is not lost . . .'

'Explain, Taskmistress, if you please,' said Lord Aldrid. Anya's heart was beating faster and faster; she could guess what Ildren was about to say.

'That training can still be given . . . and with a slave as promising as this one, it shall not take long. Such training, if suitably intensive, could be completed before the Prince's return . . .'

Aldrid interrupted enthusiastically. 'And then consent could still be given – the betrothal could go ahead.' Everyone was nodding eagerly, even Lord Sardroc. Anya knew now that all hope was lost. She slumped back against the table. Ildren merely folded her arms and waited. 'What do you say to that, my Lord Sardroc?' Aldrid asked. 'Shall we take the vote on that?'

Sardroc beamed. 'My lord, I feel that any vote would be a mere formality.' Now everyone was laughing, apart from Anya, who was devastated, and Ildren, whose face remained impassive.

Lord Aldrid rose to his feet, and held his arms out. 'Taskmistress, we entrust her to your care and close attention, and we thank you; we shall not forget this service you have done us.' Ildren allowed herself a bashful smile amid the deluge of applause.

'My lords, I am overwhelmed. Shall the slave then be allowed privileges? These could perhaps interfere with the training programme, but I am of course thinking of her special status . . .'

'We leave the details to your judgment, Taskmistress, but nothing shall be allowed to delay the programme.' Lord Aldrid had fully recovered his composure; he was now very firm, and gaining momentum all the time. 'This training must be expedited. No avenue of learning shall remain unexplored. Do you think you will be able to complete the familiarisation in time?'

Ildren placed her hand on her heart. 'I will do my best, my lord. When shall the training commence?'

'The sooner, the better.'

'Her status as the Prince's . . . under the Council's special protection?'

'She is under your protection, Taskmistress, until the Council meets again.'

'No!' Anya's mouth had formed the shape of that protest, but the word never even came out; it would certainly have been a wasted word against these strict and hardened hearts.

'Then her training shall begin now,' Ildren announced and smiled fully at last. Anya could not believe it. Lord Aldrid, the Council – these were the very people who were supposed to be protecting her, and now they had pushed her into the pit of her deepest fear. Her chest felt tight; she could not breathe; her heart felt as if it would burst. She shut her eyes, then opened them and then it seemed the scene was moving, and it was not she who was standing there; instead she was floating up above the room; and even though she could feel the hands upon her, she was somehow looking down at the forlorn dejected creature who no longer had the will to prevent that evil woman taking away her cloak, exposing her in front of everyone, removing her boots, then fitting the three gold chains of slavery once more – making the memory flood back of that first night all those months ago when, in her innocence, she had thought the chains an adornment to her body. But now, those same chains were like millstones, weighing her down, fixing her to this place forever, and this was the only way she would ever be able to escape – by allowing her mind to float free entirely from her subjugated body.

'On the table, slave.' Anya moved automatically. 'No – stand. There is much to be undone . . .' Ildren added softly. Anya was made to stand with her hands behind her head and her ankles wide apart. 'Hold up your head and keep your eyes open. Now turn round – slowly – all the way round.' Anya tried to switch her mind off as all the staring faces passed before her eyes. 'Stop!' In the centre of her field of vision now was Lord Sardroc, looking directly at her. His arms were folded and his eyes, of all those eyes, seemed to search right through to her soul. He was assessing her body as if it belonged to him, as if he had purchased it with that cruel denunciation. 'Turn round.' Anya felt relieved that she faced away from him. 'Now bend – right down. Move those legs wider apart. Further down . . .' Anya's hair fell across the table; then she felt Ildren's hand between her shoulder blades, pushing her hard, forcing her head between her calves. Now, although she shut her eyes, she could see that man again, still looking at her, looking at her blackness, laid bare for all to see. She could hear the comments – that was not imagination – the coarse whispers, and the chuckles. 'There my lords. The unique markings . . .' Ildren made Anya display her body in this degrading way to all four sides of the room before she had her stand down on the floor. Anya could not lift her head. She wanted the floor to open up and swallow her; she would never ever be able to face these people again. She did not want to, not after what they had done to her. Why could they not see through this evil woman? Were they just the same?

'Stand up straight, slave.' Anya's heart stopped. From her pocket, the Taskmistress had produced a whip, a short wooden handle with a long thin cord attached. Ildren advanced; Anya backed away. Her lips formed a silent protest. Ildren folded her arms and simply gazed at Anya, but did not speak. Anya wanted to look away, but now she could not, for those deep brown eyes seemed to envelop her. The chain was once again pressing a heavy line round her belly and her lower back – the pressure of constraint – as it had done so then, all that time ago. So many memories were stirred by that gaze, and the soft pressure there – memories of profound submission and of deep and drowning pleasure – and Anya felt her resistance softly melting; the forbidden honey trickled down her throat and formed a sinking weight inside her belly, pressing out against the cool kiss of the chain. Anya felt her body sway; in its overbalancing she took a step towards the Taskmistress. Ildren had smiled – not cruelly. The smile, those sensuous lips, had summoned Anya. And now the fingers touching Anya's chain, hooking underneath it, pulling it, sent a wave of submission through her belly. Anya could not take her eyes from the Taskmistress's face; Ildren worked so confidently, so methodically at Anya's body, as if she understood it very closely and could tell precisely what Anya was feeling. She fastened the end of the whip to the chain, just below Anya's navel, then let the handle hang between Anya's knees.

'Turn around, my precious,' she said. 'Put your hands on the table.' The deep wave inside her belly came again, as the Taskmistress stood behind her, using her body in this way. The handle swung between her legs. Anya felt it being drawn back and up between her thighs then slipped, from below, under the chain in the middle of her back; then it was allowed to hang. The cord was drawn by the weight of the handle into Anya's divide, from front to back and up between the cheeks of her bottom. Ildren placed her palms against Anya's inner thighs and eased them further apart, so the cord hung slackly; then she pressed a palm against Anya's back and steadily pulled the handle; the cord was drawn up tightly; it fitted tight against the inner flesh of Anya's bottom groove. The line of tension pressed across the tender mouth of her bottom and up against her sex. The pulling seemed to lift the bridge between her legs, making her want to stretch up on her toes. Ildren wanted Anya's thighs opened wider; she made her lie with her belly on the table but her feet still on the floor. She lifted Anya's breasts out to the sides; she stroked the velvet tips, then pulled the handle again, very firmly.

'There,' she said softly, as Anya felt it give – the leaves of flesh about her sex had split about the cord and now it bedded up against her nubbin. Ildren made Anya reach back and spread the cheeks of her bottom as widely as she could while Ildren pulled again and this time Anya gasped – the cord was cutting deeply into her, back and front, cutting her in two. 'Now stand up. Straighter.' Ildren seemed satisfied at last. 'Thank you, my lords,' she said. The room stayed silent. No one had spoken since Ildren had set about applying the restraint.

Anya was marched through the main doors and out into the corridor with Ildren holding the whip handle, keeping it tight, lifting so Anya needed to walk on her toes. The line of pressure cut her and the cord was burning hot against the flesh that moulded round it, yet the welling feeling in her belly, the promise of protracted pleasure, could not be appeased . . .

'Guard! Take this slave down to the dungeons. Have her shaved. Then she shall await Lord Sardroc's pleasure.'

The Taskmistress watched the two of them disappearing down the stairs. Her heart was thumping; her body ached; she was burning up with wanting for that slave.

Why did Ildren do it? Why did she always deny herself the pleasure? What was this compulsion that made her hand her lover over to these others – men at that – for them to abuse that body in any way they chose to? Why did she keep punishing herself like this, when all she really wanted was to have her lover in her bed?

Sometimes, she did not understand herself at all.

She shook her head and set off towards the Bondslaves' House, and to duty. Where could that young blonde virgin bondslave have got to?

[5]

The Seeds of Desire

Anya never forgot the way that Axine had tried to save her that day. She must have heard the commotion as Anya was taken out the other way, through the main doors of the Council chamber. All Anya saw was the flash of purple of her cloak; but she might have known it would be Axine, from the speed at which she came flying down the staircase behind them and caught them up even before they reached the bottom of the first flight.

'Stop!' Axine shouted. 'What are you doing? Where are you taking her? Don't you know who that is?' She didn't give the grey guard a chance to answer before she grasped him by the arm.

'Get off!' The guard thrashed out at her. She was too quick. His hand merely glanced across the soft black brush of Axine's close-cropped hair. 'I've got my orders . . .' he protested, but he sounded weak and Anya could tell he was unsure of himself.

'What has she done?'

The guard then tried to ignore her, but he had been unnerved; Anya could smell his sweat. 'Get moving, you,' he ordered Anya, pushing her onwards and at the same time, pulling the whip handle sharply upwards so the cord cut into her flesh and made her cry out. But even before the echo of the cry had died, Anya heard the guard howl. He let go of the whip. When she turned round he was already collapsed upon the floor and clutching at his knee. His face was twisted in pain. Anya couldn't believe it – Axine was standing over him, arms akimbo, with her booted foot raised up to kick him yet again. 'Now – where are you taking her,' she said, 'and on whose authority?'

Then all three of them jumped – a soft voice had sounded at Axine's back.

'She is being escorted to the dungeons as I have requested.'

Both Anya and Axine froze. They had not heard him coming down the stairs. The guard got up, and even he seemed worried. Anya had recognised the voice even before she saw the green robe and the pale blue eyes – so old for one so young in face – which once more seemed to look into her heart. His black hair shone as if it had been oiled. It was drawn back tightly and fastened at the back. His face – those thin lips – seemed hard. He had been looking at Anya while he spoke but now he turned to face Axine – and yet he addressed the guard. It was as if he used his gaze to restrain her.

'On about your errand, guard. Have the slave made ready. And instruct Thelda to take special care with that body.' Anya's blood ran cold. 'Its smoothness must remain unbroken.' He glanced at Anya again. She was shivering; each phrase had felt like ice-cold water splashed against her belly.

And as the guard led her away, though not so roughly as before, she tried to analyse those words, but the thought of what they might mean only made her even more afraid. And she was afraid too for Axine; Lord Sardroc stood unmoving still, facing her across the corridor.

The stairs seemed to go down and down. They must be below ground – now there were no windows, nothing to show it was daylight outside, nothing to mark the sunny afternoon. Where was her Prince now? If he knew her plight he would surely cross the river once again and come to save her; but he did not know. How could he? Unless he came soon she would never survive this dreadful place. But how could she escape?

Still the stairs descended, and now there were darkened passages leading off to the sides. She could hear muffled sounds and distant echoes. The walls ran damp, but the air did not seem cool as it would do in a cellar. The air was getting warmer and she could smell, not dankness, but something else – something very faint at first but getting stronger. And then she recognised it – the scent of human heat.

They had emerged into a wide low corridor almost like a cavern, cut in living rock. The air felt hot and oppressive; the humidity was making Anya sweat. Ahead of them she could see the bars – thick iron bars all the way across the cavern, and extending from the ceiling to the floor. She had heard the slaves refer to this place, but she had imagined it to be something like the guardroom. She had never expected it to be on this scale. Across the entrance was a decorated arch, with abstract swirling sculptures in the stone. Then Anya realised there were patterns in the convolutions – female shapes woven within the arms of a great tree, wrapped around or slung beneath the interlacing branches, dangling like exotic fruits.

That first image of the dungeons filled Anya with awe. Behind the bars the cavern widened to a huge room that was very brightly lit, not dark, and now she could see that there were people moving about; there seemed to be passageways leading off in several directions, as if the area was the entrance hall not simply to some prison cells, but to a whole suite of rooms – another castle almost, underground.

There were slaves, in chains like Anya's, but they also wore collars round their necks or sometimes round their waists, and then there were men – and women too – whom Anya took to be their warders, uniformly stripped to the waist, wearing leather aprons and carrying whips or straps slung round their middles. This made Anya very fearful.

Against the wall was a large desk, with an even larger man behind it. He too was bare to the waist; he glistened with sweat; his body formed a heap so fat that his hands appeared tiny and seemed to be attached almost directly to his torso, with no intervening arms. His head looked as if it had been pushed into his body. He sat immobile. Two tiny black eyes were following Anya as she approached the gate. Her guard waited. Anya tried to look away. She did not like his eyes; they seemed so strange and frightening when his body did not move at all. She touched her foot against a bar;

it felt warm. Her gaze was drawn again by the face and those tiny eyes. Behind him hung row upon row of bunches of keys, and further along the wall, shackles and manacles like the ones that she had seen upon the slaves being led from one part of the dungeons to another.

Now her guard was getting impatient. 'Turnkey!' he shouted, and banged upon the bars. The eyes stopped moving altogether. Very slowly, the fat man rose. He never took his eyes from Anya, but a tiny arm reached out behind him and selected by feel alone a bunch of keys which looked to Anya identical to the rest.

'Hold your horses! Tut-Tschh. Can't you see I'm coming?' His voice was tiny, like his hands and eyes, but he appeared to float across almost as if his body were weightless. Anya couldn't see his feet moving. The key slipped easily in the lock and the gate opened silently. He was only as tall as Anya but now his bulk filled her field of vision. She doubted if he could have gotten through the gate at all; unless there were another exit, it meant he would be a prisoner here behind these bars for life. Anya panicked; she had a sudden fear that this would happen to her too – that she would be fed and fed until she was so fat that she could not escape even with the gates thrown wide.

'Step inside, my sweet,' he hissed, and when Anya didn't move he reached a stubby arm to take her hand. She pulled away. He chuckled. He made her feel creepy. His hand had felt warm and clammy yet it had made her flesh go cold. 'Come in, my dove, you're very welcome here.' The guard pushed her in, but he let go of the handle of the whip; he didn't venture in himself. Anya found this made it even more disturbing; it was as if the guard were afraid to cross the threshold. Again that vision struck, of her never ever getting out. The turnkey chuckled again in his high-pitched voice and locked the gate behind her.

Beyond the bars, the guard had cleared his throat. 'The orders are from the Taskmistress herself. She is to be shaved and then . . .'

The turnkey interrupted. 'Ah . . . another one for Lord Sardroc.' She backed towards the bars. His hands were

68

touching her, palpating her belly and breasts as if he meant to eat her. One hand dipped into the pocket of his apron and then stretched out again and opened. 'Would you like a sweetmeat?' She jumped back as if in that simple act, her worst fear had been confirmed, as if the contents of the hand were poison. The turnkey shrugged and popped the sugar-plums in his mouth. 'Ssank you, guard,' he mumbled with his mouth full. 'We'll manage now, won't we dear?' The guard didn't need telling twice and immediately dis-appeared back the way he'd come.

'Now, my dove, do not be afraid, let's get this contrap-tion off,' he sighed, then sucked. 'Tch . . . no subtlety, these guards. Tchtch.' He unhitched the whip very quickly, but despite his apparent act of consideration, Anya did not trust him at all, and she was disquieted by the way the door had clanked shut and then been locked. There was no way she would be able to get out unless this creature opened it. Even if she could get to the keys without him seeing her, she would never know which one to use. She felt completely at his mercy and she was so afraid of what might be done to her in here; even if that vision was just a nightmare, there was still the shaving that they kept referring to; she knew it would be cruel and degrading. And Lord Sardroc – why did he want to have that done to her? In what way would he take his pleasure with her?

'Over here, my little bird; we must fit you with your collar.'

'No . . .' She did not want anything fastened round her neck.

The turnkey suddenly stopped, a look of complete sur-prise on his face, as though Anya were actually a bird and now the bird had spoken. With one hand he took hold of the chain round her waist. She watched his stubby fingers grip and twist it, then she felt the chain bite into her back with a sudden strength she had never expected from this short and thin-voiced creature. He pulled her towards him till his skin was touching hers. She could feel the oily warmth against her nipples.

He held his finger up like a stick with which he would hit

her if she annoyed him any further. 'My dear, perhaps I should have made things clearer. In the dungeons we do not permit *that word* from slaves in answer to a request.' Anya was stunned. His other hand moved to her breast; the clammy fingers began pawing her. 'Now – what is the word we prefer to hear?' She looked away. She would not say it; never. 'Very well. But there are ways, many ways; ways you would not understand, my dove – not yet. Ways you will find strange.' He chuckled, and shook his head. 'But in the end, you will come round.' His tiny eyes fixed upon her. 'They all come round, take my word, my dear. I see it every day . . .' And Anya found the assurance in his eyes was worse by far than any beating he might have chosen to bestow upon her for this act of disobedience. He lifted up her breast. To her shame, the nipple had turned quite firm; he smiled.

Anya was now more subdued but very much more apprehensive as he led her round the corner to a large embayment. The walls were covered with restraints. Some of these devices looked more sinister than the one he had only just removed from her. There were chains of all types, but these were iron chains, not gold ones like her own, and also leather collars and cuffs and waistbands – and more intimate devices, such as halters and reins, leather bodices and belts with cruel-looking attachments, and other things which she could not identify. They filled her with dread for she could not guess how they might be applied to her person.

'Now, let's look at you.' His high-pitched whisper made the skin on Anya's belly crawl. 'Do not cover up, my sweet one. Put your hands down by your side, there.' Anya closed her eyes. The warm damp fingers touched her again, underneath her breasts, then held them only by the stiffened tips and shook them. Then she felt his fingers down below her belly. She could not stop him, even though she hated it. 'Mmm . . . unusual. Such a shame to take away this bush; never mind. Thelda will soon have you clean as a whistle.' So now at least she knew for certain about the shaving, but the knowledge only seemed to make the sinking feeling worse.

'Here . . . now sit on here.' The turnkey pointed to a pole supported between two uprights. It perturbed Anya. It reminded her of the Horse, the cruel device to which the Taskmistress had tethered her and then subjected her to such degradation. 'Hurry up, my dear. I must look at you closely.' Anya placed her hands upon the pole and began to lift herself to sit upon it as if it were a high bench. 'No, no – silly girl! How can I examine you like that? Put your legs astride.' The pole was very narrow; it was difficult to balance for her feet did not reach the floor. 'Put your hands behind you. Hold on there. Good.' She closed her eyes. She could not bear the thought of him touching her again. 'Push forward. There.' Anya felt her flesh being teased apart. His fingertips were shaking, sending shivers upwards from the points of contact. She opened her eyes. She did not trust him. 'Now . . .' He wet his fingers and closed them stickily round her bud of flesh and carefully rolled it. Anya hated the pleasure that his pudgy fingertips were giving her. While he pleasured her, he quizzed her.

'Does the Taskmistress do this to you?' he asked. Anya flushed crimson at the memories. 'Answer now . . .' The weight inside sank deeper; she nodded. 'I see. . .' He wet his fingers again; her nubbin was beginning to crave the touch. 'How . . . how does she prefer to use you?' She did not know what to say. Did he know anyway? Was this just a game? The manipulation took up again, became more insistent. 'Does she like to . . . use things on you? To penetrate you?' Now her belly overturned. 'Hmm. Let me have a look.' He placed his hand against her back and forced her to bend forwards until her open sex was pressed against the pole. A wave of shame came over her again as she remembered what the Taskmistress had done to her with her chains – how she had forced pleasure on her in those degrading ways. Could he tell? How could he? But as his fingertip touched the mouth of her bottom, Anya felt herself contract; the contraction was from guilt. 'Mm . . .' he said, 'have their lordships used you in this way, too?' Again he tapped her bottom, precisely in the centre of its mouth.

'No!' she cried, but again, the mouth pulsed softly. The

turnkey merely stroked across it as if undecided, then flicked it quickly, and Anya closed her eyes again, for a surge of wantonness had rippled deep inside her. The recollections were not simply ones of degradation. 'Mm . . .' He sat her up and she was mortified by what he was staring at. 'Your body makes good seepage . . .' he observed, drawing his finger across the fluid filmed surface of the pole and rubbing his fingertips together, then, 'Push forward,' he said, smearing the fluid round her nubbin and squeezing very softly. 'Lord Sardroc has not previously used you for his pleasure?'

'No.' Anya was very frightened by the tenor of this conversation, and yet the pressure of the hard smooth wood against her bridge of flesh was stirring her. And the constant touching of her bud was slowly bringing her on. The turnkey did not seem to understand this – how close she was to disgracing herself. 'Spread your legs, my dear. Point out your toes. Good.' He had eased apart the cheeks of Anya's bottom so the pressure there became exquisite. Now he made her rock her body slowly back and forth. 'Very good,' he said, as the pressure moved against her, and he worked her nubbin until her breathing came in gulps. 'But now we must ready you for Lord Sardroc.' He sealed her leaves neatly about the tiny bursting ball of flesh. 'Get down now – quickly.'

He left her while he drifted along the wall, bobbing slowly up and down, lifting up the loops of leather, sorting them, turning back to look at Anya as if checking for her size, and gradually she realised it wasn't simply one item he was seeking. Each loop he selected was hooked over his arm or, if it was too small, over a finger, until he carried so many of these leather collars and wristbands that he looked almost like a juggler.

'There. Now let us see if they fit,' he said in that whisper of a voice. 'Sit on the table my dear; saves me having to bend.' Anya doubted he could do that if he tried. He stood in front of her with the bare skin of his belly overhanging his apron and enveloping her knees, like a goatskin full of warm water. 'Turn round.' He made her lift her feet onto the table and turn away from him while he tied her hair up and pinned it. 'There, now we can see that neck,' he said, running his fingers over Anya's shoulders and pressing his flab against her back. 'Such freckles . . . you're very sweet, my child.' Then she felt the collar being slipped round her neck. The suffocating feeling came as the thick band of leather was buckled about her throat; she thought she would choke. 'No – keep still.' He slapped her hand down sharply. Her heart was beating faster; the collar was buckled so closely that it made the suffocating feeling come again.

'Why? Why are you doing this to me?' she pleaded. He did not reply, but turned her round and fastened the bands round her wrists, very tightly, moving the chain out of the way, then round her ankles. Each wristband and ankleband had a metal catch. Anya guessed those catches must also be on her collar. 'Why are you doing this?' she asked again. 'What have I done?'

He sighed, stepped back to look at her, and brought his hands together. 'His lordship requires it, my dear,' he said, as if that explained everything.

'But why? What is he going to do to me?' She could imagine herself being fastened down, completely at the mercy of Sardroc's cruel eyes.

The turnkey only shrugged, then brought Anya's wrists together behind her back. A loud snap sounded and she could not move them apart. 'There. Now, you know,' he said. 'Does that make you feel better, my sweet little bird? Does this?' And now that her hands were helpless, he was playing with her nipples and smiling, making them hard again. She tried to move away, back across the table. 'Tch, tch – shall I shackle your feet together? Or, since these limbs seem so supple, perhaps fasten them behind your head?' He stroked his lower lip. 'We could while away the time like that until his lordship gets here – I'm sure I could amuse you.'

Anya felt the icy fear between her legs.

'Nn . . .' She formed the word; his eyebrows raised expectantly. Fortunately she could not get the word out.

'Now, I fear, we must play a rather more necessary game.

Squat, my dear, we must ready you for love.' He held a threatening finger up. 'Now – what have I warned you? That is better; place your feet apart.' Anya couldn't balance herself with her wrists still clipped behind her. Her weight was forced down between her thighs. He steadied her but insisted that she did as she was told – she had to edge her feet so far apart her thighs were aching and her sex was almost touching the table top. Then he pressed her waist down and gently rocked her; her flesh leaves brushed the surface, sending tickles up inside her. He spread her apart, then deliberately lowered her again until she suckered down upon the polished top. Her flesh had left a kiss mark there. She felt humiliated. 'Stay still.'

He left her and went over to a cupboard. It was full of jars and glass bottles of coloured liquids and small wooden boxes which rattled when he lifted them. He opened one bottle and sniffed the contents, then another, this time pushing his finger in and tasting with the tip of his tiny pink tongue; all of this left Anya in dread of what he meant to do. Then he opened an inset drawer and removed a stoppered glass tube containing something yellow. 'Ah,' he said with satisfaction, making Anya immediately very frightened of the contents. Her lips were trembling as he floated back and placed the glass tube directly in front of her.

'Capsules,' he declared and held them up. There were two in the tube, each about an inch across. 'Lord Sardroc prefers that they be applied beforehand to enhance his pleasure. No, do not fear, they will help sustain you too, my dear. They will bring you deep delight – in due course.' As he leaned forwards, his body touched her breasts; the oily dampness slicked against her as he moved, making her nipples tighten even though she hated this contact. His face was so close that his hot, sickly-sweet breath surrounded her. Anya had to look away. She looked up at the walls, at the flickering torchlight, and tried to shut her ears off from the sound of his breathing and the little grunts he made as if any movement were an effort.

'Now, look straight at me; do not move.' He held her chin so she was forced to look into his swollen sallow face and those tiny points of eyes. Then she felt his fingers there between her legs, touching, opening her leaves and – she wanted to close her eyes – a finger entered her. And her inner flesh disgraced her by closing around it, tightening and kissing that clinging skin though she did not want it to, though she wanted her flesh to expand away from this awful intimacy. The finger pulled against her as it withdrew; she felt the pulling all the way up inside her almost to her throat. Next, the capsule was inserted; its hard smoothness was pushed slowly up and up against her tightness until it would bed no deeper and it took her breath away, and all that time, even as the finger pushed that foreign body into her, she had been forced to look upon his face. Her sex was lined with a soft warmth where the capsule had stroked against her in its passage upwards; it made her feel distended; she could feel its roundness up against the mouth of her womb.

Suddenly there came a noise behind her, and she almost overbalanced with surprise. The turnkey was distracted. Anya tightened round his finger. A warder appeared in front of her with a closely collared female slave who wore a halter round her breasts. It was drawn so tightly that her breasts pushed up, and pressed so deeply through the webbing that her teats had turned deep purple. Both the warder and the slave were looking at Anya; she could not turn her face away for the turnkey still held her. But they were looking at his hand between her legs. She closed her eyes tightly against the shame.

The warder coughed. 'Lady Amalicia's slave,' he said. Anya knew that name; Lady Amalicia was the Prince's cousin, and Anya was sure she would never be so cruel as to send her slave down here. There must be some mistake.

'Take her into the training cells; you know what is required. Two hour sessions to begin with. Wait. This may be of interest to her.' Anya's heart sank. 'Open your eyes, my sweet . . .' The girl was held in front of Anya while the turnkey demonstrated. He removed his finger slowly; her tightness had not wanted to release it. Anya wanted to die. The girl looked very apprehensive. The turnkey moved round behind Anya; she had to close her eyes again as this

75

time the cheeks of her bottom were spread and then she heard the girl gasp as the capsule was pressed against her, then pushed inside, guided by the clinging finger, until she felt the wall of flesh within being trapped between the capsules; the soft warm feeling was now on both sides.

When she opened her eyes again, the two had gone; the turnkey helped her down. 'Do you feel it yet?' he asked. Anya hung her head in shame. He stroked her lower back. 'Soon it will come strongly; soon you will not be able to contain those feelings.' He chuckled softly. 'But we will help you, do not worry.' Now she was very much afraid; the warmth down there felt stronger, making her want to squeeze her thighs together and contract around the capsules, but she was unsure whether the sensation was real or merely fired by her imagination acting upon his words.

He led her from that place, crooking his finger, then pressing it against his lips and finally rolling his eyes and pointing towards a wide corridor to the right. A row of cells stretched down one side. Along the other was a plain stone wall with, every so often, a projecting block carved into the shape of a monstrous face. Running water trickled in a gutter at the foot of the wall. 'Sshhh,' he whispered, and tiptoed along. The cells were all the same – each a semi-circular arch of stone with bars extending from the ceiling to the floor, which was sand, covered with straw. Anyone in the corridor had an uninterrupted view into the cell.

What she saw in the first cell took Anya's breath. There were three people – a male and a female warder, both stripped to the waist, and a female slave. The warders had noticed the interlopers but the slave was quite oblivious. She was suspended from the ceiling. The woman's wristbands were fastened together and a rope had been slung between them and attached to a hook in the ceiling. What frightened Anya more was the way in which the woman's fingers writhed. They were the only parts of her that moved. It was as if all her turmoil were concentrated there. The rest of her body, though quite still, was tight. She hung like a straining statue, although her legs were stretched out horizontally. The female warder stood in front of her, holding her feet apart. Behind the bondslave stood the man. Anya could not see what he was doing to her but one hand was stroking her back and the other was between her legs; she could see his wrist moving. The woman's belly shuddered; the female warder bent forwards and began to suck her nipples. Anya saw the hand from behind slide upwards to press across the belly that had shuddered and she heard the woman's moan. She felt her own belly waver in sympathy with the slave's, and then her own involuntary contraction against the capsule bedded up to the mouth of her womb. A slow warmth was spreading outwards from that point inside her.

Her legs felt heavy as the turnkey silently moved her along to the next tableau. The churning wave came again. This slave was secured with her back to a post and her hands above her head, behind the post, fastened high so that with her feet so wide apart, she had to stand on tiptoes, which pushed her bottom out against the post. A female warder sat in front of her on a stool. Beside her was a bucket. Again the woman's body seemed tight and seemed to ooze with unfathomed sensuality. The air was heavy with the scent of prolonged denial. The warder's breasts swayed as she bent over the bucket and withdrew the brush which seemed to be coated in a heavy oil or paste. The globules dropped back with thickened, deadened splashes. The slave bit her lip. Her belly contracted to a hard round drum; she held her breath, and her breasts began to quiver. But the warder was waiting for something else. At last the slave pushed out her tongue and arched her legs out higher and pressed her shoulders back, which forced her belly to reach out towards the dripping brush. Then Anya could almost feel the woman's flesh being pasted – in slow wet strokes, as if the warder had all the time in the world, up one inner thigh, along the join, then up the other, working only upwards in that one place, recharging the brush, until the girl seemed to rise higher and higher upon her toes to escape the slow wet pleasuring, then finally gasped out loud, whereupon the pasting stopped and the warder waited, kneading the girl's nipples, until the brushing could begin again, using always the upstroke, always with the girl's tongue pushed out, until a curtain of paste slid down her thighs to drip upon the straw. Then Anya jumped; the turnkey's fingers had touched her belly and then had touched her back.

'What do you think, my dear?' he whispered in her ear. His fingers brushed her bottom as he spoke.

'Why. . . ?' Anya could not phrase any other answer.

He chuckled softly. 'Why not? These are special slaves, undergoing special punishment, enjoying special pleasures.' Anya's eyes widened. Would she be subjected to this treatment, she wondered? She dared not ask directly.

'The Taskmistress?' she whispered. She had to know this, at least.

'No – these are Lady Amalicia's slaves, some of her favourites.' Anya could not believe it of the Prince's cousin. Did she know what was actually being done to her slaves? Her face had always seemed so fresh and innocent.

The turnkey beckoned again, as if he might have read her mind and now, as she advanced towards the third cell, Anya could feel the swelling warmth making her pulse race; with every step, tickling feelings wormed like tendrils from the deeply lodged capsules. Through the bars she could see a male warder and a female slave. The slave was being fitted to a wooden framework, a little like the one that Anya had been forced to sit astride, but consisting of two horizontal bars, one half as high as the other, supported on uprights fixed to a base. The higher bar looked worn and smooth. The slave was made to bend over the upper bar and touch the floor. Her back then touched the lower. The warder took her arms beneath this bar and drew them back above it, then fastened them to ropes attached to the upper one. The lower bar, which passed between her back and arms, was now adjusted by moving it down and back, so that the woman's body was held in a double curve, with her back curved sharply downwards, her hips bent tightly over the upper bar and her breasts pushed out so strongly beneath the lower that they almost touched the floor. Anya could see her nipples poking out. Her feet were tied apart, to the bases of the uprights.

'Have you seen enough now?' the turnkey murmured in her ear. Anya did not listen to him; he was showing her these things deliberately to stimulate her wanting. But the scene in front of her, the capsules in her belly, were making her feel so lustful; she had to know what would happen to the woman. She had to know if it would be punishment or pleasure. Anya grasped the bars very tightly and held her breath; she knew exactly what the woman must be feeling. The turnkey understood; he spread Anya's thighs and jammed her feet between the bars so she could not move them back. Then he pressed her body against the metal – hard – so her breasts were squeezed between the bars and pushed out like this woman's were. His stubby fingers were stroking the cheeks of Anya's bottom; she could feel them but she could not move away. Her body did not want to. The woman had turned her head and briefly looked at Anya; the glance had been, not forlorn, but charged with sensuality, and suddenly Anya wanted to be in there with her; she wanted to be close to that woman, doing those forbidden things to her.

The warder had begun to play with the slave. He stood behind her, calmly playing with her. The woman could not move. Anya could see his hand pushed through her legs and pressed against her belly; then it stood away from her and stroked, just as those other fingers were deliberately stroking Anya's bottom. The warder bent forward and the woman moaned; he had kissed her back, very low down, where its curvature changed, in the tender spot; her belly had at that moment pushed down so seductively to meet his stroking fingers, which now retreated to a point between her thighs. Anya was burning up – her body burned to know just what his fingers were doing to the slave. Anya lifted on her toes; she did not care about the turnkey – that he was ugly, that he was here to punish her, that his fingers were stumpy and warm and sticky. She needed those fingers against her flesh now, in the way the warder's fingers must be against the woman. She pushed her bottom out; though her cheeks were burning bright, she had to do it. The capsules deep inside were moving – slowly turning in her liquid – the liquid that was melting from her body. But his fingers would not touch her in the way she needed.

Inside the cell, the warder stood back to stroke the slave; he stroked her bottom. Then his fingers began to probe her; her breathing changed; she murmured something, some protest or request. Anya was beside herself. She pushed her bottom out harder, to separate the cheeks; though it was wrong to do, she could not help herself, she could not help the way her body felt. Then she held her breath – the turnkey's fingers tickled in the gap at last, exactly where she wanted them, gently touching the mouth of her bottom, softly testing it.

The warder had picked up a large carved cockstem. Anya watched him fitting it below the slave's upturned bottom, between her thighs, then slowly pushing it into the yielding fleshy peach. And though her ankles were restrained, the woman lifted up on tiptoes. As she did so, the turnkey's fingers parted Anya's leaves of flesh and stroked along their edges, but did not enter her. Why did he not penetrate her? She tried to bear down hard to open herself and the feeling was as if the ball inside was sucking her, drawing her nectar from her body, and her liquid, seeping down, was making the inner walls of her sex sensitive, so hot that even his thick fingers would feel cool against her burning flesh. And now, all Anya could see was the large carved pair of bumps between the woman's legs. She was penetrated to the hilt, yet Anya had nothing – only that slow tickling round the mouth of her sex which just made her craving more acute.

Then she saw the woman's belly move, and that was even worse; the man had hold of the cockstem by the bumps and was lifting it, moving it in a circle. Each time the bumps reached the top of the circle, something pushed against the woman's belly from inside. But still the warder had not finished; in his hand was a second cockstem slightly smaller than the one bedded in her body. Anya's heart was beating so loudly that she was sure that everyone must hear it. The capsule up her bottom stirred; she wanted to close her eyes but how could she? She had to see that cockstem being dipped at first to dripping point in a bowl of oil then slowly being pushed into the woman; the only sounds were the woman's gasping, and Anya's heartbeat in her throat; the oil dripped silently from between the bondslave's legs and onto the floor. And finally Anya was forced to close her eyes, for she felt the turnkey's finger sliding up her bottom, very slowly on and up until it touched against the capsule and triggered a tight contraction against the pleasure of that wrongful penetration. And if the turnkey had brushed a hand between her thighs and lifted her, with that finger still inside her, and spread her leaves and touched her nubbin even once, she would have cried out and delivered herself to wantonness there and then. The turnkey simply waited till her contraction had subsided and then equally slowly drew the finger out.

'Turn round, my dear.'

Anya was full of shame with herself for taking pleasure in this perverse way without her being forced to do so. She did not want to face him, but he made her admit to him that those sticky fingers had given her delight.

'I have taken pleasure wantonly.' He made her say it over and over, while he held her flesh and smeared her wetness round her nubbin, round and round until her face was burning bright, until her knees were buckling and she was on the brink of pleasure, then he turned her round and made her hold her cheeks apart and smacked her till she could not get her breath. The capsules throbbed and seemed to swell so hard inside her that she could not stand up straight. Then with his fingers gripped again about her flesh and his hand about her chain, she was dragged along the corridor to the next cell, which was empty.

It contained only a low wooden bed with a mattress and some rods propped in the corner. As she waited for him to open the gate, she glimpsed a movement in the cell beyond and then she heard a groan. She jumped back – a male slave had been pushed against the bars. She could not see who was behind him or what was being done to force the sounds of deep yet needful protest, to make the muscles on his legs go cramped and to make his cockstem push so strongly upwards between the bars. But she could feel the capsules inside her swelling still, making her feel hot and heavy down there.

The turnkey led her in. 'You must await Lord Sardroc,' he said. 'You shall rest whilst the capsules take effect.' He laid her on her side on the mattress. He crossed her arms over her breasts and fastened her wrists to the catches on the collar and the collar to the bed. Then he brought across a rod and, placing it upright beside the bed and level with her shoulders, he thrust the end into the sand then tested it for firmness. He fastened her ankles round it, so now her body was held firmly, tightly bent. Finally, he pushed a finger into her at the front until it touched the capsule and made it kiss against the entrance to her womb; then he spread her cheeks and pushed the finger up the back. The capsule had moved up into her. Even with his finger pushed in to the knuckle he could not reach it. He seemed satisfied with this. Then he left her and she heard the gate being locked behind him. His footsteps retreated down the corridor.

The cell was not silent. Above her breathing and the beating of her heart she could hear noises all the time – subdued echoes along the corridor and then more distinctly, from the cell next door, the woman's softly pleading voice. Anya knew her plea was not for mercy but for deliverance. The image lay with her still – the cockstem moving, causing the woman's belly to ripple. How long would that torture last? How long would her own? She could hear broken phrases from the cell to the other side. There must be at least two women in there with the male slave, and one was instructing the other. 'Open him more fully,' she had said, then, 'No, let me . . .' and 'Quick – the cord! Wrap it round first . . .' Then she had heard a groan that sounded as if the slave's heart and soul were being drawn out through his cockstem. And though Anya could not move, she felt the ball of torment shift inside her, drawing once again, sucking at the mouth of her womb and sending out its filaments of lust deep into her body, making her try to squeeze her thighs together but, with her legs drawn up, not being able to apply the squeezing where she needed it, round her swollen peach and the pushed out burning pip between her legs. She could feel her body oozing. A slow syrup of denial was welling out of her, soaking thinly into the hairs around her sex, then turning hot and sticky. And the second ball was burning her. Her bottom felt as if it were held open while a soft fire licked inside. She shuddered, then just as quickly shivered with delight, for she was imagining a hand against her there, with her restrained in this position, splitting apart her leaves and gently oiling her nubbin whilst cool thin flesh entered her to stem the cruel burning in her bottom. And the hand she had imagined was Lord Sardroc's hand and the long cool flesh was Sardroc's cockstem. Anya's belly trembled once again beneath the sweet beguilement of that illicit thought.

Another fugitive cry of pleasure echoed down the passage. She wished that cry were hers.

[6]

Lord Sardroc's Pleasure

When Anya woke up she had the peculiar sensation that the reverse had happened, that exhaustion had finally tumbled her into sleep and she was dreaming – for the scene seemed so unreal. She didn't know how long she had been asleep; probably not long, but now she was not fastened down. A table had appeared and there were four people round her bed, although only three were visible. One was a male warder and one the turnkey; they stood near the door; it was the other two that worried her. An old woman dressed in drab and ragged clothes was bending over her. She had a hooked nose and on her chin was a whiskered mole; her hair was blue-grey with bits of straw matted into it. Anya was very frightened by this woman. She had never seen a witch before. It was the witch's bony finger that had prodded her awake.

'There, my lord,' she had cried in her cracked sharp voice, as Anya's eyelids opened.

'Have her turn over, Thelda,' was all the soft clear voice behind her had said. Anya knew that voice well, and soft though it was, it had fallen like an ice-cold cascade across her back and shoulders, making the hairs upon her body bristle, making her lower belly and her bottom tighten hard against the capsules fitted there.

'Will that be all, Lord Sardroc?' the turnkey whispered. Anya heard no reply, but then the turnkey and the warder withdrew.

The witch shook Anya and tried to lift her arm. Anya pulled away.

'You are very shy, my dear – turn over.' That voice again made Anya freeze. 'Turn over!' he said more sharply, and

84

now she felt the cold weight of his blue-grey eyes upon her nakedness. His lordship's arms were folded. His hair shone black with oil. 'Move your hands away. I hope you are not going to prove difficult, like your friend upstairs is doing . . .' He smiled.

Anya was terrified now. She should have spoken out; she should have asked him what he had done with Axine, why he was punishing her when all she had done was intercede to help a friend in trouble, but she was too frightened to speak. He stroked her cheek; she wanted to turn her head away but dared not. And she could smell a woman's heat upon his fingers; she knew it was Axine's.

He made her place her hands behind her head to expose her underarms. But that was not the worst. She was forced to part her thighs and then to bend her knees and spread until it hurt. She was so ashamed to have to do this. 'I wish to see that blackness,' he said, 'but I wish to see it in its fullness. Has any man seen your blackness in that state?' He stroked her curls; Anya shivered. She could feel the prickly droplets forming on her forehead; her skin was gathering up to gooseflesh at his words. 'I thought not. Push; push out that flesh now . . .' The backs of two fingers closed about her unresisting leaves and very gently pulled them; the pulling made her throb, and while he pulled he stroked his fingers over her belly, lifting her chain and readjusting it, making it tickle against her. 'So smooth,' he mused, and pulled her proffered leaves again.

'Have the capsules been administered, Thelda?'

'Yes, my lord.'

His fingertips ran up the crease at the top of Anya's leg and hesitated when Anya shuddered. It was as if he was trying to coax the tendrils of desire from her body; it felt as if those tendrils were licking down from inside to kiss against his fingers where they touched her. He opened out her leaves. He did it very tenderly, yet so slowly that Anya felt her body was being peeled in two. 'So black,' he whispered, and the tendrils brushed across her outspread moistness. 'So liquid in there . . . let me see . . .' He opened her out more widely and Anya's cheeks burned with shame. Her body burned with wanting, and Sardroc must have known it. He was flattening the edge of one leaf between his fingers, working round, up one side and down the other, squeezing the softness firmly into shape – forming her flesh into an upstanding ear about her fleshpot – then he quickly dipped into her and drew a thread of syrup out and wound it round her nubbin. Anya's neck was burning from the way her body was dishonouring her, but overlaying that hot shame was the fear.

'Hmm . . . I entrust her to your care, then, Thelda,' he said, pursing her leaves together again.

She realised now that what had been placed beside the bed was a waist-high bench. In design, it was somewhere between a narrow table, a short bed and a box with a padded top, but at one end were a pair of stirrups. Their presence unnerved her. 'Up here, my dear,' Thelda said and chuckled to herself as she patted the bench top. 'Sit here.' With increasing trepidation, Anya climbed onto it; she was made to sit at the end then lie back. With the bench being so narrow, her legs fell open. 'There . . . wider.' Thelda bent her knees and fitted her feet to the leather stirrups. Then she could feel those bony fingers shaking as they dug into her belly. 'Good and firm,' the woman croaked. 'You've got a good one here, my lord.'

'I hope so, this time, Thelda. I do hope so,' Sardroc said coldly.

'Ah yes, last time was unfortunate . . .' Thelda shook her head, making Anya begin to imagine all sorts of things that might have gone wrong.

The old woman next unfastened Anya's chain, then disappeared from view and reappeared with a pot and brush. She stirred the brush round very quickly in the pot and beat it back and forth, then held it up. The lather was thick and creamy. She beat it again. Anya could feel the threads of ticklish warmth extending once again from the capsules bedded in her body. Thelda stood between her legs and held the brush above her. Her belly tightened to a drum. The lather slapped down as Anya tried to squirm away; the lukewarm liquid spread across her flesh. The woman worked it against her belly, round and round below the navel, slicking down the curls into darkened swirling patterns, charging the brush again, working downwards into Anya's parted thighs, making her want to close her legs against the liquid stroking. The wetness tickled her flesh to goosebumps; the slow circles of pressure stirred down into her body. More lather was tipped upon her. Thelda brushed it into the hairs at the tops of Anya's thighs then worked it carefully into the creases. She held the leaves of Anya's sex to the side, stroking up and down them until Anya could almost feel the stroking on the inside. The constant wet brushing of her tender skin, the persistent upstrokes to the sides, were making her flesh leaves swell and Anya knew that if that stroking should continue her tiny flaming bud of lust would distend to peeping point and the brush would tickle against its tip and then she would disgrace herself. Her cheeks flushed hot at the thought of that and yet she did not really want that stroking pleasure to stop.

Now Thelda had taken Anya's leaves and gently pulled them while she worked the lather round them; Anya felt her sex squeeze hard against the capsule and it moved. That movement, in her present state of pleasured tension, made her belly overturn. Thelda stopped, turned her head to one side and looked at Anya as if waiting for something to happen. The bubbles of lather were beginning to burst, showering tickles over her skin as all her captive curls sprang free.

When Thelda produced the razor and the strop, Anya strained to close her thighs even though her feet were held quite firmly in the stirrups. But she could not bring her knees together. 'I fear you must open your legs wider, my dear. I need some room to move. And keep still – we don't want any accidents.' Anya's sex contracted away from this terrifying threat. The hand that held the razor shook and nearly dropped it.

Lord Sardroc stretched Anya's arms out behind her head, holding her hands together, then lifted her head and pinned her elbows back beneath it, so her breasts were drawn up across her ribcage; the skin was stretched out tightly and she could not move her head. 'Push down; keep that belly tight,' he whispered then bent and drew his tongue across her lips exactly at the moment that the razor touched her belly. She shivered as the cold steel cut a swath across her flesh. Now he was looking into her eyes, staring at her with a quiet calmness, holding her eyes captive as the line of cutting coldness pressed against her again, sweeping down and working in her ticklishness of crease, working towards her burning leaves. And as he kissed her the second time, she felt that delicate, very private part of her being taken between Thelda's shaking fingers and folded to the side and then the metal line of pressure against it in short sharp one-way scratches which pulled across her very nervous flesh, so virgin to this perverse treatment, to make the skin crawl and retract only to be drawn and stretched out by those fingers once again and re-tickled with light quick shaky scratches, then folded over the other way and tantalized with a slowly marching line of very uncertain pressure working first across the crease, then into the smooth and oh, so tender and easily sliced skin where her flesh leaves joined her mound. Then, with her leaves drawn straight out from her body and pulled tight, the fine hard edge was swept across each side yet again, until finally, in narrow, careful yet still shaking little backstrokes, it flicked around the hooded flesh that sheathed about her pip.

And all the while as Thelda shaved her sensitized mound, so hard with Anya's tightness, and worked the razor in tiny strokes around her hot soft leaves that lay so pliantly between Thelda's cold hard fingers, those lips of Sardroc's closed around her own to capture them, to suck upon them and subdue her, to taste her trembling sensuality – the delicious edge of fear – and to savour the first step in the pilgrimage to pleasurable abeyance that this tight full-breasted gently frightened body would be made to suffer at his hands.

Suddenly Anya's belly contracted strongly and the capsule burst inside her sex. Her body shook; she whimpered as Lord Sardroc pushed his tongue into her mouth. Then the freezing pleasure came as the contents of the capsule squirted out inside – threads of ice pushed up and kissed inside her womb. An icy needle from inside her pierced through her nubbin and it felt as if an ice-cold silken thread was being forced out through the tip, heaping cool fine squirming coils upon the surface of her smoothly shaven fleshpot. She moaned against the lips that held her down. Her belly lifted from the bench. The feeling was exquisite.

'My lord, the capsule has melted. See – her belly trembles.' Anya could not stop the shudders from the iciness inside, against her inner warmth, and now the bathing of her fleshpot in a gently pulsing pleasure.

'Good, very good. My compliments to the turnkey. His timing is excellent.' Now Anya could feel her leaves begin to swell up. She could feel them filling, so hard that the pleasure had turned painful, and so very, very cold.

'Look, my lord – her flesh lips are responding.' Anya felt his lordship's fingers palpating her, tapping her freezing puffed up leaves until they shook, then pressing them over on their side until their freezing coldness touched against the smooth warmth of her mound. He squeezed them gently and she felt that they would burst. She gasped against the pleasure.

'Now let's have her over and finish the job.' Her shaking body was lifted and turned until the bench top pressed into her belly and her sex overhung the end. Her knees were bent once more and fitted to the stirrups. The weight of pleasure seemed to drain into her there and made her flesh feel heavy, so the slightest movement made it swing between her legs. Then the second capsule burst and Anya felt as if an ice cold finger had been pushed into her bottom. The feeling came again, the feeling of a very long thread being drawn out of her, this time through her bottom; the squirming loops of icy pleasure wriggled in the groove. Then Thelda lathered her in her groove.

She felt the supple brush-head working up and down there, stroking cold thick lather across that even colder tightly puckered mouth, then twirling round and dabbing till the bristle tips pricked against it like tiny needles, making her move her hips from side to side in a vain attempt to escape the brush, which merely followed. And as this long-drawn-out and intricate creaming progressed, his lordship stood beside her, tickling her back, spreading her locks across her shoulders then gathering them up again so the hairs brushed against her skin, then drawing her hands behind her, clipping her wrists together, back to back, and lifting up her outstretched arms until her muscles ached, simply to make her breasts overhang the sides so he could play with her nipple while he waited, dipping his fingers first into the pot of lather then working the cream around the velvet tip.

Then Anya heard the stropping sound again. 'Keep very still,' Thelda croaked, and Anya felt a thumping in her throat. She felt the bony fingers pushing into the left cheek of her bottom, stretching the skin to ticklishness, and then the itching brushing scrape, first to the left side of her groove and then to the right.

'Push out, my dear.' Thelda had the brush again; she twirled the tip to a point precisely in the centre and as Anya felt her nipple rolling slowly and moistly between Lord Sardoc's fingers, the brush point peeped up inside her body and twisted round to take her breath away. Finally, the corner of the blade was teased in minute hesitant scrapes around the pouted mouth before Thelda dabbed her dry and stroked her hand across her bottom.

'There, my lord. Do you wish her perfumed?'

'No, I think not.'

Thelda now refastened Anya's chain. 'Then she is finished. Would your lordship care to check her?'

'Mm. Move her down a little – there.' The end of the bench pressed into Anya just below her navel, and with her knees pushed up so tightly by her footholds in the stirrups, the pressure was transmitted to her mound – her newly fashioned nectarine of love – and to her very swollen, cool yet slowly warming leaves which felt like they were bursting. 'Very good, Thelda, very smooth,' he murmured. His fingertips brushed up Anya's thighs, then softly round her mound. 'Just the way I like these girls. We must keep her like this now, fresh and smooth and hard – twice a day.' He sighed with satisfaction. The backs of his fingers stroked across her dangling flesh, not touching her body at all, but stroking slowly back and to across the incurved bursting edges, lifting her leaves, making them sway, then crooking a finger round the hood, yet not squeezing, as her nubbin wanted him to do, but restraining, making its presence felt whilst with a fingertip he tickled in her groove, brushing gentle downsweeps across her velvet mouth. That kind of stroking always made her feel so lewd; she wanted that finger up inside her, but all he did was hold her hooded nubbin very lightly with the undelivered promise of a squeeze and kiss his padded fingertip repeatedly against her bottom mouth. He did it till her body writhed. Then he lifted her down with a hand beneath her belly and a hand across her breast and rolled her onto the bed.

'Thank you, Thelda. You have done well; you may leave us. The slave will take her pleasure now.' Anya's heart was blocking her throat. 'And her pleasure will be to satisfy her lord in any manner of his choosing. Is that not so, my sweet?'

Anya lay upon her back; her hands were still fastened beneath her, pushing into her back and arching her belly upwards. The edge of wanting deep inside was whetted on her fear; she knew he would show no mercy; she could see it in his eyes as he waited for her to speak. He had laid her belly naked and now he would lay that belly open with his flesh. She could not form the words of a reply. She answered him in her obeisance – in the way her thighs lay open to his pleasure, in the way she now offered up the softness of her curve of neck for his teeth to browse upon, and in the way she blinked her liquid eyes – very softly, once. And though his lordship never even touched her, those fingers – those other fingers of cool delicious fear – pushed into her and probed between her open thighs, probed into the beating heart of Anya's living flesh and shed the serpent of sweet seduction into her, the slow snake of submission which slipped its slender head deep inside and insinuated its sucking tongue into her womb. Anya's breath was drawn right out of her body, for his hand had spread about and pressed softly down upon the belly that the cool snake sucked within.

'Now, what is your pleasure, my darling?'

'To sss . . ' Anya was choking. The snake was pushing upwards, sliding up her throat. Its tongue was licking out to taste the fear within her mouth, the sickly-sweet and base submission which was welling there to drown her.

'Hmm . . .?'

'To . . . To satisfy my . . . lord,' she gurgled and her freshly naked belly squirmed beneath his hand as that liquid snake, so thickly coated with saliva, withdrew and twisted tightly down again to nest within her womb.

Her lord smiled upon her, then lifted her feet. Her toes were enclosed within a single fist, and Anya was defenceless, her hands tied, her knees bent tightly and her feet held fast while her master slowly drew a finger over the smoothness of her mound, stroking lines of pleasure across the sensitized skin which felt so cool since every breath of air was free to whisper in its polished creases and caress its nudity. But her leaves of flesh were not cool now; they were hot, swollen up with blood and sealed tight about her softly burning nubbin which was yearning for the caressing fingertip to push into her flesh and kiss against it – to keep coaxing it with tiny kisses whilst his hand stayed gripped around her toes, pushing her feet down firmly against her belly, rocking her body against his finger, keeping her fleshpot tight unto bursting throughout that fingertip kissing, subduing her with delight.

Her lord released her toes and stretched her legs and spread them on the mattress, then fastened her ankles to the bedframe to keep them wide apart. He knelt upon the bed while he pressed a hand onto her mound and pushed two fingers into her. They split her like a knife of pleasure pushed between her thighs. He pushed them in just once – but to the knuckles, and Anya briefly felt those knuckles press against her pip – then withdrew them dripping with her heat. He pushed back the hood of flesh from her palpitating nubbin and held it that way, tightly back, until the tension was so deep and sweet that Anya had to push. And while she moved her hips and pushed her pink-red nubbin out so wantonly, Lord Sardroc looked upon her lewdness and sucked upon those fingers that were buttered with her heat.

His lordship now removed his robes. His cockstem curved up hard and thick and very stiffly yet not, as she had imagined it, from a smoothly shaven base, but from a dense black bush of hair which bristled part way up the stem.

He rearranged her on the bed. He untethered her ankles and made her kneel up facing him with her thighs spread and then lean back to support her body with her hands upon the bed. He clipped her wristbands to her ankles. Her body formed a smooth tight curve towards him. Her freckled breasts hung heavily, the black tips drawn out to the side by the stretching of her shoulders. And he removed her chain; now the surface of her belly curved unbroken in its tense and perfect smoothness to the double pouch of blackness, the stiffly swollen leaves of flesh so pressurised with desire, pushed out in wanton sexuality between her tight white thighs which strained so hard to keep that black pouch proffered to its master. Lord Sardroc pushed her knees so far apart that her thighs began to ache and her pouted flesh now almost touched the mattress. He took her leaves between his fingers and slowly pulled them whilst a finger circled softly round her navel. Anya felt her nub of flesh begin to slip between them and stiffen up; her leaves were oiled with seepage. Lord Sardroc pulled again – a long slow pull which seemed to pull right through her belly. He was watching her expression. She loved this pleasure but she did not want to look upon him. Her eyelids felt heavy. His fingers closed around the hood and shook it very quickly, then suddenly stopped, then rolled the leaves around the pip, then again shook it rapidly until Anya felt the vibrations through the centre of her nubbin. She knew that if those delicious tremblings were to continue she would very soon deliver herself to pleasure on his hand.

Now he spread the hood back to reveal the glistening nubbin. He flicked it with his finger, then stroked the finger up the join at the very top of her thigh at one side, flicked the nubbin very firmly, then stroked up the other crease, along the smoothly shaven skin, then flicked the nubbin once again and in this fashion – having first instructed her very clearly that her pleasure must not precipitate – with this alternating very ticklish stroking, then the sharp snap against her bursting pip of pleasure, he systematically reduced his slave to a state of ruddy-cheeked, rigid-nippled, drum-tight bellied, long-drawn-out abeyance. He then took time to smooth his palms across her tense hot body and to press his lips to those aromatic places misted with her sexual heat – her warm and fragrant underarms, the under-bellies of her breasts, those thigh joins he had only just been stroking – and to brush his lips, not kissing fully, but merely nuzzling in a suggestion of a browse, against her hot and silky darkened sex lips, full of heavy liquid, which dangled so provocatively beneath her lifted, shaking, pushed out mound and stimulated his taste buds with that burning strength of female slavish need which would force him onwards to punish her with pleasure beyond remission.

Then, having stirred his own flesh to greater ardour with her musky scent upon his lips and cheeks, and very strongly on his fingers, he took the jug of oil that had stood upon the floor and oiled her sweet tense shaking body – all the smoothly rounded sensual parts that were placed at his disposal – till it dripped. He tipped the aromatic liquid on his palm and smeared it round the right breast, gathering up its weight, reawakening the nipple, pulling it, moulding his fingers wetly round the teat and drawing the slipperiness through, working it up to a hard black stone on a soft and pliant stalk, then moving to the left breast, this time cupping the breast itself and dripping the oil upon the teat then, placing the jug very carefully on the floor, holding the breast up still and working the nipple with his other hand, pulling it till it slipped back through his fingers, pulling once again to slipping point, placing his hand across the breast and squeezing till the nipple pushed out through his fingers then trapping it while rubbing his other palm in a circle round its poked out tip. And having worked Anya's breasts to a pressurised warmth of wanting, he next

94

massaged her belly, pouring oil upon it, slipping his finger in her navel, melting her gently with his outspread hand until she was burning for that oiling to move downwards. This time, after making her spread and bear down hard between her legs and ensuring that the lips about her sex stood out strongly, he formed his hand into a cup sealed about her pot of flesh; he poured the oil to brimming point within that cup. Anya felt the line of liquid rising up against her smooth bare flesh, up around the lips, then seeping in to flood around her nubbin. And then his middle finger moved and slowly slid into her sex, then out again, splitting the cup and causing the oil to trickle down her thighs. Sardroc sat back, forming his hand into a fist with the middle finger-stuck straight out. With her body still in that tight back-curve, he made her mould her flesh around the finger then slide back and forth along it, squeezing very tightly, pushing hard against his fist, taking pleasure in this way. Then once again he manipulatd her, making her flesh leaves slip, shaking them very nervously till she gasped, then nipping cruelly till the pleasure ebbed, then massaging yet again until she was compelled to beg for mercy.

'Please . . . my lord?' His eyebrows raised. He watched her breasts swell and shudder with each softly panting breath. 'I can . . . I cannot bear this pleasure. . .'

'Very well.' He released her wrists from her ankles. 'Turn round. Kneel up. Head down. Cheek on the bed. Get that bottom up.' He slapped it with a snap. She was forced to double tightly by digging her toes into the mattress and straining till her knees touched her breasts. Her face and neck were burning at having to expose herself this way when she could not know what would be done to her. Sardroc knelt behind her. Once again he held the jug of oil. He oiled her sex and bottom simultaneously; his hand worked up and down the groove and round the mound, beside the swollen leaves, dripping oil upon her all the while. He worked his fingers into her, one at first, at the front, then at the back and when this entered smoothly, two fingers, then three. Anya found it very difficult to accommodate these three fingers. She could feel them stroking round inside her, then holding her open against her tightness while the oil was poured inside her upturned bottom and her sex. He sealed the flesh lips tightly while he pushed a finger into her bottom and curled it round to press against the oil filled sac. Then he released his hold and sat back and watched the leaves split apart and the liquid, warmed to thinness by her body, trickle out across her pip and drip upon the nipples down below.

'And how is she progressing?' The sound of that voice struck terror into Anya. She tried to bury her face, but Sardroc lifted her up and held her by her chin. The Taskmistress stood in the passageway, watching. How long had she been there?

'She is learning, but rather slowly I fear, Taskmistress.' He spread Anya's legs and opened out her dripping flesh as if to demonstrate.

'Hmm. Bring her over. Perhaps I can assist.'

Sardroc carried Anya across and pushed her against the bars. Ildren stood back. 'My lord, you must be more firm with these creatures,' she said. Sardroc placed one hand between Anya's shoulders and the other at her hips and pushed very hard until her breasts were squeezed between the bars and her sex was pressed against the bar that cleaved them. The Taskmistress smiled. She drew Anya's arms through and tied them to the bars; the same was done with her feet, which forced her belly more closely to the metal. Her body formed a cross. The Taskmistress produced a short length of thin black cord with a slip knot at each end; she fastened these loops tightly round Anya's nipples, drawing each nipple through the loop while she secured it, then testing the cord by pulling.

'There, my lord. . .' A delicious sinking fear was being drawn out of her between her legs as Sardroc spread her cheeks and leisurely oiled between them. He pressed his cockstem up against her bottom mouth. 'Push,' he said. The curled up snake of pleasure within her belly began uncoiling very slowly. 'Open your body. . .' Its tail unfurled and began sliding backwards along the inside of her bottom. The Taskmistress's fingers were touching Anya's nipples, pulling at their ends, tapping them, making them swell up hard against the tight constriction. 'Your pleasure shall be to take this cockhead into you. . .' The oily tail pushed down again and tickled at the tight sealed whirlpool from inside. The pressure of his cockstem was increased.

'This velvet mouth must yield to my requirement.' Her master's voice was soft yet very steady in her ear. She knew it would permit no refusal. He laid his hand upon her back – lightly, low down, stroking with the backs of his fingers, tickling the soft hairs. Ildren's hands had pushed between the bars to press against her belly. The pressure there, the stroking in her back, they encompassed her, seduced her, nutured Anya's need. Now Ildren's fingertips softly probed, transmitting pleasure to the pulsing flesh between her tightened leaves. The slow pressure of pleasure, the prolonged tightness, the delicious fear that dripped into her blood, the edge of wanting, the honeyed pain of long denial would surely melt her to their will.

Anya knew she was a slave – a slave of love, but a slave, too, of her desires, a bondslave to these unremitting pleasures laced with constant apprehension.

'Now push against me, make that bottom spread. I wish to feel your tightened flesh suck pleasure from this cockhead.' Anya closed her eyes. She did not want this thing to happen; she did not want this degradation forced upon her. He would have to take her; she would never do it willingly. She could feel the hard polished head of flesh pushing up against her; at the front she could feel the pressure-pleasure distending her nubbin for Ildren now to stroke, to stroke the oily pleasure into it, to make the snake tail move again inside her bottom, stabbing softly where it should not, pushing out, pushing through the eye of flesh.

'There. Spread for me. . .' The stroking came again to seduce her to forbidden pleasure; she moved her hips; she felt that snake tail probing for the tiny mouth within that cockstem, seeking out the entrance to his tube. Sardroc softly groaned. As Anya pushed, that snake, the snake of her desire, had found him and was slowly threading down his tube, distending him just as his cockhead now distended

97

her, working down inside him to curl up tight within him. And Anya could feel those tightened coils of snake inside his bag rest heavily against her; she could feel his fleshy plum held captive by her body. She squeezed to make him groan again with pleasure. Then the Taskmistress took each of Anya's leaves and pulled them till her nubbin touched the bar and made her gasp; her flesh was moulded round it, so when Sardroc moved and pushed against her, her flesh slipped up the bar, then down again, with Ildren's fingers stroking round it, so now she was defenceless; she could not control the sliding pleasure, the pressure of the oily surface up against her nubbin, the delicious splitting of her flesh which made her tighten hard around the cockstem that impaled her. The Taskmistress hooked her fingers round the cord between her nipples, and with each thrust that Sardroc took, she gave the cord a twist and increased her grip about the flesh that moulded to the bar, until Anya tightened up so much against the sweet metallic pressure in that place she brought his lordship on in hot quick spurts within her sucking body. He gasped and dragged her hips back from the bar then pulled his cockstem out of her, not tenderly, but very quickly, so it pulled her flesh and hurt her, and left her pleasure cruelly interrupted.

His lordship dressed, then left without another word. The Taskmistress slowly shook her head. Anya was in tears.

But at last his heartless usage of her body, the nightmare of degradation was at an end. Why did he want to torture her body in this way? Why did he not permit her pleasure?

The Taskmistress carefully unfastened her breasts, her wrists and feet, then entered the cell, led her to the bed and bade her lie down. She stroked her cheeks very softly, then kissed her fully on the lips. And though Anya hated this woman for what had happened, for what she had allowed Lord Sardroc to do to her, for the way she had even helped him to humiliate her, still she found that soft kissing very tender and almost reassuring, as if the Taskmistress understood her pain and fear, as if she might even care. The Taskmistress rubbed her body down with a soft towel, then

98

took an even softer cloth, moistened it with water, then worked it very gently into Anya's body, into the tender place that Sardroc had so cruelly desecrated. She planted a soft moist kiss on Anya's belly, a kiss which made her sigh. Anya's body began to glow beneath the soft warmth of those large brown eyes. Ildren gathered up her robe and sat upon the bed beside her. She reached her arm across and rested it on the bed. Her faintly spicy fragrance drifted all around.

'His lordship has upset you, has he not, my darling?' Her voice was soft and deep; her bosom rose and fell with nervous breaths. Anya looked away, but it was true; this woman understood her feelings. Each movement the Taskmistress made brushed the robe against her skin; the velvet stroked her side and the sleeve brushed across her nipple. Ildren did not force her to reply. Anya turned to look at her again and Ildren smiled at her.

'Your Taskmistress wishes to – to restrain this luscious body, my precious,' Ildren murmured, then waited for her words to take effect. Anya hesitated. Ildren raised her eyebrows and slowly parted her lips. Anya was afraid but she could not help herself; she knew this woman could bring her overpowering pleasures; her heart was beating wildly as she nodded, very slightly. Ildren smiled again. When she kissed her, Anya opened her mouth to permit Ildren's tongue inside to curl about her own and slake its thirst upon her spittle. 'You delicious thing,' the Taskmistress whispered. She secured her ankles to the bedframe, very wide apart, and clipped her wristbands to her collar. She restored the gold chain round her middle, then lifted her nipples on her tongue and moistly kissed her belly. Then Anya felt warm breath between her parted thighs; she tensed; the tip of Ildren's tongue deposited a droplet on her burning nubbin. That single touch made Anya buck and almost deliver herself to pleasure. 'Shh, my sweet,' said the Taskmistress, and placed her hand upon the shuddering belly to calm its urgency.

Ildren now took from her robe a clip – a flat-jawed metal spring clip about two inches long, which she closed around

Anya's leaves and almost made them burst; it forced her nubbin out like a tiny hot red berry. And whilst that clip squeezed burning needles of cruel pleasure through her nubbin, Ildren kissed her and sucked upon her tongue and gently tapped the weighted clamp from side to side between her legs. When the kiss was concluded, she readjusted the clip, pulling Anya's flesh leaves through more fully so it gripped against them tightly where they joined her body. 'Shh . . .' she said again when Anya softly moaned. The slippery snake of seduction was moving again, reaching down inside her sex to stroke behind her tight clamped leaves along their line of sealing.

Then she heard voices and the jingle of keys and the opening of a metal gate. Her heart began to palpitate; the turnkey stood outside. The male slave was being led out from the next cell. He was tethered by a single cord which disappeared between his buttocks.

'Do not concern yourself with that, my darling. They cannot harm you.' The Taskmistress was looking at Anya's outspread smoothness and the metal gripped around her swollen flesh. Anya's nubbin throbbed. 'Mmm . . . so tense; so full of pleasure. . .' Ildren murmured. Her gaze swept slowly up Anya's body. 'Look at me, my child.' Anya looked into her soft brown eyes. 'You are so very special.' Ildren shuddered. 'Push out your tongue. Moisten it; push it out at me. Do not be shy. . .' The sinking feeling came in Anya's belly. She opened her lips, then closed them. Ildren's eyes beckoned to her. She could hear the weight of Ildren's breathing. Now Anya shuddered as the wave of wanting overtook her and she slowly pushed the pink tip out. The feeling as she did it was as if a finger – Ildren's finger – had been pushed into her bottom yet Ildren had not moved at all. Her eyes had merely widened. But now she did move. Her finger touched the tongue-tip and Anya felt again that phantom finger enter her and wriggle seductively inside.

Ildren said, 'Keep still.' Her finger disappeared and Anya felt it search for, then find, the tip of her nub. The touching there, just at the tip, when her nubbin was so swollen and defenceless and charged with burning passion, almost made her wet herself. The finger stroked across her and she could not bear the stimulation. She moved her hips and rolled her head and tried to shake away the burden of that pleasure, but Ildren's finger just kept moving at the same very slow pace, tickling at the tip, then hesitating just too long before tickling again.

'You must keep very still and do not move your head at all. Do not move your tight sweet body. Just look into my eyes and keep that mouth open very wide. There. . .' The tickling resumed at a very light, very cruel pace, a bee's kiss of a whisper at the tip of Anya's nubbin. 'And keep that tongue pushed out at me. Do not let it touch your lips. Do not move it; keep it tight – a tight and tiny point. Arch it up. . .' Anya's breath was turning into a long slow groan of wanting that was rooted in her belly. Her head was lifted off the bed as if her tongue-tip was somehow reaching out to touch her nubbin. Ildren bent to kiss that tongue-tip but even as her lips formed into a moist and tiny sucking 'o' which pouted out to close about it, Anya's belly burst beneath the waves of honeyed wanting and Ildren felt the hot bud shower a hundred tiny pulsing kisses against the pad of her fingertip. Anya felt as if her sex had been dipped in thin warm syrup.

The Taskmistress removed the clip and massaged her while she sucked at last upon that very willing, very thankful tongue which pushed so strongly into her mouth as Ildren's searching fingers found again Anya's honeyed resonance and felt the delectably shuddering creature seep warm oil upon her fingers. And when the Taskmistress had tasted fulfilment in her slave's delicious tongue, she turned to the turnkey who had entered quietly and was standing over by the door. 'You have the capsules? Good.' She placed a loving hand on Anya's frightened belly. 'No, do not fret. We must administer these little baubles of love again, my sweet . . . a little stronger this time. We must recharge this luscious body for all the loving tasks that lie ahead.' Ildren removed the clip, then turned Anya onto her front for the infixion of this torture, placing a hard cushion underneath her belly and tying her spread-eagled. Then, when she had finished, she reapplied the clip and stroked a fingertip all the way down Anya's spine, down into the groove, down to the velvet cup. 'Good,' she said as the cup contracted back in pleasure. 'And since you have done so very well, my darling, tomorrow we promote you – to the kitchens.'

Anya was terror-stricken; those words were like a knife-blow in her belly. 'You have the male slave ready, turnkey? Good.' Ildren then departed.

That night, Anya's sleep came fitfully. Her mind was kept in turmoil by Ildren's parting threat – the certain tortures that would await her at the cook's cruel hands – and her body slowly burned with the hot and itchy stimulation deep inside her and the unrelenting tightness of the clamp that slowly sucked upon her flesh.

In the early hours, she was woken by frightening sounds from down the passageway – sounds of punishment, slaps of thin soft leather against moist flesh, slow slaps at first, and moans as the slaps came faster, and then a woman's strangled cry as pleasure was drawn forth by that means, followed by a softly panting afterpleasure overlain by sobs, then echoing footsteps retreating into the hollow distance. Then Anya's belly shuddered as her capsules burst inside.

[7]

Strange Ways

It was morning. There was no way of telling that directly, for the dungeons seemed to stay uniformly lit, but Anya knew from the way her body ached, from the way the aches grew stronger by the minute. She felt so stiff she could not move at first. Her arms and feet had been unfastened but she could still feel the wicked clamp between her thighs.

Thelda removed her collar, then made her sit up while she removed her wristbands and anklebands. She next removed the clamp. The pain down there, as the circulation was restored, was excruciating. It almost made her double over. Thelda clutched the pot and brush again.

'Lie down. Spread your legs.' She shaved her very briskly. Anya found the coolness of the lather soothing. She was much less worried this time; the steel slid much more smoothly against her. It tickled her.

'Up, my pretty,' Thelda screeched. 'You haven't time to dawdle.' The cell door lay open. Thelda took her out and led her to a low dark dripping place to attend to her toilet. There was no privacy; Anya had to squat while Thelda stood and watched her. Then she was taken to be bathed. The room was small, with a wet and slimy rough stone floor, some stone benches and tables, and four stone-lined cisterns set into the ground. She was made to sit upon the side and then lower herself up to the neck in water so cold – like a mountain spring – it sucked the breath right out of her. Thelda pushed her under.

Suddenly Anya lost her footing. Her feet could not find the bottom. The water wasn't contained by the cistern; it was flowing across underneath the flagstones and the current was dragging her sideways; all around was blackness;

the shocking coldness stopped her breathing altogether. She panicked, bumped her head against the stonework and flailed her arms up as she surfaced, smacking Thelda on her great hooked nose. Thelda jumped back, slapped her face and dragged her out by her hair; she took a brush and whacked her hard across the bottom till she squealed, then let her stand there shivering and dripping on the slippery floor. Finally she relented and dried her with a rough hessian towel, rubbing especially cruelly and hard in between her legs. 'Let that be a lesson,' Thelda said. And Anya's flesh was swollen up to burning – and yet she had the satisfaction of seeing that Thelda's nose was just the same.

Then Anya was taken to a small room across the way, sat at a wooden table and given breakfast – a mug of lukewarm water and a dried up crust of bread. 'Wait here.' Thelda left her unattended while she went to get the turnkey.

The water in the cistern had tasted fresher than this. The bread was days old. As Anya bit into it, it cracked and most of it fell onto the floor, but she wasn't really hungry anyway. She looked about the room. The door was closed, but she hadn't heard it lock. Was anyone on the other side? Perhaps she could escape? She got up and went over to it, reached for the latch then changed her mind. It would be impossible; she could never get to the outer gate without being seen and even then it would be locked. The floor felt cold against her feet, yet it was covered in straw. A cool draught of air was blowing across it, but it did not come from underneath the door. Suddenly she saw something move under the table, and she screamed for she thought at first it was a huge rat. The rabbit sat up and calmly looked at her while it chewed the piece of bread. As Anya moved towards it, it loped across the floor and disappeared into the corner. Anya followed it. At the foot of the wall, partly concealed with straw, was a large hole – wide enough for a fox, at least – where the stonework was collapsing and the dirt floor fell away to blackness. She could hear running water down there. It must be the outflow from the cisterns.

'What was that scream?' Anya was startled by the voice. Standing at the door were Thelda and the turnkey.

'I – I thought I heard it too,' said Anya.

The turnkey looked uncertain, then a smile of satisfaction spread across his face. He held his finger up. 'Ah, yes,' he said, and cocked his head. 'That would be the punishment.' Anya's jaw fell open. He held his hands out apologetically as Anya backed away. 'We have a difficult slave down there, my dear.' He pointed down the passage in a direction Anya had not been taken. 'Perhaps you heard her in the night?' Anya's blood chilled. 'Mmm . . . perhaps you ought to see this one before you go upstairs. Yes.' He chuckled. 'Very instructive . . . seeing how they come round. Hmm?'

Anya was very frightened as the turnkey led her even deeper into the dungeons. They passed a place where several slaves were chained to the wall, some facing outwards, some away. One slave, a girl, was chained by her collar very close to the floor. She was kneeling with her bottom pushed up higher than her head. 'Her lord will be here very soon; he prefers to take her this way, after breakfast and after supper,' the turnkey explained. He stopped, then spread her legs, as if checking her. He removed something from his belt and it disappeared between the girl's thighs. 'I have to ensure that she is ready – in the right frame of mind . . . disposed, as it were, to pleasure.' He placed one hand on her back, near the base of her spine and pressed; his other hand was moving in a gentle pumping action in between her legs. The bondslave softly murmured. Then his hand was withdrawn; it contained a small ivory tusk, now glistening, on a chain. He patted the bondslave on the bottom. 'Very good, my dear,' he pronounced. 'I feel sure his lordship will be pleased with you this time.' She buried her head in her arms. All of this made Anya very fearful of what treatment might be reserved for herself.

Next, they turned a corner and came upon the slave who was being punished. Anya's heart rose up inside her throat to choke her, for the girl was tethered on her back to a Horse – that cruel wooden beast of pleasure – placed in the centre of the corridor. Her feet were tied apart, fastened by ropes to hooks in the ceiling. A warder stood between her legs. He held a strap; it was like the one that had been used on Anya when she was a prisoner in the guardroom, but it was larger, a broad tongue of thin black leather. The sight of it, when she knew what he would do with it, when she knew what it felt like to be punished in that way – there – with the degradation overlain with pain and aching wanting, made a shiver kiss her coolly in between her legs. She was imagining what it would be like to receive that punishment now, to feel the persistent slap of the leather tongue against her newly shaven mound.

Anya was made to stand beside the warder and to witness the woman's shame. The man looked cruel and heartless. The slave was balanced with her hands beneath her hips, which were thereby lifted and kept more open to the warder's ministrations. Her nipples looked inflamed and swollen, as if stiffened by prolonged working rather than by pleasure.

'She has failed to satisfy her lord,' the turnkey whispered. 'So now she must be acclimatised to pleasure.'

Anya's eyes widened. 'Pleasure?' She could not believe this treatment could be construed that way.

'Yes indeed – but after the manner her master has decreed. Now watch.' He turned to the warder. 'Proceed with the pleasuring – to completion, if you will.' The woman's belly tensed. The skin between her thighs was shiny; the hairs were wet. Then Anya realised why. The warder balanced the strap upon her belly, then scooped his fingers into a pot on the floor and spread the woman's flesh back, then massaged the nub that nestled there, rubbing firmly, using his fingertips with the measured assurance of long practice, aware of the woman's progress, yet forcing the restless stirrings of her pelvis to align themselves with the rhythm that he set. He glanced at Anya several times while he worked the woman; those looks sent thrills of illicit delight through that selfsame place between Anya's thighs. He would stop to recharge his fingers, deliberately taking his time, working at his own speed, while the woman's heavy breathing testified to her pressing need for the lubrication to continue, then apply the jellied gobbet in the same place as before, making wet sounds of sucking pleasure that Anya found unbearable to hear, until the woman's breathing snapped and shattered into little gasps of forepleasure. Her belly tried to thrust against his fingers, which had not varied their pace at all, but now they slowed and then gradually withdrew as she tried to push out her sex to follow them. The warder then pushed two fingers of each hand into her, opening out her sex and holding it that way, watching the woman while she shook her head from side to side and panted; he waited.

'Now?' he asked the turnkey.

'Wait.' The turnkey took up a position at the woman's head, then beckoned Anya over. He gathered up the woman's breasts and squeezed them so the nipples pushed out stiffly, then nodded. 'Go ahead,' he said. The warder carefully removed his fingers, sealed her lips together so they stood up straight, then lifted the leather tongue and cracked it down smartly upon her fleshpot. Her belly bucked but it was Anya's cry that rent the air. The turnkey smiled and whispered, 'Do not be misled. . . Soon her body will see this punishment as pleasure. Pleasure can be made to come in strange ways. . .' He laid his hand against Anya's bottom. 'These ways do not come naturally; they must be learnt, my child, and tested.' His finger probed into the groove between her cheeks, searching out the place of inner need, making her blush, even as she spread to take him, quelling her softly with that kissing fingertip.

The warder now teased apart the slave's flesh again to re-expose her nubbin, oiled it with the jelly, worked it systematically up again until her belly looked as if it would burst, then sealed the leaves against the woman's tender whimpers and her soft protests, and stayed his hand until her belly shuddered before he slapped down hard against her hot oiled flesh, then spread her out again, oiled her up to grunting point and snapped cruel delight again in between her outspread thighs. The slaps were getting closer together; the strap kept cutting short the woman's pleasure so she could be worked back to the brink once more, and the working time was getting shorter. And throughout the slapping and the slow wet working, the mouth of Anya's bottom gently sucked the turnkey's fingertip. The turnkey did not move; he did not instruct her to do this; her body had no choice. How could her body do other than respond to these seductions? Anya wanted pleasure, not in that way, with the strap, but certainly there, where the slave was being pleasured.

'Please?' the woman moaned this time as the warder held the strap above her while he continued to work her to the very last second, not closing her leaves at all to protect her sensitive nubbin from the smacking, making Anya cry out once again.

The turnkey withdrew his fingertip, took Anya by the hand and pulled her away. He had done it deliberately; he knew she did not want to go. Her face and neck were hot. She could feel her belly liquifying; she felt all swollen up as if it had been her upon the Horse. And had it been, her pleasure would surely have proclaimed her depravity long before now.

'Her warder is very skilled,' the turnkey declared, after they had progressed some way, as if he had read her thoughts. 'Her lord has directed that she be trained this way. The treatment we apply depends on the slave and, more particularly, on the whim of her master; but in this case, her passion will in time be made to blossom by the simple act of slapping that intimate place. That is the purpose of the exercise.' She could feel the blood draining from her face at the thought of that. 'The stroking will not be required.' The turnkey brushed her bottom softly with the back of his hand. 'The smacking will take over and deliver her to delight.' Anya was shaken, and yet a shiver had tickled her again, for she was recalling her own cruel treatment at the hands of the castle guards – how her punishment in that throbbing place had, it was true, very nearly brought about her pleasure; certainly it had secured her degradation.

They had barely rounded the corner when the turnkey suddenly stopped her and turned his head to listen. Her eyes widened; she could hear the sounds from down the corridor and they were coming very quickly. He looked intently at her, as if searching for some sign. It made her very frightened – of herself, and the peculiar feelings that were churning round inside her. He placed his hand upon her belly, fitting it smoothly against her, then looked at her again and nodded very solemnly as if he had sensed that inner conflict, but how could he? How could he know what she was feeling when she was in turmoil, when she did not understand herself? He removed something from his belt and held it up. It was the small ivory tusk. The very fact of him holding it in that way made the feeling come again; her belly was sinking down and down beneath the delicious weight, the pleasure of submission. It was clear that he knew this. He pressed his hand against her – against her belly – softly. She could hear the sounds of punishment and the moans.

He made her turn round – he merely twirled his finger round in the air and she immediately obeyed – and stand with legs apart and hands against the wall, low down, below the level of her waist. He wanted her bottom raised. Her back curved smoothly downwards. He spread her cheeks and held them that way with his fingers, placed the tip of the tusk against her, just inside, and waited. She felt her bottom kiss it.

'Wait,' he said. He must have seen and understood that first hesitating kiss of complicity. Anya held her breath and then in the distance heard the rapid smacking sounds being submerged at last beneath a wailing moan of long denied female pleasure, and then the tusk began to move. 'Good. . . take it very gently.' Her legs began to shake as the tusk was very slowly pushed inside, so deliciously slowly that it drew her breath away from her in shudders. 'There . . . you see. Strange ways.' And her cheeks burned bright with shame as her body softly pulsed around its smooth white stem, and then she felt the gold clasp round its base touch against her tender rim. The turnkey left her like that, braced against the wall, and stood beside her, just brushing her bowed-out belly with his fingertips, until the sounds of pleasure in the distance had completely ebbed away. Then he took hold of the tusk once more and Anya tightened hard against it when it was withdrawn.

'There. . .' he said again. Again she felt ashamed to have him underline her lewdness.

After that he took her on a long journey through wide dry sandy corridors and low damp passageways, making Anya begin to worry where she might be being taken. They must still be very deep within the dungeons, but the kitchens must surely be upstairs. At last they came upon a large wooden door with an iron grille set into it. The turnkey peeped inside. 'Have a look,' he said. Anya had to stand on tiptoes. The room was very large and was full of machines – wheels and frames with many ropes and chains attached in complicated ways. There were stocks and wooden bars and poles, and ropes that dangled from the ceiling. A fire burned in a large brazier in the middle. A hot humid current of air flowed out through the grille.

'The Chamber of Correction,' he announced, and Anya was very frightened, for she was certain then of what she had guessed – that these machines were used for cruelty. 'For slaves who persistently misbehave.' The room seemed empty, which was some little reassurance at least, until the turnkey pointed upwards. Anya gasped; at first she thought they could not be real. Attached to the ceiling, fastened to horizontal frames drawn up on ropes and pulleys were humans – naked male and female slaves – slung in such a way that they were facing downwards. Several of the slaves had weighted cords or chains dangling from between their thighs. The male slaves' cockstems stuck out rigidly; the females' thighs were fastened apart.

Anya heard a sound; someone out of sight was moving about. Suddenly she saw her, and her heart missed a beat, for it was the Taskmistress who now stepped into the middle of the room, carrying a small table with a number of objects on it. She set it down and began winding down one of the frames that had a male slave attached. Anya recognised him too – it was the same slave she had seen being taken out last night from the cell next to hers. It made her very fearful indeed; she wanted to be away from here. Maybe she would be next.

'Correction will soon resume,' said the turnkey. 'Their lordships and ladyships will then be down to supervise.' The Taskmistress had lowered the slave to shoulder height; she was speaking to him, but she also had hold of him; she was doing something to him. The frame slowly rotated, then Anya saw that the slave now had a collar round his cockstem, close against the base. The Taskmistress seemed to be questioning him, but all the time she was working him, rolling his flesh between her palms like pastry. 'I can see you are enthralled, my dear. . .' Anya's mouth was open; she was shaking her head. She was horrified. 'But we don't want you arriving late for kitchen duty, upsetting Cook, now do we?' He winked and Anya felt an even colder chill descending.

The turnkey led her up two flights of steps, unlocked a gate – again it was too narrow for him to pass – and simply pushed her out. 'Hurry along,' he chuckled. 'I'm sure they are expecting you.'

[8]

Kitchen Duties

Anya was out of that dreadful place, but the single passage-way that lay ahead held no consolation. It must be a back entrance to the kitchens, she assumed. She could hear the clatter of the pans, and the shouting was getting louder. Perhaps she could sneak through in the midst of the turmoil? But as she approached the corner she realised that idea was foolish. The place was full of servants, all of them dressed while she was nude. And yet they seemed to be ignoring her; each of them seemed intent on what he himself was doing.

She peeped round the corner and surveyed the scene. She was scared to enter; the cook might be lurking near and Anya was afraid she would remember her from that first night and punish her in the cruel way she had threatened; only by Axine's timely intervention had she been prevented from doing it then. There was no Axine to save her now; she was on her own.

The servants were busying about, preparing food, carry-ing tubs of vegetables and baskets full of meat and bread, sweeping up and cleaning the stoves. The smell of fresh bread was drifting in from the bakehouse – the delicious smell of soft bread rolls, baked quickly in a very hot oven to make them crispy brown on the outside. Anya loved that smell. A short way ahead of her, two large cauldrons steamed. Into one of them a kitchen boy was dropping dumplings; the second tub was being stirred with a giant paddle by a boy who stood on a stool while a third boy tipped in a trayful of meat. He then recharged the tray from a nearby table at which a servant was chopping up the carcass of a sheep; another servant helped him. These

112

preparations must be for the midday meal for the lords of the Council.

Then Anya saw that she had been mistaken, for not everyone was clothed; once in a while a slave wearing only chains would pass, bearing a tray; not a large wooden kitchen tray but a small serving tray carrying gold or silver plates of the kind for use upstairs. These slaves must be waiting on the lords and ladies of the castle. The servants appeared not to take any notice of them. This gave Anya an idea: if she could collect a tray, perhaps she could pretend she was delivering it upstairs and could make her escape without anybody noticing. Once she got out of here she would find Marella and then she would be safe. She could trust Marella more than anyone. Marella would hide her; Marella would help her to escape from the castle altogether. She would break free and go in search of her Prince.

She looked around; the tables were heaped with grimy, food-encrusted pots and pans and there didn't appear to be any trays or anything else she could use. So much for her plan. Then she spotted a large jug and a pair of mugs on the nearest table. Beside the jug was a loaf of bread and a wedge of cheese. It made her mouth water. She waited till no one appeared to be looking in her direction then took a deep breath, closed her eyes for a second then quickly stepped across. Glancing round, she broke off a piece of cheese and popped it in her mouth before she picked the jug up – and very nearly dropped it, for she had thought it empty. It was full of beer. She lifted it awkwardly and balanced it on her shoulder, using one hand on the handle above her head and the other supporting it at the side, in the way a servant girl would do, even though she felt very conspicuous and exposed that way, with both her hands occupied. It made her conscious of her breasts and, in particular, the bareness of her belly. She would have to take the risk; if necessary she could drop the jug on the floor and perhaps escape in the commotion.

Now her heart sank, for the way ahead would take her past the servants cutting meat, and both of them had turned and were looking towards her. They seemed to be looking straight at her, making her almost panic and want to run. Behind her there was no way out, except down to the dungeons. She would brazen it out. She walked towards the men without hurrying, trying to look purposeful as if she were on an errand, but keeping her eyes down as she passed them.

'Stop!' the gruff voice said. A hand now barred her way. She looked up into the questioning face of the servant with the knife. He looked powerfully built and threatening, but it was the way he held up the blade that really frightened her. It was wet with blood.

Anya frowned. 'Out of my way,' she said with mock assurance; she didn't want to show how scared she really was.

'And where do you think you're going?'

'Upstairs.' She set her jaw and held her head up.

'With our beer?'

Now she was sunk. She turned to get away; the other servant blocked her retreat. He was smaller than the first one; his smile looked evil. She raised her leg to kick him in the groin. 'Look out!'

He dodged aside. She had forgotten to drop the jug; the man behind her effortlessly lifted it from her shoulder and at the same time grabbed her by the hair and pulled her off balance. He calmly took a swig from the jug and passed it to his friend, who had more difficulty holding it. When Anya tried to struggle and kick again, the strong one pulled her hair the harder.

'Well, well, Mago, what have we here?' the small one chuckled, putting the jug down on the table. 'Look, this chicken has been plucked, it seems.'

Mago released her hair and pushed her up against the table. Her hands were held behind her back. 'And shows her true colours, at that,' he said, shaking his heavy jaw. 'Did you ever see a one like that, Thrinn?'

'No, I surely did not. Hold her still.' She struggled. Thrinn stood up and shook a finger in her face. 'Move that foot up just once more . . .' He held his hand out; Mago handed him the knife. 'And it's one more dainty morsel for the stewpot.' He chopped the knife down hard and split a piece of meat on the table clean in two. Anya jumped. She was terrified. People were now beginning to gather round. Another servant joined in the assault. Anya's feet were kicked apart, then Thrinn began to maul her. She couldn't move to stop him; the strong one had her hands pinned together behind her and drew them up and backwards till it hurt; the third one held her feet apart. Thrinn took the knife, wiped the sheep's blood on his sleeve and pressed the blade flat against her belly. Anya shivered, shut her eyes but then she heard a screech, followed by a metallic thud and then the clatter of the knife blade on the floor. Suddenly her hands were freed. Thrinn lay in a groaning heap at Anya's feet. Before her stood the cook, who clutched the ladle as if she meant to use it again. Everyone began to back away.

Cook's face was livid; the veins stood out from her neck. She looked as if she might burst at any second. She had one eye shut and her head cocked to one side. And with her small size and rotund shape, her outfit and demeanour, she reminded Anya of a very irate white hen who had just unearthed a grub that tasted rancid. Cook was the most dangerous woman, for her size, that Anya had ever met. She never knew quite how to take her, quite what she might do next; she alternated so rapidly between warmth and cruelty. And now she appeared ready to beat her servants senseless.

'Don't anybody move.' Those on the outer fringes of the circle froze as Cook's cock-eye swept round and caught them. She held the ladle ready against anyone who might defy her. 'You!' She pointed at Thrinn. Anya tried to edge her foot away from him to avoid incrimination. 'Up!' Now she pointed to the knife on the floor. 'Is that yours?'

Thrinn began to tremble. She knocked him down again. 'And you!' She clubbed the cowering Mago twice and made him whimper. Anya started to shake; surely she was next? But no.

'What have you been doing to this girl? Speak up.' No one dared to. Anya was able to breathe again. 'This slave is not for your amusement,' Cook stepped towards her and tickled her under the chin, '. . . are you, darling?'

115

Anya swallowed and managed to shake her head. Cook looked intently into her face. Would she recognise her from the last time? Anya hoped and prayed she wouldn't. Suddenly, Cook's eyes widened and Anya's hopes faded. The finger of accusation was held up. 'You didn't encourage them, did you?'

'No!' Anya was affronted.

'We get girls like that down here you know, wayward types, flaunting themselves – their lordships let them do as they like and then send them down here, cavorting with my servants. So nothing ever gets done. Does it?'

'Ouch!' She had kicked Mago in the shin.

'Good-for-nothing slouches . . .' She was staring hard at Anya again.

'No. I never did any such thing.' Anya thought she'd better make it clear.

'Hmm. Well, I hope not.' Cook sounded a little less aggressive, then suddenly sharpened up again. 'But mind – I'll be keeping an eye out. Cook has ways of bringing wayward females back to heel, you know.' She stood back and looked at Anya, bobbing towards her, then swaying back again, as if attempting to plumb the depths of her lubricity. Then her mouth fell open; she looked horrified. Anya thought at first she had been recognised, then realised where the woman was looking. It made her very ashamed but also very frightened. The cook began to shake; she was turning a very deep shade of purple. 'Oh!' She pointed with the ladle. 'Oh! You brazen little hussy!' she cried, then nervously smoothed her apron down as if that would some-how help atone for the immodesty that now confronted her. 'How dare you? How could you? In my kitchen, in that state, flaunting your anatomy?'

Some of the servants began to snigger, whereupon the cook turned on them, flailing the ladle wildly about her head. 'Away! Get away from here! Off about your duties.' Anya wondered if she ought to try to make a bolt for it, but the woman spun round and threatened her again.

Anya crouched and held her hand up. 'Please,' she cried. 'I am innocent – '

116

'Hmmph!' Cook folded her arms.

'This was not my doing. It was forced upon me.' She bowed her head. 'Lord Sardroc has instructed that I should be kept this way . . .' and she felt the tears welling up inside her.

'Not in my kitchen, you shan't,' Cook declared sternly. 'The servants are bad enough as it is. No . . .' She pursed her lips then tapped them with a finger. 'Hmm – I've got just the thing for you,' she said.

It was a pouch, made of a very thin supple leather on a double loop of leather string. Anya thought at first it was a sling-shot; she had never seen anything like it as a garment. She couldn't believe it was meant to fit about her person until Cook made her step into it, drew it tightly up and fastened it about her waist. 'There,' she said with satisfaction. She checked the fit. The cord descended at the back between the cheeks of Anya's bottom; the pouch closed snugly round her sex, like an ever-present hand, but smoother, more intimate than a hand could be, moulding much more perfectly to her flesh, making her feel very strange indeed. Cook tightened and then re-fastened it. Now it was like a second skin against her smoothly shaven mound, fitting in the parting, making her flesh leaves stand out, separating them, making them swell, arousing her, and making her enjoy the sensation when Cook's fingers stroked against her and briefly slipped into the crease. 'There,' she tested that the cord was snug between the cheeks, 'a little modesty never hurt.' Now Anya knew for sure the creature was demented.

'And now this . . .' which was a halter, in the same very thin skin. It had been oiled until the leather flowed between the fingers – Cook's fingers, for she spent some time rubbing it absent-mindedly between finger and thumb before fitting it tightly round Anya's breasts. Then she rubbed it once again. There were tiny holes cut into it; too small to take Anya's nipples, but as the leather skin was stretched tighter, her nipples squeezed until they burst through it. The constriction made them feel as if they were being sucked. They were swelling up against the constant stimulation. Cook stood back but this time scowled at her as if she disapproved. 'Hm . . .' she said. 'You're sure you didn't lead them on?' But despite Anya's renewed protestations, Cook was unconvinced. She kept stroking Anya's firming nipples with an attitude of mild dissatisfaction.

'Well, don't let me catch you making sheep's eyes at my servants again. Is that clear? Or I'll . . .' Anya shrank back. 'Never mind. You'll find out.' Anya could guess; it made her very scared. 'Now, get your apron on, and you can make some use of yourself. We've plenty of jobs for flirtatious slaves like you.'

Anya felt worse than naked now, even with the apron Cook had found her. It covered her belly and her breasts, but it rubbed against her captive nipples; it extended to her knees but, apart from the string tied across the middle, it left her bare at the back. She was taken to a corner of the kitchen.

'Porridge pots,' said the cook with peculiar satisfaction as Anya's gaze worked up the heap that extended nearly to the ceiling. How could that much washing-up be produced in just one morning? 'They've let things slip, I'm afraid,' the woman added, shaking her head. 'As long as they can find one that hasn't been used . . .' She shrugged, and tentatively scratched her fingernail in a deeply crusted pot. 'Too busy dallying about with the slaves.' Then she frowned and her colour began to darken. 'It's friends of yours that's the cause of this – coming down here, cavorting when they're supposed to be here to help me. I hope you're not going to prove to be a problem that way?' Now she had one eye closed as she peered at Anya in that very unfriendly way.

Anya knew she had to try and calm the woman down. 'No – I like work,' she said quite truthfully, picking up the bucket from the huge stone sink. 'Where can I get warm water?'

'Oh,' Cook seemed quite surprised. 'Er . . .' She turned and pointed down the aisle. 'Down there,' she said and watched Anya get the first bucketful from the vat. She shook her head as if she couldn't believe that a slave was actually doing something useful, then left her to it.

Anya sighed with relief, then looked with trepidation at the mountain of pots and pans. She didn't mind doing the washing-up, but she had never tackled anything like this. It took about a dozen bucketfuls to fill the sink. All the while, the servants were interfering with her as she passed, brushing against her, tickling their fingers over her bare bottom. The women were as bad as the men, but she didn't dare protest too loudly in case the cook should overhear. One of them, a large strong girl with plaited hair, made her bend over the sink while she investigated Anya underneath the apron. She seemed fascinated by the way her nipples poked out through the leather; she kept touching them, and stretching them, not roughly, but softly. Then she traced the line of the cord from the base of Anya's backbone, down between the cheeks, running her finger underneath and round the front, slipping her fingers inside the pouch and touching her unashamedly, searching out her hard hot nubbin and working it until Anya began to moisten. The girl stood her up and turned her round, then laughed and sucked her finger before she ran off, leaving Anya's heart racing with guilty excitement at what she had let her do. She looked about, fearful that the cook might appear at any second. When nothing happened after a minute or two, she turned and got to work, but she couldn't put aside the thought of what had taken place, and the feelings there were undiminished.

She extricated a pot from the pile. It was large enough to boil a pig's head in. The porridge had dried hard round the rim and run down the outside, where it had burnt through sticky brown to crispy charcoal black near the bottom. It looked as if it had been used and re-used without ever being cleaned out and had then been left for weeks. She would never get it clean. She had only a wooden pallet with which to scrape it and the water was already going cold. She tried; the porridge on the inside turned to gummy jelly which sloughed away in slippery lumps an inch at a time, only to reveal another crust below. She scraped and rubbed; she clawed it with her fingers, swirled the water round and hacked the incrustation with the sharp edge of the pallet, making the pot clang, trying to crack the stupid armour-plated sheathing, getting hot and bothered with the greasy and now saturated apron pressed against her upper thighs and belly, and the fusty smell of disentombed porridge slurry suffocating her. The sink was full of watery gruel with disgusting slimy lumps that bobbed beneath the surface, and after what seemed an age she still hadn't finished the first pot. She flung it down; the gruel spattered up into her face. She threw the pallet at it and then she couldn't find it in the murky depths. This was hopeless.

'Everything all right, my dear?'

Anya shot round and tried to cover up the mess behind her. Cook was smiling sweetly; it made her look so strange.

'Oh . . . yes, thank you.'

'Good.' Cook leaned sideways to try to see round her; she looked uncertainly at the undiminished heap of pots. 'You seem a little slow. I want them done by noon, mind.'

'Yes ma'am.'

'Hmm.' Cook looked intently into her face again, making Anya very anxious that she might be remembering, or might be able to read Anya's recent lustful misdemeanour simply in the colour of her cheeks. The woman opened her mouth to speak, then thought better of it. Anya pretended to be working busily as she watched her disappear from view.

This was her chance. She had nothing else to lose. If she stayed, the servants would never let her be and in any case she would never finish even two or three pots by midday and then she would be punished and degraded by the cook. She knew this woman of old. Anya had witnessed what she had done that day to the male slave – for no reason at all – and she was sure the cook would have no hesitation in doing it to her.

She knew that beyond the kitchen was the bakehouse, then the broad staircase out to the Great Hall and the courtyard. Cook had this time gone past Anya in the opposite direction; whatever might lie between Anya and the stairs, it couldn't be her. She acted quickly. She took the apron off and stowed it underneath the sink, then picked up the empty bucket and walked quickly towards where the exit ought to be. She was right, for now she passed the bank of ovens and she could see the long table where she had taken supper on that first night. It was empty; the exit was beyond it. She speeded up until she could see the stairs; she heard a sound behind her, but didn't look back. There was just one aisle, between high cupboards, that she had to negotiate before the race to the exit. She broke into a run – and tripped, letting go of the bucket. In that split second, a man stepped out in front of her and caught her. It was Mago.

He clapped his giant hand over her mouth. Thrinn's foot had tripped her as she passed; he had been hidden behind a heap of sacks. But now he was behind her, tying a gag between her lips while Mago clasped her arms to her body, pulling her hard against him and crushing her knees together so she couldn't kick out.

'What have we here, then?' said Thrinn. 'I wonder if Cook knows she has a chicken on the loose?'

They must have guessed her plan. They must have been watching her all along, otherwise they would never have been able to ambush her like this. She wanted to beg them not to hand her over to that evil woman. Thrinn turned her round to face him while Mago held her. She could never break free from that iron grip.

'Now, which is it to be, my dear? Rough or smooth?' He stroked her breasts, through the leather, then stroked her nipples with the backs of his hands. He forced her thighs apart and cupped a hand around her captive sex. He ran a finger up the cord that divided her at the back, lifting it and letting it snap against her, then trying to insinuate a finger underneath it and into her. She shook her head and tried to pull away; she would never agree to that with these disgusting creatures. 'Oh?' He kept his hand against her at the front, but turned his head to one side and listened. 'Do I hear Cook now?'

There was a crash at the other end of the kitchen, then a scream of pain, followed very swiftly by Cook's distinctive wild tirade. Anya's eyes opened wide in terror. 'It sounds as if she's coming this way; are your chores complete, my dear? They'd better be. Maybe we can get back into Cook's good books, Mago, returning this *wayward hussy*?' Anya's cry of protest was stifled by the gag. 'I wonder what Cook has in store for a girl like this? Hmm, I wonder, now? Perhaps she'll allow us the pleasure of drawing this sweet thing off?' His middle finger pressed firmly against the crease of her fleshpot.

Anya felt faint. The memory came flooding back – of how, that evening, the male slave had been forced to take pleasurable deliverance in so cruel a manner, of how the cook had ordered that he be drawn off thrice per day – and now these servants had confirmed the worst, that this wicked treatment would be applied to a female – to her – probably in front of everyone. She knew she would die; the shame would kill her.

'Quick! She's coming,' Mago shouted; sure enough, Anya could see in the distance the small white fireball heading straight towards them. But before she had a chance to panic, she was dragged sideways. Thrinn and Mago started running. Anya found herself running too, and it wasn't because they held her arms; she was running as hard as she possibly could, as they were, to get away from Cook. They shot alongside the sacks, between some dangling sides of beef, setting them spinning, then past wooden crates full of live and now squawking chickens, to a small doorway in the wall. Mago lifted the latch and opened it, flung Anya in and followed her inside.

It was soot black in there. Anya fell to her knees. The wooden floor felt dusty; the air was dry and smelled of grain. Thrinn came in with a lamp. Now Anya could see that the room was small and it was full of sacks stacked very neatly on their sides, in sloping ranks almost to the ceiling. The dust was grain meal that had spilled onto the floor. Thrinn put his finger to his lips while he listened at the door. Mago held Anya by the chain at her waist; even though she was gagged and couldn't breath out through her mouth anyway, she held her breath until her lungs were bursting. Still Thrinn waited. His eyes looked frightened but excited.

At last he tiptoed over, hung the lamp on a hook in the ceiling, then went carefully back to the door and opened it a fraction, looked out through the crack, then closed it, leaned against it and heaved a sigh of relief. And Anya found herself doing exactly the same even though she was far from out of danger, even though she knew these men would force her to their pleasure. But in some strange way, their mutual fear – the fear that made the wily Thrinn and the powerful Mago cower down from a woman who was half their size – and that dash to temporary safety, had drawn a bond between the three. Anya didn't understand it; she didn't understand why she no longer hated them in quite the way she had done before. They had threatened to turn her over to the cook, after all. But in the end, they hadn't. Perhaps that was it. Intent as they were on using her body, despite the fact that they were bad, and they had gagged her and carried her away – perhaps they were not cruel.

But – cruel or not – they tied her. They fastened her wrists together then slung the end of the rope over a beam below the ceiling and secured it, so she was stretched up in the centre of the room. They brought across two sacks and placed them upright, one in front of her and one behind, so they could sit upon them while they played with her. But they didn't get that far. Mago's hand stretched out to roll the pouch down from her flesh, then shot back so quickly that he toppled over backwards. A second after that she heard the cry of dismay from Thrinn as he jumped up, lurched past her and scrambled up the heap of sacks. It could only mean one thing, and the look on Mago's face confirmed it. He began to whine. Anya had to force herself to turn, but she knew well enough what she would see. The cook stood at the door; for once she didn't have her ladle; she clutched a rolling pin; her hands were covered in flour. Anya allowed the twist in the rope to turn her back again. She hung limply. All she could do was to close her eyes, waiting for the onslaught to descend.

'Layabout!' Her eyes snapped open. 'Good-for-nothing!' Cook was kicking Mago in a slow circle around Anya's feet. 'Snivelling little swine,' she cried, which surely underestimated his dimensions, Anya couldn't help but think, if not his inclinations. 'Always chasing randy little slaves . . .'

Anya jerked. Those words were quite uncalled for, and she would have said so, had she not been gagged and too afraid to blink.

'You! Don't look so innocent.' Anya's eyes were wide with fright. 'What do you mean by it? Leading my servants on like this?' Now Anya did protest into her gag. Cook pulled it down sharply. 'Well?'

'But I didn't . . .'

'Hmmph.' Cook pointed her rolling pin at Anya's exposed belly, then tapped her nipples with it. 'Well, what's the meaning of that then? Where's your apron? Shameless hussy.'

'But . . .' And yet it was true she'd cast the apron casually aside.

'And those . . .' She flicked her finger against each of Anya's stiffly trapped nipples, then made her spread her legs. Anya had to go on tiptoes since she was still fastened by the rope. Cook thrust her fingers down inside the pouch. Anya was mortified, for her flesh was burning from its tight confinement and the treatment from the servant girl, and now from the men. 'Oh! Now you've asked for it. Now you'll get your just deserts.' She took hold of Anya's hair and began to march away with it, until the scream reminded her the slave was still attached to the ceiling. Now she tried to jump to reach the knot around the beam, but every time she bent her knees and propelled herself up, she failed to leave the ground. The action only served to pump more blood into the woman's cheeks. Eventually, the luckless Mago was coaxed to her assistance with a kick and Anya was untied.

Cook closed her eyes and swayed unsteadily. When she opened them again, she looked at Anya, blinked, then stared around the room as if uncertain of her surroundings and what she was doing there. She looked down at the floor.

'Right boys, tidy up these sacks, then off about your work.' The two servants stared at each other, then watched her warily while Mago put the sacks away and Thrinn crept down from the safety of the heap. 'Off you go then. Shoo!'

Anya turned uncertainly to follow. 'Not you!' Cook's hand shot out, grabbing her by the ear. 'We've a lesson or two for girls like you, with ideas above their station.' She tugged Anya's ear cruelly, pulling her head down until she was staring into Cook's blood-veined yellow eyes. 'Pleasure – that's all you slaves are interested in, isn't it?' Cook's breath smelled of aniseed.

'No.' Anya's protest was weak from fear – and guilt.

'Yes! So pleasure is what you're going to get, my shameless one. More than you bargained for – pleasure till you can't stand up.' Anya felt the blood draining from her face. 'We'll have the servants draw you off.'

'No! Please!' Anya sank to her knees.

'Hmmph. And then we'll see how innocent you are.' She was dragged out to the long table in the kitchen. 'Right. Strip off.' She stood there. Servant men and women began to gather round. She couldn't do it. Cook beckoned one of the girls. 'Ulla! Over here.' It was the one that had mauled Anya. 'Strip her.' The girl was grinning slyly. Anya was turned round while Ulla undid the halter round her breasts; it fell away but caught upon her nipples, which had swollen up so tightly that they wouldn't pass through the tiny holes. Cooked turned her round so everyone could see her. 'See,' she said, 'look at this for innocence.' The servant girls began to giggle, the men to laugh. Cook took the trailing end of the halter and jerked it hard until it freed. Anya cried out in pain and shame. 'Now that.' Cook pointed to the leather pouch. Ulla worked quickly. This time, as if she'd learnt her lesson from the cook, she whipped it sharply from between Anya's legs so it pulled against the tender flesh to which her moistness moulded it.

'Now, let us see the state of that innocence. On the table. Spread.' And Anya had to open her legs before all the staring eyes while Cook examined her. She probed at Anya's open flesh, she pulled her leaves apart and palpated her nubbin. 'Hm. Seems very hard to me,' said Cook complainingly. She pressed it into Anya's body and Anya could feel it slowly pushing out again. Cook pushed it in again and watched with horror as it thrust out even harder, though Anya was willing it not to.

'Hmmph. Innocence indeed!' She took hold of Anya's flesh and worked it, twisting the pip round one way and back the other, then rubbing very quickly as if she were trying to burnish it, then pressing it in again and getting more irate as it got larger and more firm. 'One more chance, and then – ' She didn't finish, but Anya was very frightened nevertheless – and also very aroused, for Cook's fingers, though not gently applied, were bringing her on. Cook held a fingertip against her nubbin and very rapidly shook it. 'Mm.' She wet her fingertip and did it once again. Anya could not hold out against this calculated pleasuring much longer. Her lower belly cramped. 'Mm. Lift your legs. Wider . . .' The woman now picked up the rolling pin and rolled it across Anya's flesh, from side to side then deliberately up and down across her bursting nubbin. Each time, after she had rolled the flesh leaves flat, she plumped them up again. Then when she was satisfied and Anya was gasping, she spread them and had Anya hold herself open while Cook stood back to admire her handiwork.

'Innocent. Ha!' she said. 'Who would like to draw this innocent victim off?'

Everyone it seemed.

Anya was lifted up and stood upon the table, so all would get to witness this terrible degradation. The table had holes in it at each side, into which a beam on legs was fitted. Anya was bent over the beam and her wrists were tied to her ankles. It was Ulla who sat behind her on a stool. She had many advisers as to how she should go about it, but more significantly, she had a long white feather with a finely pointed tip. She laid this down upon the table together with a second toy, a pair of metal balls attached by a short length of very fine cord. Her speculation about this latter instrument caused Anya very much concern. 'The first drawing must be very deep and slow,' was Cook's instruction. Anya shuddered even before Ulla touched her, but when she did touch her, it was very clear to Anya why this girl had been selected to perform the humiliation. It was obvious she knew exactly how to elicit lust from a woman without precipitating pleasure.

Ulla began by smacking her. She did it in a way that made Anya very ashamed, for it provoked her flesh into wanting it to continue. The smacking was carefully meted out in order to arouse her. It was a punishment worse than pain; it was a punishment with pleasure falling just short of fulfilment. The girl spread apart Anya's flesh, folding back the leaves as if she meant to touch her there. Instead she separated the cheeks of Anya's bottom and, keeping the skin stretched taut, smacked it in the middle with a finger. The sudden stimulation caused Anya's flesh to tighten, bringing her leaves together once again. The girl – keeping the skin still very stretched – now stroked her fingertip down the groove, stopping at the bridge of flesh then trailing back again so the fingernail scratched across the very tender rim. Once again she coaxed open the softening leaves to expose their liquid surfaces, spread them back against the bare skin of the mound then held the cheeks apart and smacked firmly down again, making the leaves contract once more. This time they felt more sensitized. Anya could feel them kiss against each other then finally cling together. The stroking down and up the groove was carefully repeated, then the opening, the pause and then the smack of delectation.

The girl continued this precisely worked-out treatment until Anya's flesh had gone so soft and pliant that the lips no longer closed but remained spread back against her mound where they had been put. Now the attention was turned to stimulating her nipples, again by smacking, only this time with a small strap, as long and broad as a woman's thumb, but certainly much thinner. Once again Ulla did not simply slap them up to greater firmness, but worked at them methodically, gathering them on two fingertips and stroking with the thumb, then supporting the upturned breast with the nipple on her palm while she trickled spittle over it, then rolled it in the pool of wetness, then smacked it sharply once, alternating the procedure between each breast until the nipples had swelled to hard black balls and she deemed it time to progress the pleasuring one stage further.

The girl took up the feather and with its finely drawn-out tip she traced the line of separation of Anya's leaves of flesh, using nervously tickling downstrokes towards the poking pip, but deliberately not quite touching it, then round the softly incurled edges, teasing out the pink and black wafered fins, which immediately curled back from their heat, tantalizing them, stroking cruelly then stopping while Anya's feet were edged further apart to make the beam press more definitely into her belly and thereby pushing her mound out and render her flesh more open to this tickling. The feather tip, now wet with Anya's syrup, and drawn by the stroking to a finer, stiffer point, was probed around the joining of her flesh lips, then beneath the hood, so Anya could feel it trapped against the slow pulse of her nubbin, pricking round its base, flexing, drawing round its outline in a half circle of cruel delight, then flexing the other way and drawing a fine line of sweetly cutting pleasure back as if to slice her nubbin free and let it push out even harder. Her body dripped desire; her liquid welled and gathered at her burning tip for the feather point to flick away then kiss her, tip to tip, then stroke around her once again.

'Push,' Ulla instructed, and Anya pushed hard enough to turn her body inside out. And as she forced her body open in this fashion, the tip of the feather entered her and stroked her just inside before she gasped and closed up once again. 'Push!' Ulla encouraged her once more and this time Anya grunted and the feather stroked seduction deeper into her so that when she closed she caught it and it had to be withdrawn against the pressure of her body.

The girl put the feather down and picked up the metal balls which were connected by the cord. She wet one, and moistened round the mouth of Anya's bottom before pushing it into her. Its coldness caused her to contract tightly. The cord, with the second ball suspended from it, was lifted and allowed to dangle part way down her upturned back, before the cord was pulled gently but firmly until the metal ball inside was bedded up against her tightness. Ulla pushed two fingers deep into Anya's sex, curling them round towards the front to push her nubbin outwards.

'Tighten,' she said. Anya squeezed and tried to draw the fingers deeper. The ball moved up her back a tiny fraction, drawn by her contraction, and swayed against her. The feather was taken up again. Now the ball was set in motion, rolling like a pendulum in a cool path of pressure from side to side across Anya's lower back, while the tip of the feather tickled very short quick strokes over the end of her pushed-out nubbin.

Anya was quite helpless against the systematic pleasuring – she could not move to bring it on, she could not hold it back. When the pendulum slowed and finally stopped, the feather tip did too, while Ulla set the pendulum off again so the tickling might continue. And after four such oscillatory, dancing, tickling sessions, Anya's body could take no more. It was as if every nerve within her belly was connected to its own spider-thin silk drawn tightly through and knotted on the outside of her nubbin, and the knot that held those myriad strands of pleasure was now being cruelly teased until every nerve cried out for its deliverance. The girl withdrew her fingers carefully, but continued feathering Anya's minute silken knot until she gasped out loud. Then she ran the feather tip round and round until Anya finally grunted; Ulla stopped with the tip still bowed against her. Anya had the feeling she was poised high in the air, her whole body balanced on that wicked point of pleasure, and any second now the slightest movement would cause her skin to split and she would impale herself on the long thin slowly flexing needle of sweet delicious pleasure. She could feel her last surrender coming on.

The girl carefully relaxed the pressure, took the tip away and lifted the pendulum over, fitting the weighted cord precisely to the divide of Anya's sex so it balanced precariously up against her nubbin and, as Anya's pre-spasms came in tiny shudders that shook the weight and tickled the cord against herself, Ulla moved round to the other side and licked slow wet strokes in the small of Anya's back. The transmitted pressure of the licking shook the weight to make the cord resonate just enough to bring the pleasure on. And gentle though the licking was, and unmoving though the finely drawn yet vibrating weight of cord that buzzed against her nubbin, still that style of pleasure almost made the slave black out.

Something about that deep deliverance seemed to bring the cook to life. 'There!' she shouted. 'What did I tell you?' to no one in particular. 'Just like all the others – only interested in one thing.'

When Anya was unfastened, she was so cramped that she could hardly stand. 'Well, we'll cure you of your waywardness, young lady, however long it takes.' Cook turned to Ulla. 'She must be punished – every hour on the hour. Twenty lashes.' Then she shook her finger at Anya. 'Now – get dressed and get to work.'

Anya was made to serve up the dumpling stew, ladling it out into great tureens for dispatch to the masters, before she was given food and drink. And in the middle of her meal, as she sat at the long table where she had suffered the degradation, Ulla brought the stool and placed it next to her. The other servants began to grin and nudge one another.

'Please,' Anya begged, but it was no use. Cook stood by with arms folded. Anya had to pull down her leather pouch to her knees and bend across the girl's lap, in front of everyone. The rough material of Ulla's dress brushed against Anya's shaven mound. Her flesh was still hot and swollen, and the threads tickled against her cruelly. However, Ulla was unsatisfied with Anya's posture. She made her readjust it several times; she wanted Anya's flesh spread wider. In the end she pulled the pouch completely off and Anya had to hold it in one hand and grip the leg of the stool with the other while Ulla spread her cheeks then finger-smacked the mouth of her bottom, counting out the lashes. While her fingertip snapped shame against the hot little mouth, her other hand was progressively introduced between Anya's thighs, spreading apart her flesh at first, then holding the leaves open, then entering her with two fingers, keeping the walls of her sex apart, then finally searching out the hardened nubbin, squeezing it at every smack. 'This waywardness must stop,' she said, in imitation of the cook, but loving every minute of it. 'It must be worked right out of this hot hard flesh.' When the twenty lashes were up, Anya was made to stand up and hold her flesh open while Ulla examined her. Then she had to thank her before she put her pouch back on.

Throughout that afternoon, in between gutting fish, peeling turnips, plucking fowl and polishing the stove, she was punished in that way, as Cook had promised, on the hour. The stool would be brought, Anya would be made to bend and suffer the degradation. Though exactly twenty lashes were administered each time – for Ulla counted them quite clearly – she would sometimes prefer to take her time, making the lashing finger fall at unpredictable intervals after long pauses during which the stimulation was maintained, until Anya was so wet that the fingers would make liquid sounds if, as commonly happened, they chose to probe inside her. Any servants standing nearby would stop whatever they were doing to watch and comment on the proceedings – how her body writhed or jerked, how wide she spread, comments on her bareness and her blackness – and all the time, the stimulation in the same spot, and the slow smacking with the servant's quick wet fingers, were making her rim of flesh swell hot to burning. It was on the third such punishment, surrounded by chicken feathers floating in the air, with her pouch of leather down around her ankle, with her cheeks spread very wide indeed and the girl's knee pushed into her belly just above her sex, forcing her nubbin out strongly, with a fingernail scratching lightly back and forth across it, and on the seventeenth smack – with a finger so wet and whipped so quickly down that the fingertip pushed inside her – that Anya disgraced herself and groaned out loud and kicked her leg and came. Her pouch was thrown across the kitchen floor, so then she had the degradation of having to retrieve it amid all the jeers and, as she bent to pick it up, the furtive touchings of her gently pulsing flesh. After that, Ulla tried every time to prolong the stimulation but always managed to stop short of the deliverance.

The lashings continued until late into the evening, when Anya was bathed; she had to stand in a large shallow pan while Ulla washed her down. She found the washing very soothing and relaxing. Then she was put to bed, in a tiny room beside the bakehouse, with only a straw mattress on the floor. The door was bolted from the outside. She took her halter and her pouch off, pulled the blanket up around her and cried.

Yet despite her exhaustion, she didn't fall asleep. She couldn't. All the events of that day raced through her mind; the things she had witnessed in the dungeons, the woman's punishment and then her own. But at the back of everything, all the time, even when she'd been forced to bend across the beam to be degraded in that way, was that other image, of the slaves suspended from the ceiling in the Chamber of Correction, and of one of them being lowered into the waiting arms of the Taskmistress. She knew that the Taskmistress would do this to her too, if she got the chance. She didn't feel safe from her even in the kitchens; she was sure the Taskmistress had directed all of this. The other slaves she had seen down here were not being subjected to the cruel abuse that she was being made to suffer. She had been set apart for special degradation, otherwise why was she locked in here instead of being allowed to sleep in the dormitory with all the other servants – and slaves – on kitchen duty? And why had Cook arranged for that shameful torment every hour? It was exactly the kind of wicked stimulation that the Taskmistress might devise, and this was yet another reason why Anya could not sleep. She knew the hour would soon be up and Ulla would bring in the stool – the stool with three legs, one of which had a piece cut out of it and one a large knot in the wood, half way down, which Anya would grip so hard that her hand hurt, while those strong fingers of Ulla's delivered shameful pleasure between her legs and between her buttocks.

Then Anya heard the latch. She pulled the blanket over her head although, with only the corridor light filtering through the window in the wall, the room was nearly dark. Her tears flowed silently. The sinking feeling came between her thighs. Someone sat beside her on the mattress.

'Anya?' the voice whispered. The blanket was drawn

back. Even in silhouette, Anya knew those finely drawn features and that closely clipped hair.

'Axine!' She threw herself at her and clasped her arms around her. And now she sobbed out loud – giant sobs that carried all the pent-up hurt, all the anguish and misery of the last two days. 'I hate it, Axine. I cannot stand it any more. Get me out of here. Please!'

'Shh . . . shh.' Axine held her tightly, stroking her curls, pressing her delicate fingers protectively round her head, brushing her fingertip across the lobe of Anya's ear, and combing the hair back from her face. She kissed Anya's tears, taking up the liquid drops of hurt upon her soft cool lips. 'Shh . . .' She kissed her lips to Anya's. 'You must be strong . . .' She caressed them with her sweet breath, just brushing across them, brushing that cool confidence across Anya's hot salt swollen lips. 'You are strong, I know it.' This time she parted her lips and closed them briefly against Anya's pouted lower lip, pulling gently, then stroking softly from side to side, barely touching the skin at all, tickling the faint and downy hairs on Anya's upper lip. 'You must not weaken . . . that is the test.'

'The test?' Anya was recalling what had happened at the Council meeting. That was the test – or trick – and she had failed it.

'These trials are the Taskmistress's way of proving you.'

'She is trying to degrade me.'

'No. I have heard what happened at the Council. She is trying to prove your worth, so nobody again may call it into question.'

'But she is trying to turn the Council against me.'

Axine stared at her in disbelief.

'She wants to rule Lidir,' said Anya. 'She wants to control me and when I am made Princess, she will do away with the Prince.'

'No . . .' Axine looked troubled; she was looking at Anya as she would at someone who was disturbed in mind. She stroked her hand across Anya's brow. Anya knocked her hand away.

'It's true! She does. She is evil. She is a very evil woman.

133

Can't you see how devious she is? Why can't anybody see it? Is everyone blind?'

'But it was she who came to the rescue when Lord Sardroc tried to discredit you in the Council. Wasn't it? She was the one who suggested a way in which consent to the betrothal could come about.' Axine waited.

Anya frowned. She had been sidetracked by the mention of that name.

'What – what did he do to you, Axine?' Anya put her arms around Axine again. 'You tried to save me from the guard and he took it out on you, didn't he? Did he hurt you? Why did you not run away?'

Axine turned her face away and didn't answer. Anya could see she was upset. She ran her fingers through the bristles of her hair, then touched Axine's cheek. She had thought that Axine would be crying, but she wasn't. Anya kissed that unflinching cheek and Axine turned and smiled.

She placed her hand on Anya's. 'I have to go. You must get some sleep now.'

'Axine – what will happen tomorrow?'

Axine slowly shook her head. 'I don't know. You might be moved upstairs. But whatever it is, you must have strength.' It made Anya want to cry again, all this talk about being strong; it was what the Prince had told her before any of this was dreamt of . . .

Axine kissed her one last time, on the tip of her nose, then stood up and walked swiftly to the door.

'Axine?'

'Yes?'

'Why did you come here tonight?'

Axine was silent for a moment or two. 'I had to see you,' she said finally. 'I had to know that you were all right.'

Then she was gone. Anya lay there thinking about it. Axine was a true friend. Anya would bide her time, let Axine into her secret and Axine would help her to escape. Anya slept soundly that night.

[9]

The Library

Next morning, Anya was already awake when Ulla came to get her. It was definitely morning for she could hear people moving about and shouting, and the sounds of the cauldrons being filled with water. She didn't feel exhausted any more. She had been thinking about her plan, imagining herself in the courtyard at the castle gate, with Axine distracting the guard while Anya slipped out unnoticed. They would never catch her then, once she crossed the clearing and made it to the forest edge. The forest went on forever, almost; that's what she'd thought as a child. It was certainly very large. It was said that you could travel from one end of Lidir to the other without ever leaving the forest. But where was the Great River? She had never heard of that before. Who – that she could trust – would know? She ought to have asked Axine.

Ulla didn't have the stool this time. 'Get up,' she said brusquely. When Anya moved her thighs, she could feel the bristles beginning to re-establish themselves and prickle her.

Ulla's sleeves were rolled up. She had bronzed arms, like a girl used to working in the fields rather than in the kitchens. 'You won't need those today.' Anya had begun to step into the loops of her leather pouch, and now she looked up questioningly. But Ulla was not forthcoming; she had the same unsparing look that she had had yesterday, each time she had taken pleasure in bending Anya across her knee. 'Come.' Ulla held Anya's wrists behind her back with one hand while she led her out, firstly to be washed then to be set down to breakfast at the long table. Anya was very hungry, and even though the bowl before her was full to the

135

brim of what she thought she hated most, she finished every spoonful. Somehow, although it defied reason, she had acquired the taste for it – coarse thick salty porridge, laced quite liberally with ripe goat's milk and honey. While she was in the midst of eating, licking round the thickly coated spoon, Cook passed by, staring straight through her and totally ignoring her. She didn't even notice when Anya dropped the spoon. Cook was very strange; Anya couldn't understand her.

When she had finished breakfast, a tray was placed before her. Her eyes lit up, for it was a silver tray, which must be destined for upstairs. 'For Lord Sennax in the library. He lives there,' Ulla said.

'He *lives* in the library?'

Ulla nodded gravely as if she disapproved. 'I will take you up there.'

'Oh.' Anya's plan would need modifying yet again. Why did Ulla have to spoil it by going with her?

'But you must take it in to him. I will wait outside.' The way that Ulla had said that made Anya suspicious. Why was Anya needed at all? Why couldn't Ulla deliver it? Surely a hefty girl like that couldn't be afraid?

The tray contained an empty bowl, a cloth and a large mug of hot spiced milk; even though the mug had a cap over it, Anya could smell the scent of cloves. Also on the tray was something unexpected, a bunch of large black berries. Anya immediately recognised what they were, although she had never seen them before.

'Are they. . . ?'

'Grapes.' Ulla nodded with assurance.

Anya had tasted raisins once, and wine, of course. She had had wine quite often, but never grapes. Grapes were very rare. The Prince had told Anya all about them and had promised her some when they came into season, but she knew that season to be far away. 'But how?' she asked.

Ulla tapped a finger against her nose. 'These are the very last . . . we store them in the cellar with the wine. Very sweet . . .' She pulled one from the bunch and popped it in her mouth, then did the same for Anya. The grape felt like a cold glass bead; she bit it and the sweet sharp liquid burst upon her tongue. But as she chewed the skin, the sweet taste turned to bitter, like oak leaves, and made her wince as she crunched the tiny wormwood flavoured pip. Even so, she found the taste of grapes to be bewitching.

'Ah, no more. They are needed for Lord Sennax; they help to keep his strength up. And so does this . . .' She lifted up the cap of the mug and dipped her finger in; it came out thickly coated. 'Extra creamy. He is very frail.' Then Ulla looked away. Anya wondered once more why Ulla should be so unwilling to take the tray herself, if he was indeed such a weak old man. Was there something else, perhaps, that Ulla wasn't telling?

It was many minutes before they reached the library, and Anya understood now why the mug of hot milk had a cover; it would be barely warm by the time Lord Sennax got it. Nevertheless, Ulla had walked so quickly that Anya had difficulty keeping up. She tripped on the broad stairs leading up to the Great Hall, but Ulla managed to catch the tray in time.

The library was situated in a part of the castle that Anya had never visited, far beyond the Bondslaves' House, in the south wing. Few people ever talked about the south wing. She had heard that some of the older lords and ladies lived there – Marella had told her this much – but she had never met any of them. Marella was always very evasive about the details; when pressed, she would only shake her head and murmur, 'I'm sure I don't know, my dear . . . we don't go there very often, you see,' and immediately change the subject. There seemed to be some mystery about it. The Prince's cousin, Lady Amalicia, was the only person Anya had met who actually lived there, and she certainly wasn't old. But Anya still hadn't visited her suite. She had been invited, but the Prince had refused; Anya thought this was probably because the cousins did not get on, although she had found Amalicia to be very pleasant. Of course, there was now the nagging suspicion about the slaves Amalicia had supposedly sent down to the dungeons. Anya would give her the benefit of the doubt on that, at least until she got to know her better, when she might ask her about it directly.

The south wing seemed very quiet; the air smelled slightly musty. They didn't meet a soul before they reached the large panelled door of the library.

'Is his lordship in there? Shall we go in?' asked Anya.

It was clear that Ulla wouldn't budge an inch. After the haste that Ulla had shown up to this point, this made Anya concerned. But Ulla looked worried.

'I'll come back for you later on,' she said.

'But it will only take a minute for me to leave the tray off, won't it?'

'Lord Sennax may wish that you keep him company for a while. He likes to talk about his books.' Once again, Ulla hadn't looked at Anya when she said this, instead allowing her eyes to glance up at the ceiling, at the door, then finally at the floor.

It was therefore with a degree of trepidation that Anya opened the library door, which creaked as if it had never been used since the day it was built, and stepped inside. She left the door ajar, and not merely to avoid a repetition of that anguished sound.

The air in the library was so still and cool that Anya could almost feel her body gliding through it as she walked. It was totally silent in there. She could not hear her footfalls on the carpet. A roughly central aisle, with embayments placed on either side, led off erratically into the distance. The first pair of embayments each contained a large table and a lectern, with shelves of books behind, shelves extending high up to the ceiling. All the books seemed to be arranged neatly, as if they were rarely used. On the ceiling was a painting of a winding path above the aisle, with branches over each embayment. A different scene blossomed from each branch. The first one on the right depicted crowds of people of all shapes and sizes and manner of dress and tone of skin. To the left were animals – common ones, rabbits, foxes, horses and the like, but also strange creatures like the ones on the tapestries in Lord Aldrid's bedchamber. The striped horse was there, and an even stranger fantasy; as large as a deer, it had a deer's head lacking horns, a rabbit's hind legs, a mouse's tail, and an extra, smaller head projecting from its belly. Each scene bore a scroll on which a cipher was painted. There were ciphers carved into the wood above the shelves, which were packed with leather-bound books and parchment scrolls. Some of the books looked too large for one person to lift. Anya knew the ciphers and the scenes must refer to the contents of the books and, quite probably, each book had its own special resting place. She would have loved to open some of these books and look at them, especially those in the left-hand bay, for she knew that books often contained interesting paintings arranged so as to tell a story. In fact she owned a book. The Prince had given it to her. It was full of pictures of horses and she had always kept it beside the bed. She loved to weave stories around the pictures and tell them to the Prince. But she would probably never see that book again. She felt the sadness surging up from deep inside. She might never see her Prince again . . .

A noise cut through the silence. It sounded like a sharp intake of breath – a woman's breath, but how could it be? It had come from much deeper into the library, but it was difficult to tell how far. Anya crept slowly along, checking each embayment before proceeding to the next pair, following the changing scenes, from mountains, rivers and waterfalls; great armies in battles; wise men grouped around a table; to a tableau entirely composed of ciphers of all kinds. She couldn't hear the sound now, so she moved more quickly – too quickly – and too late she noticed the scene upon the ceiling. It was an exotic garden, full of naked women being chased by men with rigid cockstems. She might have guessed this one would be occupied. To make things worse, she announced her presence with a sneeze, brought on by the dust that filled the air from the many books that lay open, strewn upon the table. Lord Sennax stopped what he was doing and slowly turned round. The young slave on the table hid her face.

Lord Sennax did indeed look frail. His blue robe, faded to pale washed grey, hung limply from his bones. His hair was pure white, his beard was long and wispy, and his skin reminded Anya of the pale yellow parchment of an old manuscript which had been rolled and unrolled countless times until it was creased and cracked. His eyes stared out from deep, hollow sockets and his long thin shaking fingers, angled downwards from the outstretched hand, looked as fragile as a spider that was long dead from starvation.

He waved the spider. 'Aah. Put it down, my dear.' His voice was like the rustle of wind through drifted autumn leaves. Anya placed the tray beside him on the leather-topped table; with all the books, it was difficult to find a space. The girl stayed turned away. 'I'll be with you in a moment . . . Yes.' Anya bowed and backed away again, for Lord Sennax was turning his attention once more to the girl. The two of them had not even separated at this inter-ruption. The girl knelt with elbows on the table and hips low down, perhaps to make it more convenient for his lordship, who was standing while he penetrated her. His hands returned to grip the chain about her hips. 'Why not have a browse for a minute or two?' Anya did not need telling twice. She backed round the corner. Her heart was racing after what she had witnessed. Would she be made to do that too? The thought of it – she could never face it, not with a man like that . . .

She sat on the edge of the table in the next alcove while she regained her breath. The shelves here had many more scrolls than books. She glanced up, and then her eyes widened, for the painting on the ceiling was a very familiar one. It was the emblem of Lidir, showing the castle and forest and the Princess in white. That picture made her heart quicken; it always did. She hoped that one day, she might be strong and fearless, and as wise and kind as the Princess was said to have been.

The sound of the girl's breathing was getting louder again. Behind the unsteady sound was pleasure. But how could the girl be taking pleasure from this? Anya got up and stood against the shelves to listen. As she moved closer to the end, her foot dislodged a scroll which began to open as it rolled across the floor. Straight away she could tell it was a map – an eagle's view of a landscape. Perhaps the landscape was Lidir? She knelt down to look at it. There were many ciphers on the map. On the bottom edge was an image of the sun. A tiny drawing of a castle lay in the middle, and all around it, minute trees were figured, but below the castle and trees, running across the parchment, was a wavy blue line with many branches. It had to be the Great River. Below that were pointed shapes – mountains – and at the bottom, a great swath of blue with ships, and a winged fish flying over it. This could only be the ocean. The ocean was even bigger than the forest – it was said to extend all around Lidir – and yet this map showed it only at the bottom, which was very odd. Anya stared harder and harder at the map, frowning until her eyebrows met, as though, by staring long and hard enough, she would see into it as if it were a magic crystal and divine her Prince's fate. She knew he was in that parchment somewhere, below the river, in the mountains, perhaps beyond. She closed her eyes and tried to picture his surroundings, but she could only see his soft green eyes and his strong and gentle face.

Now she was brought to earth sharply by the girl's throes of pleasure. As she held her breath and listened to the gasps, Anya could almost feel the young slave's passion. She waited a decent interval until the softening sighs had ebbed to silence, and she was sure the pleasuring had finished, before getting up and creeping round the corner. She stopped short. It had not finished. It had only just begun. The girl was on the table still, but sitting back on her heels now, facing Lord Sennax. Her knees were spread apart. Lord Sennax was unfastening the chain about her belly; as it slid away, he sighed. The girl was shaking; soft shudders rippled upwards through her breasts. She looked anxious as her chain – the symbol of her identity – was being taken away. Lord Sennax tried to calm her; he pressed both hands flat against her newly naked belly, then lifted, moved and pressed again.

'There,' he said. Her lips began to tremble. He opened her with his thumbs, pressing one to either side of her sex to split the thin, pale pink wafers very gently apart to reveal the

141

deep moist pink within. He maintained her in this open state with one hand arched across her flesh while he dangled the chain down her belly, through the arch, until it touched against her and she shivered. His lordship picked up. the cloth from the tray and carefully folded it. 'Lift, my sweet,' he said. The girl looked timidly at him. He touched a finger to her cheek, then held up her chin. 'Lift.' And as she raised her hips, he placed the cloth on the table in between her thighs, so when she lowered, her sex now rested upon it. She watched him take up the mug of milk and tip some in the bowl. Now she was breathing very rapidly. 'Shh, my dear, do not be afraid.' But she shuddered as he cupped first one breast in the tilted bowl and then the other. The milk formed a creamy circle round each teat, but then the circles broke into two parallel lines, disappearing underneath each breast then running across the outswell of her belly. Lord Sennax stood back and waited until the runnels had progressed down to her navel before he bent to lick them up, then suck upon each breast in turn.

He had no teeth; Anya shivered to see her suckle him. He raised his head and whispered in the girl's ear. Her nipples were now wet with his spittle. She held her breasts up while he drew the tips out in a gentle milking action, forming them into bulbils. This time, when he lifted up the bowl, the girl bent forward, taking her breasts in her hands and dipping each of them in, coating them with the thick and creamy milk, for him to suck again. But he waited longer, until the rivulets ran down and seeped into the creases at the tops of her thighs, before he licked back up the lines and sucked upon the nipples. Now the girl had closed her eyes, for while he sucked, his fingers lay upon the cloth that lay between her thighs, touching her very lightly, exploring her tenderness. Anya watched those thighs spread wider, then lift and move then settle back as her warm young flesh gave succour to his covert explorations.

When he raised his head, Lord Sennax turned. Anya had been spotted. She retreated, afraid she might be scolded on account of this unheralded interruption. 'No, sit down my dear. Come, sit beside me.' The girl tried to turn her head away; she was terribly embarrassed. His lordship removed his fingers and stroked her belly to soothe her. 'Shh . . . Look at me, my darling, there,' he said, and the stroking progressed upwards to her breasts, lifting up the nipples, then down again across her belly.

Anya sat uneasily on the chair to his right. The table was strewn with open books and unfurled parchments. Lord Sennax picked up the bowl again and dripped the milk low down on the girl's belly, dripping while his fingers massaged her gently between the legs. 'Shh . . .' he whispered while the droplets fell, some upon his fingers, some upon her flesh, pausing when her breathing became too uneven, then dripping the milk again and working her until her belly shuddered once, whereupon he stopped and stroked her belly with the back of his hand, pressing firmly, lifting as he pressed, so her sex was lifted too, only to fall back again to kiss the moistened cloth. Then he took the cloth away, doubled the thickness and, spreading her more completely, he replaced the cloth so it pressed against her fully open sex. He picked up the bowl and dripped the milk precisely into the open join between the girl's legs, holding back the flesh hood as he did so, and whispering to Anya, 'She will not be much longer. Will you, child?' The girl covered her face. Anya could smell the cloves on his breath; she could see the deeply bedded points of his eyes above the sunken cheeks. It made her very sorry for the girl, who seemed so young and tender to be forced to take pleasure in this way at the hands of a man who, at such an age, ought instead to be concerned only with his books or with lying abed and resting.

'She is very new to pleasure, you see.' But that only made it worse. He stroked the girl's inner thighs and her body rippled. 'An untapped spring of burning passion. A tabernacle of desire,' he murmured. 'Can't you feel her heat?' Anya could smell it. He sighed, then spoke gently to the girl. 'It is time to turn around, my dear, time for this vessel of love to deliver its delicious self to pleasure once more . . .'

143

The girl was kneeling on all fours, hiding her face again, facing away from Lord Sennax. Her feet hung over the edge of the table. His bony hand stroked down her thigh and onto the back of her upturned calf. She shivered when his fingers reached her ankle and began to massage it. The girl's toes began to curl. Anya's eyes began to widen. 'If I have learnt one thing . . .' he trailed away. His fingers continued massaging, rubbing very lightly and quickly to one side of the ankle, then the other. The heel of his other hand pushed slowly upwards from the base of the girl's spine for a measured few inches, then lifted, moved back and pushed upwards again. It imparted a gentle rocking movement to the pouch between her legs. The girl's back curved downwards in response, until her nipples brushed the pages of the parchment beneath her.

'Yes, my lord?' Anya had spoken for the first time; she had to know what it was this old, old man had gleaned in all his years of study. His lordship had assumed the expression of a craftsman working lovingly, putting the finishing touches, smoothing out the curves, fitting his fingertips to the soft and flowing rounds and hollows, concentrating, oblivious of anything other than the perfect living sculpture in front of him. Two fingers rubbed across the middle of the sole of the slave girl's foot, softly polishing, working the pleasure gently in. The heel of his hand stroked reassurance up her back. At last, the craftsman frowned as if Anya's drifted words of long ago had finally settled on his ears.

'If I have learnt one thing in this endless quest,' he began again. 'If life has any purpose, it must be this . . .' His hands moved underneath, across her low slung belly, then divided, one to whisper gently from one nipple to the other, and to pinch beneath them softly, the other to delve within the hollow of her thighs, opening her, spreading back the flesh. 'And, my dears,' he encompassed the two women with his profound address, though only one of them was listening. The girl was in an entirely different world, as Sennax pulled softly at her sex, testing her, then wet his fingers in the bowl and slipped them up inside. 'The greatest thing a man can do, the pinnacle of man's achievement,'

Anya's eyes widened, for she was hanging on these words, 'is to bring a woman pleasure – slow, profound pleasure, tailored to her individual needs, of course, but within this constraint – pleasure to completion.' Anya found herself nodding in agreement. His lordship had now got into his stride. 'And if a woman's body shall require that completion more than once on an occasion, then it shall not be denied.' Now Anya realised that, frail and unattractive though this ancient harbinger of delight might be, still that simple philosophy had struck a chord in her belly. 'And a woman must never be forced,' he continued, his fingers making softened sucking sounds against the slave-girl's milky moistness.

'But – ' Anya protested, for the girl was hiding her face from shame; she had already been taken once, yet Sennax had kept her on the table.

His lordship took her meaning. 'She is very shy . . . that's all. But shyness is no proscription to the embrace of pleasure – on the contrary, shyness is a sauce to the delight.' While Anya considered this, Sennax withdrew his fingers, lifted the bowl of milk and placed it on the table, between the girl's thighs. 'She is almost ready now.' He made her lower. Anya heard the sounds of splashing, the milk dripping back into the bowl, the soft wet sounds of flesh. The girl's breathing began to get stronger. He lifted her up again, spread her sex and worked his fingers in once more.

'Would you wish to take your pleasure next, my dear?' Anya didn't know what to say. She had never even been asked before in quite this way – not by anyone in the castle. She was completely at a loss. 'Think about it. Have a browse.'

She should never have opened the book before her, but she did. Lord Sennax concentrated on the girl, whose hips were beginning to move against his fingers. Anya didn't get beyond the first painting – which showed a living outstretched cockstem with a woman's lips reaching up to suck upon the underside of the plum – before the girl's pleasure came, but very slowly, drawn out by Sennax's careful working. Anya sat as tight and still as a statue. She couldn't watch this happen. She tried to stare fixedly at the pouted lips upon the page and the swollen fleshy plum while the girl heaved and shook and whimpered and Sennax murmured, 'Sshhh . . . very good. Now squeeze against me tightly, squeeze those shudders from that delicious belly . . . Shh . . . Now wait, stay that pleasure,' then moved his hands from between her legs and held her knees so wide apart she sat upon the bowl. He poured in the rest of the milk from the mug and then reached in beneath her. 'Open, my child,' he whispered, 'let me squeeze you as your body drinks . . .' and amid the liquid sounds and whimpers, the girl cried out and Sennax brought about her pleasure, making Anya flush with hot desire and shame. Her senses had been overwhelmed by those images – the picture on the page before her, the sounds, soft protestations beneath the weight of pleasure, his lordship's robe brushing her knee, the pressure of the cushioned seat against her sex and now the heavy scent of spiced milk mixed with the distillation of female passion. Anya closed her eyes. She could hear Lord Sennax whisper something to the girl, a question, judging by his tone of voice. Then she heard the movement. She opened her eyes. The girl had dismounted from the table. Her cheeks were flushed. She stood there while Lord Sennax restored her chain, wiped her breasts and belly with the cloth, then wiped between her thighs and drank the contents of the bowl.

'Until tomorrow, my dear.' He kissed her hand.

'Thank you, my lord,' she said, then curtsied to him, turned and left.

Anya's heart was beating in her throat; her palms felt clammy; she was staring again at the picture in front of her while the waves still swelled and dashed against her belly, the waves of wanting, and the waves of shame for permitting herself to think of taking pleasure in this way, with this frail old man.

'Ah yes,' his whisper broke her silent reverie, 'the pictures. The forbidden tomes.' Lord Sennax sat down beside her and when Anya didn't move – her body was a shaking statue – he lifted up the book and held it open, with the spine supported on the table edge, and watched the young girl's eyes glance away from the page and then, as always happened, sink slowly back again, drawn by the sweet seduction of those images. He turned the page, and watched her bosom swell, the delicious swell of smooth and flawless youthful roundedness, the tender fleshy dark brown tips provoked to pleasured tautness by those shameless revelations, but most of all the eyes – the eyes, expanded now to liquid drowning blackness. How many of those eyes had Sennax drowned in? How much pleasure had he witnessed through those long years? How much had he given? And when his old decrepit body was finally taken by the soil, what then? Would his soul live on in those memories of pleasure inveigling those sweet young minds, seducing them with softened echoes of their fervour at his hands? Would he be remembered for the passions he had wakened?

Sennax chose another book, a smaller one. 'Take it . . . take hold of it, my child.' Anya's fingers shook as they closed upon the smooth soft leather cover – almost like a living thing between her fingertips – and she felt Lord Sennax's fingers touch her belly, long cold fingers, curling, resting against her, drawing sustenance from the warmth of her skin.

'Do you like grapes, my child?'

Anya was sitting astride Lord Sennax's knees, facing the table. She had been afraid to place her full weight upon him, until he insisted she should relax. Now she could feel his bony thighs pressing against her. His long beard tickled her shoulders. His cockstem bedded deeply in her belly; she could feel the head inside her, swollen so hard against her from the long thin bony stem that she felt as if she were pegged down to his body; when Sennax rocked, the two of them moved as one. His bag, which he had suggested she might touch, felt dry but faintly oily, like the dried up skin of an apricot. The sweet sharp scent of grapes ascended from between their conjoined thighs.

The grape was being rolled very slowly round her outturned leaves, guided quite precisely by Sennax's bony fingers, before being gently pressed against her nubbin then lifted away and slipped into his mouth. Her flesh was dripping with the grape juice trickling down it, for every third or fourth grape would be carefully held in place until Anya had absorbed the picture fully – the image now before her showed a slave-girl held upside down between two guards, who held her legs wide apart while a bejewelled lady smacked her fleshpot – then Lord Sennax would draw back her hood and burst the grape against her nubbin, then smear the pulp around it.

When they reached a picture of a knotted cord being drawn from a bondgirl's bottom, Anya's sudden catch of breath made Sennax hesitate. 'Lean forward, my dear,' he said and Anya gasped before he touched her, for she knew what was coming. He made her press her breasts against the leather surface of the table but hold the book before her and look upon the image while he touched her, holding his fingertip against the velvet mouth, making her push out while he stroked it, then pressing a grape against her, pushing until she expanded just enough to take its width, then making her strain to hold it in position within the entrance to the tube of flesh while he stroked her back and, reaching round, very lightly touched her nubbin. 'Hmm . . .' he observed with gravity when Anya finally could bear no more and tightened so the grape slipped out and rolled across the floor.

'Sit up. Proceed with the lesson, my child.' The next picture showed a woman's bud being fitted with a pearl. It made Anya's sex tense, to see this torture set out on the page, this image of the cruel clasp of denial that had been fastened to her nub of pleasure by the Taskmistress all that time ago.

'This image is familiar to you?' Lord Sennax asked.

'Yes, my lord.'

'Your flesh was fitted with the pearl?' He lightly touched her once, in that place. She shivered at the recollection. 'It gave you pleasure – the denial, I mean?' Now she bowed her head. Her heart was beating faster. His words had caused a churning feeling deep inside her belly. 'I see . . .' It was almost as if he could read things that lay hidden from herself. His fingers traced the edge of her flesh; her neck arched back; he took the leaves and pulled them once, then allowed them to retract. 'I see.' Now, under that gentle provocation, she could feel herself distending; her petals of desire were expanding, tickling as they did so, brushing against the long curls on his belly. He held the leaves apart, pulled out gently from her body, holding them very still that way, making her aware. She shuddered with delight.

'Hmm . . .' He made her turn the page. Now she wanted to squirm away, but he held her very firmly, bringing her leaves together, so they kissed against each other, then peeling them very slowly apart. The pictures showed a woman's sex being pierced with a needle. 'This is new to you?' She could only nod. 'Many girls have this treatment, if their masters so decide. Some choose it for themselves.' Anya cried out as if that needle had been pushed into her flesh.

'No!' She could not believe anyone would agree to this torture.

Again he pressed the leaves together, more tightly this time, then very softly peeled them back apart.

'Indeed. See – we make three incisions.' His lordship demonstrated on her person. 'One here, above the hood, from one side to the other.' He took hold of it at the very top, where it joined her body, but squeezed so gently that it made her sex contract, then he lifted back the loose skin to expose her swelling pip. 'Hmm,' he said, 'and the others here . . .' He took the flesh leaves by turn and nipped them just below the level of her nubbin. He sealed her flesh again. 'Go on, turn the page.' But she was fearful now of what torture might be revealed next. 'There. There are many little baubles that can bring a girl delight . . .' The first was a short string of tiny gold beads attached to the hood of flesh and dangling down across the figured stiffly poking nubbin. Anya did not need this one explaining; it would brush across it with every single movement that the woman made. 'It helps to ready a girl for love,' he said.

Now he peeled her stickiness open yet again and held her that way. 'No, do not squeeze, my child. It is too soon for that.' Anya felt her cheeks begin to burn. His fingers pulled her flesh back so her pip stuck out. He made her turn the page again. 'The bridle . . .' And now she wanted him to touch her nubbin. She needed to have it touch against something.

'The bridle?'

'Mmm,' he said. As his fingertips pressed the inner surface of her leaves, his thumbs stretched back the hood. 'The lover controls the progress of pleasure by means of the bridle.' It was a tiny rod of gold which passed between the pierced leaves and pressed against the underside of the nubbin, with a tiny chain looped between the metal ends. 'When the chain is drawn up, the rod rolls across the nubbin. When the tension is released, the nubbin pushes up and rolls it back.' His lordship demonstrated. He took a gold pin from his robe and, holding back the hood again to make her push out strongly, he stroked the bar upwards once across the burning pip. Anya gasped. He stroked it down again.

For the next picture, his lordship sleeved her hood back down across her nubbin. Then he squeezed it through the hood, very gently at first but gradually increasing the pressure while he explained. 'The clamp passes through the flesh leaves and presses the two small gold discs together with the bud trapped in between. This is normally a prelude to lovemaking, a pressurised denial of the kind I think might appeal to you . . .' He gave her flesh a firmer squeeze. Anya's belly was slowly liquifying under the thrall of this pageant of persecution.

The final picture that Anya's belly was able to sustain without disgrace was of a ring, a tiny split ring which had been fed through all three incisions so it formed a gold band encircling the nubbin. Lord Sennax wet his fingers and, applying the very tips in the form of a small wet mouth which softly milked her nub as if it were a nipple, explained. 'The lover sucks the nubbin outwards through the ring,' whereupon Anya groaned and squirmed and tried to push against the fingertip mouth even as it retreated.

The book held one more secret. The back cover was thicker than the front one; it carried a small hinged lid which folded out to reveal a slim compartment, lined with fur. Bedded in the fur were the very jewels that were figured in the pictures – the clamps and minute rings and chains. Anya's heart was pounding as Sennax took her hand and lifted up her finger; he touched the fingertip to the pearl, and Anya shivered; then he touched the same fingertip very lightly to her bud of flesh – the living pearl between her legs – and she closed her eyes, for all the memories came flooding back of that endless night of cruel torment suffered without release, and her reward – her deliverance into the evil clutches of the Taskmistress, to be used simply for her entertainment and her pleasure. Her belly shuddered at those recollections.

His lordship closed the lid and turned the book round. Projecting from the spine was a small loop, large enough to accommodate a finger. Anya took it to be a page marker slipped down the spine. Sennax pulled it out slowly; it was the knotted leather cord.

Lord Sennax now withdrew his stem from Anya's body, so he could deal with her more easily. He positioned her with her legs planted on the floor as wide apart as was comfortable and her belly flat to the table in such a way that the edge of it pressed into her above her sex and the hood was drawn back sharply, thereby developing her nubbin to full erection. He instructed Anya as follows: 'Endeavour to prolong your pleasure, my dear, for this will be beneficial. But you may inform me when your pleasure becomes too much to bear, and I will disenthrall you.' The final preparation was for him to pluck a grape from the bunch on the table, and have her bite the grape in half.

Sitting behind her, Lord Sennax carefully spread Anya's cheeks and inserted the cord quite fully in her bottom, until only the loop projected. He took up the grape, pressed it lightly against the tip of Anya's bud, rotating very gently while he slipped his middle finger in the loop. 'Now – do not let your bottom tighten. This is most important. The pleasure will be enhanced if the muscle stays relaxed.' The knotted cord was pulled out at an exactly even pace which, like the soft and now side to side brush of grape pulp against her bud, but did not vary however much her belly cramped or however much she moaned. To Anya, the feeling was as if her nubbin was being drawn out into a long thin thread and pulled out through her bottom. 'Good.' She bit her lip very hard and could not help but tighten. 'No – relax against the pleasure. Excellent, my child.' The cord slipped out; the grape was removed and eaten. His lordship had her bite a second grape, which tasted now of blood. 'Hold still. Do not tense.' The cord was reinserted. This time, when the grape was reapplied and the cord slipped, knot by knot, he squeezed the grape as he rotated it, so the juice trickled out and the pulp sucked upon her bud, until she thought that she would die of the delight. 'Aah, my lord, I am very, very near . . .'

'Can you bear it any more, my dear?' He held the cord taut and worked the pulp against her nubbin. The next knot slipped through so slowly that it almost made her spasm.

'Ah . . . No . . . If it should please my lord – my pleasure is coming.'

Lord Sennax held the grapeskin against her, pressing to keep her at the point of pleasure, then very carefully slipped the last remaining knot through her flesh without triggering her delight. 'Good,' he said, taking the residue of the grape away and dropping it in his mouth.

'Mmm . . . delicious,' he declared while Anya's nubbin pulsed with cruel rebuff. 'Good. Stand up.' He wiped her with the cloth, the very cloth that smelled of milk and young girl's pleasured heat. Anya opened her mouth to speak, but Sennax held his hand up. 'No – do not thank me. It is you who deserve the credit. You have done well, my child. And you have made an old man happy.' He smiled benignly. 'You may go now. I expect another visitor soon.'

'But – my lord?'

'Yes?' His lordship was already poring over a parchment.

'You said you would – you said . . . about giving a woman pleasure?'

'Yes indeed. But pleasure, as you may know, my child, comes in varied guises. What you may not know – though I believe you may suspect it – is that for you, the deepest joy is in denial. That is very clear to me. I recognise the signs.' He twitched his beard in affirmation.

Anya was dumbfounded.

'But please feel free to call back any day, and we can explore your case more fully. And there are plenty more books you can enjoy.'

Anya didn't know what to believe. She didn't know what to make of Lord Sennax's words. She didn't know what to make of herself. Was there any truth in what he'd said?

Ulla had looked at her strangely when she came out of the library, but hadn't said anything to her; she hadn't asked her what had gone on in there and, as if she'd recognised something was troubling Anya, she had left her alone that day to go about her duties in the bakehouse, kneading dough and measuring out the flour for the bakers. Anya found the work helped a little, but the nagging fear was there in the background all the time. There were no more punishments; she was thankful for that, but when Ulla put her to bed early that night, in the same small room, she could not settle. The fear came back again, but this fear was worse than anything she had anticipated when she lay in the Prince's bed those short few days ago. The premonition then had been of loneliness and danger when the Prince was gone; the loneliness was still there, and the danger was ever present, but now there was something else. She was frightened that the castle might in some way be taking over – not just taking her body, but taking her soul. Her mind was being haunted by those images of power and seduction, pleasure and pain, and now, without the immediacy of those intimate attentions, without the edge of fear, without her body being touched and stimulated, her body burned. She was burning in the flames of her denial. Her body needed that caress – the delicious caress of pleasure, the sweet deliverance. She turned onto her front and spread her body, spread it out upon the mattress, pressed her breasts against it, let its roughness take her flesh; she sucked her fingers, imagining those fingers were the Prince's flesh, then she used them for her release, making her fingers bring her long, repeated, gasping pleasure.

Lord Sennax was wrong. She hated the denial; she hated this place and all it stood for. She had to escape before it was too late.

That night, Axine came to her again.

'Axine, I want you to do something for me.'

Axine put her hand on Anya's. 'You know I would do

anything for you, Anya.' She sighed. 'But I cannot get you out of the kitchens. It is not permitted. I am not supposed to be here with you. They do not know.' She drew a fingertip down the back of Anya's hand, following the line of Anya's middle finger.

'I am leaving the castle.'

Axine's finger stopped. She didn't speak. In the darkness, Anya could see the profile of her slender body shake. She could see Axine's small breasts rise and fall with the quickness of her breathing.

Anya tried to continue in a measured tone. 'I am going to find my Prince.' She had almost faltered. She gritted her teeth. 'Nobody shall stop me. I want you to help me, Axine.' Axine had still not spoken. 'I want you to help me get through the castle gate. There is no one else I can turn to, no one I can trust.'

Axine's hand spread and pressed against Anya's. 'But it is very dangerous beyond the castle walls.'

'How could it be worse than this?'

After a long while, Axine spoke again. 'You are sure about this, Anya?' Her voice was heavy. Her hand was shaking.

'I am sure. I must go. If I stay, I will die. Inside, I will die . . .'

'No! Don't say it.' Axine put her arms around her, and Anya could feel the cool wet silent lines of sadness on Axine's cheeks, mixing with her own hot tears that Axine tried to kiss away.

'Then you must go. Now,' said Axine. 'You must not wait.'

'You will help me?'

Axine stood up. She squeezed Anya's hand again. 'I will bring you some clothes and food. I will be back as quickly as I can.'

Anya sank back with relief, then, just before Axine got to the door, suddenly remembered. 'Axine? How far is the Great River?'

'Two days' ride, maybe more, to the south.'

'The south . . . Is that towards the sun?'

[10]

Lady Amalicia and Lady Elinor

When the door opened again, Anya was ready, but she got a terrible shock, for it was not Axine at all.

'Ulla!'

'Shh. Come quickly.' But where was Axine? She couldn't ask; she had no choice but to follow and hope that Ulla was here to help.

Ulla took her out and up the stairs, but past the exit to the courtyard. Anya became suspicious when they passed the Bondslaves' House: they were heading for the south wing again. She stopped in her tracks and Ulla nearly pulled her over.

'Where are you taking me?' Ulla didn't reply. Anya was sure now that this had nothing to do with her plan, nothing to do with Axine. What if Ulla were taking her back to the library in the dark? She did not want to go. She broke free and ran but Ulla caught her and twisted her arm behind her back, took her by the hair and dragged her, though she did not have to drag her far. They had reached a door and Ulla knocked on it. Anya tried to get away again. When the door finally opened, Anya was on the floor, kicking, with Ulla on top.

'Oh dear,' the voice said softly, 'I hope I'm not interrupting.' Anya stopped kicking. She felt foolish and embarrassed in front of this woman who seemed so unperturbed.

Ulla got up. 'My Lady Elinor,' she curtsied, 'this is Anya. Lady Amalicia requested that she be . . .'

'Taught to wrestle on the floor?' Ulla fell silent. 'Are you going to get up then, Anya? You can't be very comfortable down there.'

155

Now Anya felt more foolish still, but the woman smiled gently. Even so, she seemed to carry a serene authority. Ulla seemed in awe of her, but Anya was not afraid. She found her calmness reassuring. Lady Elinor had wavy auburn hair. She wore a pale lilac silken bedrobe which enhanced her figure. She was taller than Anya by a hands-breadth, tall and slim, but with full, rounded breasts. Anya could see the shadow of her acorns through the silk. They were prominent, with dark surrounds. The woman took her hand. She had cool hands with long fingers and precisely manicured nails. She wore many rings, mainly bearing rubies and emeralds, and a turquoise necklace and earrings. She looked at Anya's turquoise ring and smiled, then lifted Anya's hand, holding it flat to her neckline, below the necklace, where Anya could feel the swell of her bosom. 'Look – it matches,' she said and widened her eyes. Anya liked her; she seemed self-assured but kind.

Lady Elinor led Anya in, closed the door without admitting Ulla, and locked it. Then she dropped the key in the pocket of her bedrobe. Anya found this to be the first disquieting action she had witnessed from this woman.

Unfortunately, the night was young, and there was much yet to befall which Anya would find unsettling. But comparatively, it was true. Lady Elinor was quite mild. Lady Amalicia was frightful.

The bedchamber was furnished in soft pink. The deep pink carpet felt like sheepskin under Anya's feet; it extended part way up the walls, which were draped in their upper reaches with white and pale pink satin curtains. The ceiling was deep cerise. Lady Amalicia's bed had four columns and a canopy with rose pink satin curtains drawn up high by braided purple velvet ropes interwoven with gold filament. Standing across the chamber from the bed was a long, low reclining couch, covered in pale mauve velvet, with the back, the sides and all the edges smoothly rounded and closely upholstered. It was skirted once again in pink satin. Lady Amalicia's dressing-table, however, was draped in white; it had a matching chair and an upright oval mirror, edged in gilt, extending almost to the ceiling. Delicately

painted roses adorning the edge of the glass formed a frame
to Amalicia's lovely face, for Lady Amalicia, in a light and
almost floating pale cream gown which fastened at the
neckline in a bow and parted down the middle to her navel,
sat upon the chair in front of the mirror, admiring her
reflection.

Amalicia was Anya's age, possibly slightly younger.
Amalicia was attractive. She had pale, pale skin, translucent
almost, without a single blemish. She was slim. Her cheeks
were rounded, with a hint of palest blush. Her lips were
bright vermilion. She had breasts of alabaster, capped with
bright red beads on stalks, as if her nipples contained glass
balls which had been sucked out strongly to the tips and
could not be retracted. But her breasts remained unblem-
ished by any freckle; her breasts were purest white with
very faint pale blue lines meandering delicately below the
surface. Anya knew this clarity of skin to be a symbol of
perfection – it was not at all like her skin, which was tainted
by the swaths of freckles on her shoulders and breasts, and
the blackened flesh between her thighs. And Amalicia's hair
was blonde and curled in dangling springy ringlets. Her
eyes were deepest blue, but bright, as if a light shone from
behind them. Yes, Anya saw purity in this face, and a body
such as Amalicia's signified perfection.

Standing beside Amalicia, rolling a lock of Amalicia's
hair tightly round a stick to form another curl, was a dark-
haired bondslave, but she did not wear the gold chains. She
wore instead a thin woollen top which contained her
shoulders, was shaped closely to her breasts, and fitted
snugly to her belly, where it ended just above the navel. She
wore nothing else. Anya had never seen a bondslave dressed
like this. When the girl turned to attend to Amalicia's fringe,
Anya could see the outcurve of her tightly rounded golden
coloured bottom reflected in the mirror alongside Amalicia's soft white face.

A male slave sat upon a low, skirted cushioned stool at the
end of the bed. His cockstem was erect. He bore the expression of one who is waiting patiently for something which
has suffered interruption to be taken up once again.

Amalicia noticed Anya through the mirror. Her eyes lit up. She turned. The bondslave, who by accident retained a hold on Amalicia's fringe, was jabbed with Amalicia's elbow. She edged away and stood with her head bowed; her fingers fidgeted anxiously with the combs and brushes on the table top behind her until Amalicia threw her a withering glance. Her head hung even lower. Anya had been taken by surprise by Amalicia's abruptness. Then a brush which was balanced uncertainly at the edge of the dressing-table fell onto the floor as the girl attempted to make a final readjustment. Amalicia didn't turn towards the girl this time, but reached out at waist height with a finger and thumb held ready. The girl stiffened, then squealed. Amalicia held up a small black curly lock between her thumb and finger. She smiled sweetly. Anya was frightened; this was not the Amalicia she thought she knew.

'Anya!' Amalicia threw her head back and parted her bright red lips to show her small bright teeth. Her little pink tongue peeped out and touched her upper lip and then retreated. 'At last! How good to see you. How good to know that after all this time,' she flung her hand up ostentatiously, 'you are available to visit me.' She turned her head to one side, and looked at Anya coyly. 'But it's not *Lady* Anya now, I understand. How sad.' Amalicia pouted her bottom lip. 'It's plain and simple Anya. Come over here, my plain and simple one. Let me have a look at you. Let us determine – if we can – what hidden charm our cousin managed to grub out of this plain and simple country girl, shall we, Elinor? This vagabond from the back of nowhere?'

Anya was very scared indeed. She had never witnessed such a contrast between a person's public and private personalities. And she felt like crying. Why was Amalicia being so spiteful towards her? What had Anya done to deserve it?

'Don't be so harsh with the girl,' said Elinor. She was sitting on the bed, toying with the male slave on the stool.

Anya stepped forward very nervously.

'You think I'm too strict with these creatures, Elinor? Perhaps you're right.' She turned to Anya. 'Hmm. Chains become you, darling,' she said, slipping a finger beneath the chain at Anya's waist and running it round her belly. 'They surely do. Such freckles.' She touched her nipples. Her cold white fingers pressed them to the side, then lifted them; she began picking at them with her long red nails, as if trying to get beneath the surface, to lift the colour off, expressing disesteem and denunciation in every peevish pick. 'Such deep dark titties too,' she glanced down, 'and so black . . . You've been shaving. Hmm, you want to shave more closely dear,' Amalicia shook her finger, 'your stubble's showing.' The fingernail scratched through the bristles. Anya was mortified by this degrading treatment. 'But showing off that blackness. Tut-tut . . .' She frowned. 'I'll bet you would get on well with my mother.' Anya looked quizzically at Amalicia. She had never heard of Amalicia's mother. 'Oh, you haven't met my mother, have you darling? Not yet? I'm surprised. She's usually falling over herself for the fresh-faced types; likes the simple look. Rather partial to black, too, the Countess. Isn't that so, Elinor?'

'The Countess is a woman of taste and refinement, Amalicia. Never forget it.'

'Hmmph . . . And my cousin. Well, well. You know, there's something about my mother's side of the family, Elinor, something weird. It must be in the blood.' Amalicia's eyes narrowed down to slits. 'How appropriate then that he should plump for a sooted fleshpot. I'll bet he couldn't get enough of it. It would match his blackened heart!'

'No!' Anya stood back with her hands protecting her flesh from any more abuse. But how could this woman be so evil as to revile her Prince that way? 'No. It is not so!' she snapped. She was trying to hold back the tears. 'He is sweet and kind and gentle.'

Amalicia laughed. 'And – do not tell me – you would defend him to the last?' Anya held her head up defiantly. 'You would – let me see – you would sacrifice yourself to save him?' Amalicia was mocking her, but that sacrifice was no less than the Prince himself had risked on that fateful day to save her from the guards. 'Mmm . . . a loyal slave. Very touching. A doting little concubine.' Anya did not flinch; she would not let these words destroy her. Amalicia turned to Elinor. 'And this slave then, for her loyalty, has her privileges safeguarded by the Council, I assume?'

'Why no,' replied Elinor demurely, as she squeezed the cockstem and stretched back the skin and rubbed her thumb around the end, then pressed the male slave's belly. 'The Taskmistress assures me that the Council are quite definite on this point. Her training must be thorough, no line of exploration left unessayed. No special treatment, so I understand.' She made the male slave lean back until his head rested on the floor; his cock stood straight up from his belly.

'So.' Lady Amalicia sat back and curled one of her springy locks about her finger, as if she were considering. 'So, a slave – bereft of privileges – who takes it upon herself to answer back. . . ?'

'. . . Must surely be reminded of her station.' Elinor calmly wet her fingers and massaged the cockstem briskly. Anya's blood turned cold.

'Indeed.' Amalicia picked up a broad flat wooden comb, flexed it, then smacked it sharply down on Anya's right nipple. Anya screeched and jumped back. 'Step forward, my dear,' said Amalicia. 'There!' She smacked the left one hard. Now Anya was fighting to hold the tears back. Her nipples were stinging unbearably. 'Perhaps you will choose your words more carefully in future, my dear?' She smacked her again, harder, on each nipple. 'Could you do that? Hmm?' She kept smacking until she had forced Anya to reply, with head hung low and nipples burning fiercely. 'Yes . . . my lady,' she mumbled weakly. Then she could feel her lip begin to tremble. Why did the woman want to do this to her? She could see Amalicia's smiling face begin to dissolve. The tears were coming; she could not stop them.

'Amalicia, you cruel thing. Come over here, my darling.' Elinor released the cockstem, then pulled Anya to her breast and used her lavender scented kerchief to dry away the tears. Anya could feel the heat of Elinor's bosom against her ear. She could hear her heartbeat, which was slow and steady, a reassuring warmth of calm against the hot defeat. Elinor lifted up her face and kissed her. She kissed her softly at first; she kissed her slowly, until Anya opened her mouth to Elinor's kisses, then she kissed her deeply. Anya's head lay back while Elinor probed her open mouth, searching out her tongue, pushing against it, sucking, drinking underneath it.

Elinor kept Anya on the bed, safe from Amalicia, while she washed her. She used a small white china bowl with pale pink roses painted round the rim, which was shaped so it fitted against Anya's inner thighs as she knelt up to be washed. The male slave had been allowed to sit up, so he could watch. He was directly opposite Anya; his cockstem was stiff and bobbing with his pulse. She looked away, not wishing to face him, to where the girl was attending to Amalicia's hair, curling it once again. Amalicia looked into the mirror at her soft white face, fringed with shaking ringlets, and those bright orange-red lips which Anya hated now, for their hardness and their cruelty. Anya could smell the rose scent faintly as the water trickled across her bristly mound then trickled back into the bowl, then more strongly as Elinor separated her flesh to let the rose scent kiss her tenderness. She turned to look at Elinor as the woman worked. She could see Lady Elinor's eyelashes flutter as those eyes caressed her body, as her fingers gently entered Anya to press the cool rose kiss inside her hot salt flesh. She could not stop her flesh from clinging to Elinor's fingers. Elinor smiled, as if she understood, but she did not shame Anya by looking at her face. Anya did not mind this woman touching her. Her body did not object when Elinor's fingers opened her bottom and entered there; Elinor did it tenderly. And when she had finished, she dabbed her dry with a soft pink cloth.

Anya had enjoyed that intimate touch. Her body was not burning now from cruelty and frustration; she felt suffused by a gentle warmth, a warmth that aroused her, not with harsh insistent need, but an ever present kiss of softness. Her flesh expanded in a slow, relaxed pleasure. Elinor sprinkled her between the legs, shaking a tiny brush above her inner thighs, showering her with essence of roses. She could feel the spirit misting coolly, then she could smell its strength of sweetness as it drifted up her belly and over her breasts. She opened her mouth to breathe it in. It intoxicated her. Elinor spread the cheeks of Anya's bottom and sprinkled there too, and Anya felt her face infuse with warm embarrassment. The woman simply smiled. She made Anya kneel up higher, then took a long cord of leather, about half as thick as Anya's little finger, but very supple as if it had been soaked in oil, and smoothly rounded, as flexible as a snake, and fastened it in a slip knot round the very top of Anya's leg. Then she pushed the knot tight, to bed it more definitely to the crease. The knot touched against Anya's flesh leaves, lifting them slightly to the side, making its presence felt whenever she brought her thighs together. Elinor took the other end of the thong and fastened it to the column of the bedpost, placing Anya so she faced into the room, so she could see the male slave, Amalicia and the girl. The snake of leather curled up from between her thighs and lay uneasily on her belly, moving with her breathing before slipping over, round the side, to the tethering post behind. The satin curtain brushed against her ear.

Elinor directed her attentions once again to the male. She knelt down in front of him and edged his feet back at each side of the stool, making his body roll forwards. Then she insinuated her fingers underneath him at the front, coaxing out the bag, which preferred to remain retracted against him. She took each tight bump upon two fingers, closed the thumb against it, and pulled. His cockstem swayed. She drew out the bumps, against the resistance of his tight bag, forcing the skin to stretch. He tensed, pushing out, trying to follow to relieve the ache, lifting up on tiptoes, until his belly lifted from the stool. Now Elinor had him at her mercy, with his body formed into an arch balanced so finely that if his straining toes should falter and relax, the firmness of her grip would stretch his cords to snapping point. And only then, beneath the weight of the tight fear and aching pain, did she finally wet her lips and push them over the end of his cock, sealing round the head and taking deep, steady

162

sucks until his body shook in straining pleasure. She released his bumps, but she did not release his cockhead from her lips before she had wound a thin cord round him at the base, pulling each loop tightly, encompassing the cockstem and the gathered up bag and drawing the end of the cord through the last loop to secure it. Elinor sat back. The slave was then allowed to lower himself. The cockstem stood up more rigidly than ever, but Anya could see that, without anybody touching it, it was still swelling. The veins were pumping up to knotted hardness, until she thought that they might burst; then the pulsing was translated to the cockstem as a whole, which shook in slow and strident thumps.

There was a clatter. The bondgirl had been holding up a looking-glass for Amalicia to admire herself, in the double reflection, from the back. Now Amalicia's eyes closed down to slits. The bondgirl was too afraid to pick the glass up. She watched wide-eyed as Amalicia opened a drawer and removed something, showed it to her and placed it on the table top. The girl shrank back. It was a strap, a small one, on a handle with gold thread wound round it and a purple tassle at the end. The girl cringed as she bent to pick the mirror up.

'Leave it. Your fingers are too clumsy.' The girl stayed in her half stooped posture. Amalicia brushed the strap across the girl's cheek, across her lips and down her neck. She was shaking. Amalicia forced her head back while she stroked the strap down the centre line of her neck, then slapped it lightly back and forth across her breasts, until her nipples pushed out through the thin material of her top. 'No. We will have to find a more secure grip altogether.' She pointed with the strap to the table top, then suddenly swept her arm across, clearing everything aside. Anya jumped as combs and brushes and bottles cascaded onto the floor. She couldn't understand how anyone could be so vindictive as to punish the girl for a misdeed which paled to innocence against the destructiveness of her own deliberate act. It was all a game, that was it; a cruel, spiteful game in which the bondslaves were the toys, and Amalicia would do what she

163

wanted with them, punishing and degrading them simply for amusement.

Lady Elinor spread her hand upon Anya's thigh to calm her, but Anya was not reassured, so she unfastened the cord from the bedpost and lifted Anya onto her lap. She opened Anya's thighs and bent her knee, then rested a hand against her without moving it, with the heel lightly but definitely against her mound and the fingers curling over, barely touching Anya's leaves, casually grazing, but with authority, as if the hand lay upon a favoured pet asleep across her knee. The scent of roses drifted up again and this time Elinor closed her eyes and breathed it. Anya had not resisted any of this; she felt safer this way, on Elinor's knee, with Elinor's arm around her and Elinor's warm bosom pressing into her side.

The girl was on the dressing-table, kneeling with her back towards the mirror. She had already spread her thighs apart in readiness. Amalicia held the strap. The girl waited until Amalicia gave the signal, a minute nod, then sat back and began rolling up her woollen top, which seemed so tight against her that it was reluctant to move. She rolled it with increasing difficulty until it reached her breasts, when she could not roll it any further. She pulled once and failed; the second time, her breasts burst through from below and then it formed a pressure band above them, forcing their fullness down and to the sides. The nipples were strong cones capped by tightly rounded pips. Amalicia touched the girl's thighs, then laid her hand against her, lightly, in much the way that Elinor's lay on Anya.

Elinor now adjusted the slip knot against Anya's crease, tightening it once again, pressing the knot against her, then folding the loose end of the leather into a loop. She was preparing Anya's body for what it was about to witness. She was trying to arouse her even as the bondslave was being punished. Anya knew this to be what Elinor intended. It would be the kind of thing that the turnkey had done to her in the dungeons while the slave was being smacked. Anya knew it, and she hated it. She hated the surging dizziness that came, as if she were on a cliff-top,

164

gulping too much air; she hated the feeling that was coming in between her legs as the loop was held there, then swept from side to side across her leaves very gently, once for each time the strap descended across the bondslave's pushed out breasts; she watched the smacks fall on the side, underneath or directly on the nipples. When the girl's gasps came especially strongly, Elinor would stroke her fingertip up across the tip of Anya's nubbin. And Anya hated it when Amalicia chose instead to lift a breast up by the nipple and slap the undersurface, for each firm slap of Amalicia's was matched by Elinor's sudden fingertip slap of Anya's nubbin. The pleasure of that finger-slapping frightened her, for it reminded her so vividly of what had happened to the woman in the dungeons; she was so afraid they might be trying to train her pleasure to come about in this degrading way.

Amalicia next began to slap the bondgirl's belly. She made her lift up, spread and push out. Amalicia would smack her three times at the navel, then bend and kiss the girl between the legs, in a short quick kiss with pouted lips which would nevertheless make the girl moan, then she would smack and kiss again. While this treatment continued, with the girl leaning further back until her head touched the mirror in her attempt to push her belly forwards, not to meet the slaps so much as to greet the quick wet vermilion kisses, Lady Elinor took the end of the leather cord and moistened it, then fed it by slow degrees into Anya's sex, hesitating when the groans from across the room came very deeply, making Anya tighten too strongly for the thong to slip inside, then opening Anya's flesh more fully and guiding the rope along the flesh walls with her fingers, wetting them to make its passage freer, and advancing the sliding snake until Anya could feel it coiling inside and pressing against the mouth of her womb. But Elinor did not desist until all the slack was taken and the cord passed straight across from the knot at the top of Anya's thigh, across one leaf, then up inside her body. As Anya tightened, the cord depressed a notch into the leaf, leaving a tight lobe of flesh beneath the main body of the leaf, like an earlobe on an ear. And, as if it were an earlobe, Elinor stretched and rubbed and played with it while the punishment continued.

Amalicia had stopped the strapping and kissing when it was clear the girl could hold back no longer. She had made the girl turn round, still kneeling, but with her bottom pushed out. Amalicia picked up the mirror. 'Now, it is time to test that grip, my dear,' she said. Anya shivered, and Elinor sensed that fear in her slave, for she lifted Anya's chin and kissed her, sucking gently on Anya's lower lip, tickling Anya's extra earlobe while she sucked, seducing her to pleasure in this way. Then, when Elinor had released her captive and now very swollen lip, allowing Anya to look once more upon the scene across the room, she took up again that too-light stimulation, this time with the heel of her hand high up against Anya's outstretched thigh and the curling fingertips resting with the weight of tiny birds' feet, lighter than any throb that lifted Anya's leaves against them. And, like birds on a bough, the fingertips gently pattered as they rearranged their stance. They did not grip or squeeze Anya in the way her flesh needed.

Amalicia held the girl's flesh open and began to push the handle of the mirror into her sex; Anya gasped so loudly that Amalicia turned to look at her. Throughout the slow insertion, Lady Elinor's fingers maintained the bird's foot patting, and when Anya could no longer bear it and pushed her hips out hard against the fingers, they immediately withdrew to lie instead with the same tormenting lightness at the top of Anya's crease.

The mirror was now fully bedded. It had been inserted so the silvered surface faced Amalicia, for Amalicia to admire her face reflected between the girl's legs as she sat behind the girl and pleasured her more fully. She wet her fingers and reached underneath the mirror. 'I want this mirror kept very still,' she said while she worked the girl between the legs, working, Anya knew, from the sounds the girl was making, at her nubbin. 'Spread those thighs a little wider. There . . .' The girl had sucked in her breath so deeply that Anya had almost felt the touch. 'What a hard little knot of pleasure, my darling,' said Amalicia. 'Let me soften it.' She spread the girl's bottom cheeks with her other hand and poked her little tongue out, checked it in the mirror, then stroked it carefully up and down the groove then dabbed it in the centre, in small dabs and flicks, alternating with the bondslave's tense short gasps, which nevertheless were becoming longer and deeper by the minute. 'Now keep that mirror steady,' Amalicia warned and this time used her fingertip to tap against the rim of the bottom, while round the front, against the squeezing there, the girl emitted tiny cries of pleasured protest. 'Still, my sweet. Good. Let that pleasure draw. Mm. Still now; let it take you slowly . . .'

Then Anya felt the thong of leather sliding very slowly out of her, pulled by Elinor's finger, as she separated Anya's flesh and gently held her nubbin between a finger and a thumb. She did not squeeze; there was simply the constant, lightly-holding pressure of the pads to each side, holding the nubbin steady against the pleasure of the slippage, the delicious deeply pulling slippage of the well-oiled snake, as steady as the looking-glass between the bondgirl's legs when the bondgirl delivered her flesh without a single shudder, but with a cry so deep and guttural as if her belly had been impaled. The tip of the thong slipped out of Anya and slid wetly across her thigh, followed by a thick droplet of her honeydew. Elinor gathered it on her finger and licked it absent-mindedly. She was thinking of something else. Anya's flesh was warm no longer; it was burning hot with wanting and now Elinor was putting her aside, leaving her to seethe with lustful thoughts, tying her to the bedpost and turning to the man again.

Amalicia had removed the mirror, wiped the handle on the girl's top and, after collecting a jar from the few remaining on the dressing-table, led her to the couch. She spread open her robe to expose her own pale thighs, then made the girl lie face down across her knee, not permitting her to roll down her top first, but keeping her with her breasts pushed out so that they hung down, one against the velvet and the other squeezed over the cushion while Amalicia played with the girl's bottom. She placed the pot in the middle of her back, scooped out the cream and worked it deeply in between the upturned cheeks. She paused to turn the girl's face towards the room and instructed her to keep her eyes open. Anya could see Amalicia's fingers entering the girl part way, then more fully as Amalicia whispered and the girl reached back to grip and pull her knee up to the level of her waist before the fingers withdrew and recharged with cream.

'Elinor – do you think my nightcap might be ready yet?'

Anya glanced at Elinor, who glanced at the male slave sitting stiffly on the stool. The slave moved uneasily. 'Mm. Let me check,' said Elinor. She took him in her hand and squeezed, then frowned, then pressed her fingers underneath him. His cockstem wavered. 'Hmmm. Tighten up, my pet. Squeeze.' He bit his lip and his plum visibly expanded. Elinor pressed her thumbs deep into his bag. He groaned. She made a ring from her finger and thumb and slipped it tightly over him and pulled the skin back hard. While she held him thus, she rubbed her palm against the undersurface of the plum. Finally, she pushed the tip of her little finger into the tiny mouth held open by the pulling, drawing out a long clear string of liquid. She tasted. Anya felt queasy. 'Yes, I'd say so,' Elinor declared.

'Would you be a dear then, Elinor?' Lady Amalicia held her glistening fingers up, flourishing them apologetically. 'I'm afraid my hands are full – aren't they darling?' The bondslave shifted on her lap. Amalicia gave her dangling teat a playful little squeeze before she spread the girl's legs again and reapplied her fingers. 'But she loves it, don't you dear?' The bondslave shut her eyes tightly as Amalicia entered her again.

Lady Elinor got off the bed and collected a glass from a small table by the side of Amalicia's dresser. She didn't collect a bottle; she didn't pour anything out. Anya didn't expect her to. She was well aware what degradation was about to be enacted and she did not care to witness it at all.

However, she had no choice. 'Would you hold this glass a minute?' Elinor asked. What could Anya do? Throw it down? Refuse even to touch it, refuse any part in this wicked debasement? And now, to make things worse, the man was on the bed, kneeling on all fours, with Elinor behind him, his calf not a handsbreadth from Anya's foot, even though she had already moved that foot away. She would not look. How could they make her? She felt so hot, with everyone so close. It was so hot in here, so sticky. The glass was delicately fashioned, with the rim constricted slightly then flared out, like a tulip. She felt very thirsty – and that brought home again just what these women were proposing to do. How could they do it? She hated them. She put the glass down beside her. Elinor noticed this, but didn't chastise her. Instead she gently edged Anya's knees apart and planted her feet to the bed, edging until her sex was pouted out so far it brushed the bedspread. She checked the knot, pressed it up against her, and very carefully separated Anya's leaves. And, with greater gentleness still – so carefully that Anya was forced to hold her breath against the feeling – Elinor insinuated her fingers and withdrawing them wet, smeared the wet round the male slave's plum and milked him till he moved his hips, forcing Anya to flush deep crimson at this public attestation to her lust. 'Modesty becomes you,' said Elinor. 'It shall yet be tested to its limit.' And with that, she forced Anya to hold her flesh leaves open.

Elinor then took up the glass; dipping her finger once again into Anya's body, she oiled the inside of the rim. She unwound the tourniquet from the upturned cockstem, rubbed the incised flesh, then looped the thong around the base once more and pulled; the cock moved back and pointed down between the slave's legs. She fed the head into the glass, twisting against the tightness of the fit until it slipped around the plum and held. She released the glass and then released the cord. The glass remained tightly in position, its weight pulling the cockstem down somewhat against the force of the erection. Elinor began to pump the glass up and down around the cockhead. She turned the slave round so Anya could see more clearly. Anya had to watch as Elinor's fingers, the very fingers that had entered her, now entered him as Elinor advanced his pleasure slowly, making him spread his knees until the base of the glass was resting on the bed, then working him that way, her fingers still inside him, while she gripped him round the base and milked in short bursts interspersed with squeezes to the thick tube on the underside of the stem.

And while this happened, Anya had to hold her lips apart. She could feel her flesh distending, her nubbin poking out with lust. Elinor kept looking at her, checking to see that she was doing as she was bid. Only once did she touch her; she left the man groaning with two fingers still inside him and the glass bobbing uneasily, and touched Anya lightly around her out-turned leaves and on her nubbin. She made her fully unsheath her hood and push very hard, and stay like that while Elinor used two hands to the slave, one around the cockstem and one tightly round the bag, pumping very roughly until he nearly spasmed. As his body pulsed gently down again, she rubbed a thumb up and down the tight, arched bridge from his bottom to his bag and commanded that he squeeze. Anya could see his tubes tightening and relaxing. Each time they tightened, Elinor drew her thumb down, flattening them, pushing the seepage through. The inside of the glass was smeared as if a snail had wandered round it. 'And you may tighten too, my darling . . .' Elinor waited until she had complied, and Anya could feel her juices seeping like the man's were; they were seeping down her bottom. She dared not look, but she was sure her open flesh must be dripping on the cover.

In time, the man began to gasp and whimper. 'Wait,' said Elinor. She sat back on her heels and drew him, on his side, onto her lap so he faced Anya, then tucked his knees up tightly to his belly. The glass was still attached to the end of his plum; a pale milky droplet of seepage moved about inside it. Elinor held his cockstem at the base, pulling back, with her fingers tightly round it. She raised his upper leg and held it crooked in the air.

'Look at her open flesh,' she said. Anya was horrified. 'Pump,' Elinor said. 'Keep pumping while you look upon her.' With that, she released the constriction of her fingers at the bottom of his stem and stroked his bridge again, pressing as he pumped, not stopping until he cried out with the pleasure, whereupon Elinor quickly lifted his leg higher yet and proceeded to slap him in that place, wetting her fingers and slapping firmly with a measured stroke upon the hard tight curving bridge. 'There . . .' she sighed, as she slapped and the bondslave shuddered, 'keep those juices coming.' She kept slapping at that same unchanging pace as the glass pumped up and the cockhead inside slowly disappeared behind the billows of milting fluid. She rubbed the bridge, back and forth, massaging with her knuckles, and then she rubbed his belly. She made him kneel up while she unsheathed him very carefully, so as not to spill a drop.

Amalicia temporarily removed her fingers from the girl – whose face was flushed although her body seemed reluctant to release them – to take the glass from Elinor. Anya's jaw fell open as Amalicia sniffed the contents, closed her eyes, then threw her head back and allowed the viscid gobbets to drip into her mouth. She pushed her tongue into the glass to clean out every drop. 'Hmmm . . . A little thick, perhaps?' She licked her bright red lips. 'I think we may have rushed it, Elinor. We'll keep him simmering a little longer next time.' The male slave winced.

Elinor held a tray in front of Anya; it bore a jug and a large pewter mug. She poured the slightly cloudy liquid out and offered it to Anya, who naturally beheld it with suspicion. 'Do not be alarmed, my dear. Taste.' It was very sour but also sweet with a faint taste of cinnamon. It was quite refreshing. 'Lemon squash,' said Elinor. 'Help yourself.' She placed the tray upon the bed. Anya drank the mugful greedily, for she was very thirsty. And she was also very trusting, she realised after she had downed a second mugful, poured out a third and begun to drink it. Above the rim, across the room, she could see Amalicia's sinister smile. What if they'd put something in the squash, something to make her sleep, or worse, to make her body acquiesce in whatever perverse pleasures they were planning? She put the mug down quickly. The drink had a slight aftertaste, a bitterness. Was that just the lemon peel? Was she beginning to feel something? How could she even tell with all the stimulation she had received and all the things she'd witnessed?

In fact there was nothing untoward in the lemon squash. There did not need to be. Lemon squash was quite effective as it stood, for the purpose here intended.

Amalicia dismissed the man. 'The ladies will retire,' she said, as Elinor ushered him out. This made Anya anxious about how many were to be accommodated in Amalicia's bed.

And although Anya had reason to worry, the actuality turned out rather worse than the expectation. Amalicia lifted the girl off her lap and deposited her face down on the couch, with her legs kept wide apart and her flesh outspread on the velvet. She brought the pot of cream across and placed it on the bed, causing Anya great concern. She went over to her dressing-table and removed what appeared to be a long thin rope; Anya saw it had a ball attached at one end. It reminded her of the device which Ulla had used on her in the kitchen, but in this case there was only a single weight, and the cord was very much longer. By now, she was getting frightened. She kept looking from the pot of cream to the ball and cord that now lay on the bed. Amalicia's fingers tickled shivers into the top of Anya's thigh; the knot was being undone.

'Stand up, modest one. Turn round.' The sinking feeling came in Anya's belly, aggravated by the liquid she had foolishly consumed; there was now a dull pressing weighted ache, low down in her belly. Her bladder felt full already. 'Bend over, on the bed.' Anya did not want to do it. Everyone was watching; Elinor was on the couch beside the girl, probing her gently, and both of them were looking at Anya, waiting for this degradation to be performed.

'Bend over!' Amalicia said more loudly. Anya did so, burying her face in the bedclothes. 'Oh no, my dear, this will not pass for modesty . . .' Amalicia angled Anya's hips to the side, so the women on the couch could see quite clearly still, but now she turned Anya's head, laid her cheek down and made her look at them.

'There, you shall adjust to shame, my dear.' Amalicia parted Anya's legs. 'Now – hold your fleshpot open.' She forced her to use a finger of each hand to hold her body

172

wide. She took her time, leisurely buttering the ball with cream while Anya looked across at the cool calm face of Lady Elinor and the flushed and anxious girl who slowly wriggled as Elinor's fingers found their mark between her outspread thighs. The ball was pushed against the mouth of Anya's sex. She kept tightening, even though her fingers tried so hard to keep her open. Amalicia was too rough; Anya was sure the ball was much too large. Eventually Amalicia lost her patience.

'Spread,' she said. Anya tried. Finally, Amalicia put the ball down, opened Anya's buttocks and whipped two fingers down between them, smacking so hard against the tender flesh that Anya screamed. The bondgirl jerked with shock and Elinor had to stroke her back then lift her hips and bed more fully into her to soothe her.

This time, when Amalicia pushed, the ball slipped in. 'Ah . . . now we know,' she said pointedly. Anya was mortified. What did the woman mean?

By this means, Anya was refastened to the bedpost. She was made to stand, facing it, with her breasts pressed to each side of the post, brushing against the curtains. Her hands were tied around it but the cord attached inside her was drawn up tightly in between her legs and fitted to the parting of her flesh, then tied high up on the column. Her feet were left free, so the choice was Anya's – whether she cared to remain on tiptoes, or preferred to rest her heels upon the floor and thereby cut her flesh in two. Amalicia checked the fit; she sealed the flesh lips round the cord, then opened Anya's buttocks one last time and stroked her finger down the groove and scratched her nail across the rim. Then, she tested Anya's belly; she knew exactly where to touch her. The drink had been part of Amalicia's cruel plan – Anya knew it then, for Amalicia's fingers pressed and probed, low down on Anya's belly, just above the mound. And with the thin cord cutting her, it made her want to pee. Amalicia kept feeling her until Anya tried to wriggle free and cried out with the burning pain as the cord cut even deeper.

Amalicia brought across a large bowl of cold water and a

cloth. The cloth was wiped down Anya's breasts. It was dripping; it had not been wrung out. The water ran down her front in cold meandering trickles. The cloth was next recharged and wiped against her belly. Amalicia was working deliberately slowly, applying the cloth lightly, so it tickled coldly, and squeezing it out against Anya's skin so the water ran down freely. She got the cloth very wet and squeezed it out between her thighs. The coldness running down her legs made her belly tighten and the feeling came again, the feeling that she would wet herself. 'There . . . does that feel good?' Amalicia said wickedly. She knew what the washing was doing to Anya. Now Anya jerked, for the cloth had been squeezed out on her shoulders and the rivulets were cutting down her back. Amalicia parted the cheeks of Anya's bottom, and Anya pleaded as the cloth was squeezed against the small of her back and a continuous trickle ran, uncertainly at first, then more smoothly, down the groove, across the ticklish mouth, then underneath to trickle down her right leg and over her inner ankle.

Amalicia did not dry her. 'I can't seem to find my towel,' she said. She left her with the droplets drifting down by stages, gathering, collecting on her skin, warming as the night progressed. At intervals one of these stray meandering pitiless blind instruments of Amalicia's torture would break rank and run, tickling down between her breasts, at the crease of her thigh or down between her buttocks.

And while her flesh was cruelly cut, and her bladder slowly swelled to a pressured weight of bursting, and the trickles chased each other down her skin in warm wet lines of persecution, her eyes were forced to witness what was happening on the bed – how the young slave-girl was carried across by Elinor and deposited there to be used by the women for their amusement, as if she were a doll. She saw how Elinor rolled that single article of clothing, the wollen top, right up to the young girl's armpits to expose her breasts more fully, then turned her on her side, gathering up the material into a fold between her shoulder blades, holding her that way while Amalicia played with her nipples, stroked her breasts and slapped them, then pressed

174

her face against them to suck them with those bright red lips. Then she saw how, without releasing her grip, Elinor rolled beneath the girl and forced her body into an arch to present the girl's belly in a tight up-curve. She watched Amalicia open her knees so all could look upon the girl's thickened, pale pink sex lips peeping from a dense and curly bush, and below her sex, between her outspread buttocks, the gently pulsing bright pink pushed-out mouth which must have suffered so much torment and distension from these women's wicked fingers.

Amalicia opened out the girl's fleshpot. She moved to the side to spread her sex with four fingers, two from each hand, then made her press her feet into the bed to lift up her hips so she could look inside. Then she used her thumbs to sleeve the hood of flesh fully back until the hard red nubbin stood out. She kept the girl in that position for some minutes, during which Anya's body burned, for she knew exactly what that girl was feeling from the degradation and heartless unfulfilment; her own body itched and prickled from the droplets that were mixing with her sweat, and the cord of torture rubbing up against her flesh whenever she made a move. Then she saw Elinor's hand reaching from underneath to spread the bondslave's bottom so her middle finger could stroke it as it pulsed, while Amalicia's thumbs began to squeeze against the nubbin. She knew then that she never would survive this night. These visions would surely kill her if she were not permitted that deliverance to pleasure very soon.

The bondslave soon began to plead, shortly after which the women desisted, tipped her back onto the bed and rolled her body back and forth between them. Amalicia then decided that the girl should bring Amalicia pleasure with her mouth. She lay back diagonally, towards Anya, while the girl knelt down and sucked between her thighs and Elinor tickled the girl's belly and her breasts. As Amalicia's pleasure rose, then ebbed, she reached back and, probing between Anya's legs, searched out the point at which the cord traversed her nubbin and worked this point, pressing the lips around the cord, rubbing cruelly, until Anya did not know whether she would come or scream or wet herself. In fact, she screamed, as Amalicia came first and squeezed the pip as if to burst it.

Amalicia ignored the outcry and sat up. The girl was turned onto her front, with a pillow placed underneath her. Elinor briefly left the bed and came back bearing a single glove fashioned from a dense white fur. Amalicia pulled it snugly over the fingers of her left hand. She brushed the gloved hand up the left inner thigh of the bondslave, then up the right. She separated the girl's thighs more definitely. The girl's pouch overhung the pillow. Amalicia stroked the pouch, then gathered it in the fur as if it were a mouse within a nest and stroked her bare finger upwards in the groove of the girl's bottom. The girl shuddered with the tickles of the fur against her tenderness; her bottom mouth contracted with the pleasure.

Elinor left the bed and went over to the dressing-table while Amalicia peeled the girl open, smacked her thighs with her bare fingers, high up near the creases, smacked her buttocks till they bounced, then slowly, with frequent pauses in which she stroked the mouth of the girl's bottom with the fur-sheathed thumb while the girl's body readjusted to the greater depth of probing, she worked the furry fingers into the slave's ever widening fleshpot until all four fingers had disappeared from view, and the brushing of the bottom still continued, counterpointed now by very soft mewling sounds and gentle undulations of the bondslave's hips and thighs, interspersed with short quick slaps upon her bottom cheeks. As Anya watched and tightened helplessly around the ball pushed deep inside her, she could feel her body weep slow pleasure against the warm numb weight of bursting pressure filling up her bladder, the itchy scratch of the cord against her nubbin, and the brush of satin curtain folds against her yearning breasts. And seeing the girl being spread this way and brushed relentlessly in that place made Anya try to open out her buttocks and push out her tightened mouth out and imagine she was being taken, brushed and penetrated with those dominating fingers – tortured in that rather different fashion.

Elinor returned with a very thin gold chain and Anya's heart almost burst right through her breast, for attached to the chain by a small gold clasp was a small white ivory tusk. Her breathing came in giant drowning gulps when Elinor fastened it at the back, to the chain round Anya's waist, then parted her buttocks and directed the chain against her while the tusk swung freely in between her thighs.

Sitting on the bed, Elinor placed the strap with the purple tassle on the girl's back and with her free hand, Amalicia took it up. Elinor reached beneath the girl, and easing her breast out to the side, began to play with the nipple.

Amalicia held the strap aloft; Anya held her breath. She gasped out loud when Amalicia brought the strap down with a sudden slap, precisely in the centre of the bondslave's bottom, against the tight pink mouth. The girl jerked but did not utter a sound. The strap came down again. The girl was breathing deeply, trying to control herself as the glove still moved within her, filling her, spreading her, pushing her onward, searching out her need.

Lady Amalicia turned to Elinor and nodded. She held the strap again but waited. Then Anya realised that Elinor was getting up again and coming over to her. Anya's belly sank and sank into that bottomless pit of forbidden wanting; as Elinor sat behind her, Anya's sex contracted, forcing the ball to press against her bladder. She felt that she was bursting. If Elinor were to touch her she would surely wet herself. And now, she could feel those cool fingers of Elinor's reaching round from behind, reaching to press against her belly, pushing into her, even as the cord cut her till her flesh was numb. She watched Amalicia's gloved fingers working, making the girl begin to shift her hips as the strap above her followed. The strap cracked down, and Elinor pressed hard against Anya's belly, making her gasp and almost leak. Then on the bed, the thumb of the glove stroked the swollen mouth of flesh that had only just been struck. Anya felt the cheeks of her bottom being spread and the chain being lifted; the tip of the tusk pressed against her secret mouth. She felt the very tip insinuate itself into her living flesh; then, each time the strap slapped down, the tusk was gently twisted, pulled out of her and then pushed in again, but only to the tip, until the girl began to moan and Amalicia turned her over, keeping her fingers still inside but curving upwards now to push the flesh around her nubbin outwards. Amalicia put down the strap, wet her fingers and worked the bondslave's nubbin till she panted then quickly took up the strap and smacked it. And as the working and the smacking progressed, the bondslave's hips gradually lifted from the bed to greet the smacks, and Elinor worked the tusk slowly into Anya while she alternately squeezed her pip and pushed her fingers into her belly and when the young girl's pleasure came in a long continuous moan that lasted through four wet workings and three firm slaps, but was precipitated by the fourth, Anya closed her eyes and felt warm wet liquid seep at first, then spurt and spray against the bedpost, then trickle over Elinor's squeezing fingers, down the cord and warmly down her leg and ankle, under-neath her upturned foot, tickling along the sole and in between her toes to soak at last into Amalicia's lovely deep piled carpet.

'Good,' said Elinor, as she felt the first uncertain spurts, and pushed the tusk more firmly in to lift the slave higher on her toes. 'Let your pleasure come, my darling.' Elinor left the tusk inside Anya as she dried her fingers with a cloth and watched her twitch on tiptoes. 'Do not be ashamed to take your pleasure in this way.' But Anya was so numb and hot and shivery and keyed-up, so vanquished by the pain and fear and cruel humiliation, that she never knew whether her pleasure came or not.

And as she shuddered for breath and pressed her head against the bedpost, which was wet with her disgrace, she heard a knocking at the door. Someone was admitted and she heard an all-too-familiar voice which made her hope that this was all a terrible dream.

'Oh, no! Your beautiful satin sheets . . . and your carpet, Amalicia. What on earth are we to do with a naughty girl like that?' asked the Taskmistress of Lidir.

[11]

The Chamber of Correction

Ildren surveyed the room one last time. It was at once familiar and yet different. The bondslaves festooning the walls and ceiling moved gently, sighing, adjusting to the languor of the warm still night. But now one star outshone all the others, and the vision still made her belly quaver; she could scarcely dare to look a moment longer at the heavenly outspread body suspended from the rafters. She quietly closed the door and left her lover – for the present – to her private dreams and made her way through the dungeons, up the stairs and into the calm seclusion of her apartments.

But Ildren was not calm. How could she be, with the moment so close at hand, the moment she had been working towards for all this time? Her plan was slowly ripening, like a delicious fruit that Ildren very soon would pick. She could almost taste the nectar on her tongue. She looked across her sitting room to the place in the corner and the instrument of pleasure she had kept reserved for this singular incumbent, ever since that fatal winter's day when Ildren had miscalculated. Yes, against her better judgement, she had tried to rush things; she had played her hand too precipitately, with insufficient preparation of the ground, and she had paid the price in anguish and in torment. That would not happen this time. The foundations had been laid with careful calculation. All the events of the last few days – Sardroc, the cook's wild crew, the old goat in the library, Amalicia's little gathering and above all, the isolation every evening – had been designed not to break her lover's will but to point up, by way of contrast, Ildren's finer qualities, of loving care and unswerving physical attention. Tonight, when she had been forced to tie that delicious body to the frame, the surge of love had almost overtaken her; she had wanted to fall upon her knees and kiss that sweet body there and then. Only the memory of that cruel setback had stayed her lips.

But one more day and her lover would be hers again; one more day, but the hardest day for Ildren, in which she would have to kowtow to that evil pervert, the Countess, while Ildren's lover was abused and punished before her very eyes. Ildren felt a teardrop welling; it seemed so heartlessly unfair. She could not bear the thought; she got up slowly, walked over to the corner, lifted up the pot of honey and dipped her fingers in. She stroked them round the broad polished tip of the Rod and up and down its firm smooth reassuring length.

Whenever she looked down, Anya felt dizzy. The scene below her swayed and, at the same time, rotated very slowly. She was floating, falling without getting anywhere. It had terrified her at first, when the Taskmistress had fastened her arms and legs to the frame with a broad band round her middle, and she had been lifted, frame and all, slowly into the air. But now the feeling was different; each time she opened her eyes, it took her breath away. She was no longer afraid. She soared like a bird, wafting on the warm air currents out above the giant room, looking down upon the mysterious devices of punishment and pleasure. When she turned her head to the side, she could see the others who floated – slaves like herself, some drifted off to sleep, but most wide awake, each slave grappling silently with his or her own peculiar torture. The men had collars round their parts, knotted cords spiralling up their stems, or weights attached directly to their flesh or rooted deep inside them. Many of the women had thongs around their breasts and had their nipples pulled out through ornate constrictions fashioned out of gold. Their legs were bound wide apart, with chains dangling from between their thighs or looped from back to front. Anya knew – for she had witnessed the fitting – that some of the women had clasps, tiny weights or other stimulants between their thighs, clamped to their lips and nubbins. Down below, fastened to the walls, their bodies outspread in a brutal travesty of love, were other slaves whose torture was worse yet. They would writhe gently against their centres of attachment, and every once in a while a moan of subdued pleasure would escape to torment Anya's ears as the night warders, one female, one male, made their rounds, selecting slaves apparently at random, some several times whilst others not at all, and applying one of the devices shackled loosely to the chains about the warders' waists. In addition to cockstems of various shapes and sizes, there were sticks and straps and feathers, brushes and tiny padded pincers. But the most effective device of all was the knotted cord, which would cause the girls to whimper and the men to overflow. Anya had witnessed two men spill beneath the repeated pleasuring by this means. Both of them had been brought back quickly to erection by the female warder smacking them with her bare hand applied between their thighs and beneath their cockstems. In one case, she had bent the slave across her knee, lifted up her apron and then trapped his stem between her thighs while she spread his legs and smacked him. When she lifted him up his cock was rigid. She took him in her mouth and sucked him for some minutes and then re-attached him to the wall.

Now the male beside Anya was lowered. As far as she could tell, he had not transgressed in any way, and his stem remained stiff. Nevertheless, through the open framework Anya could see the female warder oil her fingers, push them into him and by means of this handhold cause his body to sway while she used a leather strap to smack the undersurface of his plum. She smacked him till he pleaded, then she milked him, with her fingers delving deeply up inside him, till he moaned. When she was satisfied with her efforts, she tightened the leather cord around his cockstem and his ballocks and then wound him up again, his flesh still twitching and a large thick droplet of his seepage gathered at the end.

Anya was afraid the male warder might select her. So far he had always passed beneath her without looking up but,

181

even so, she was not free from torment. Her flesh throbbed as if a thick vein pulsed within her nubbin; her nipples felt like they were constantly being sucked; the mouth of her bottom felt as if a hot slim cockhead were being pushed into it. Before she had racked her up, the Taskmistress had applied to each of Anya's parts a wicked salve, smeared lightly with a fingertip around her nubbin, on her nipples and slipped into her bottom. 'To sweeten your dreams,' she had said, as she stood up, looked at Anya with her soft brown eyes, and touched her tongue to Anya's upper lip. 'To concentrate the mind upon love – for tomorrow, my darling, the lords and ladies will be down to select the slaves for their amusement, and to pleasure or punish them, at their whim.'

So Anya's dreams were not sweet, and they were often snatched away again by a bondslave's groan of denial or sudden cry of pleasure. She dreamt of many things and many cruel tortures, torments in which Lady Amalicia's face loomed large above her with her twisted bright red lips, brighter than the drops of blood upon the pin she was using to prick upon the surface of Anya's squeezed out nubbin, and dreams in which her bottom was impaled on Sardroc's cockstem and she was carried round the room, then lifted up on that living stake, her hot thighs held open by his cool strong palms, while Ulla placed a stool before her, wet her fingers and slapped her on the nubbin without respite until she finally came. As Anya cried out from shameful pleasure in her dream, she heard what she thought at first were the jeers and murmurs of the kitchen servants as they watched her take release in this perverse way, until she opened her eyes to a new ordeal.

It was morning in the Chamber of Correction, and their lordships exclaimed in surprise and joy as they beheld, in bright-eyed spellbound eager fascination, the enchanted walls and ceiling of this grotto of delights.

And as the slaves were taken individually or in small groups to be placed upon the rack, fastened to the wheel, to have their flesh separated on the pole or merely to be dangled by their hands before their lordships to be punished, to partake of pleasure or simply to bestow it (according to the dictates of wicked inspiration), Anya recognised, as soon as she walked through the door, the lady who would choose her. In that instant, she knew the lady would abuse her till she bent her to her will. She knew that woman would be devoid of any mercy whatsoever. Yet, restrained as she was, the certainty sent a thrill right through her body, from the root of her tongue, down into her belly, out across the tight-stretched muscles of her inner thighs and up into her bottom. The feeling was exactly as if she had lain down freely on the lady's bed and spread her legs out wide to lay her body open for whatever was to come. Had the lady asked, she would have done it willingly. She would have watched the cool slim hand unglove and slap her burning thighs and smack pleasure on and on into her pulsing fleshpot. It was a feeling her mind did not understand at all and yet her body took delight in.

The lady wore a black silk gown and grey silk gloves. At her neckline was a string of pale blue pearls. Her hair was mostly grey, but with strands of palest gold; it could at one time have been red, like Anya's. She stood erect. She had a fine bone structure; she must have been beautiful once. In a way, she still was. Her eyes were alert; they appeared to dance about the room, taking in her surroundings quickly but efficiently. Anya had noticed her eyes hesitate a fraction as they looked up in her direction. This was how she had known the lady would choose her out of all the others. For a second, their eyes had met. It was in that second that Anya had experienced the feeling. Again the feeling came, for now the lady was talking to the Taskmistress, who was slowly nodding. Even the Taskmistress seemed to treat her with respect. Then Anya had to close her eyes – the Taskmistress was coming over. She felt the sudden jerk as the frame was lowered. It was as if a giant hand had reached into her breast and squeezed around her heart. She could not get her breath. The frame was tilted upright on the floor. Anya was outspread before the lady. She had been selected.

'Open your eyes, precious one.' The lady had bright green eyes. Her voice was clear and musical. 'You are very

183

beautiful. I can see now why my nephew kept you clois-
tered . . .' Anya frowned; then the realisation slowly
dawned. This must be Amalicia's mother, the Countess.
Yet she did not seem to resemble Amalicia in the least. The
lady stepped forward and stroked Anya's cheek with her
gloved hand, then drew a finger across her lips. The lightness of the silken touch felt so beguiling. The finger drew
back the other way, very gently. 'Very beautiful,' the lady
murmured. Anya closed her eyes again, briefly, and she felt
her belly sinking, for now she could not prevent her lips
from opening to the slim silk tip and closing round it in a
short and secret kiss.

The lady began to remove her left glove, holding it up
and pulling each fingertip in turn, systematically easing off
the tightness of the fit. 'I shall use your body,' she said,
'subjecting it to pleasure . . .' her eyes pierced into Anya,
'. . . and to punishment.' She waited for the words to take
effect. Anya tried to swallow her heart, which kept pushing
up into her throat. 'I shall not ask for your agreement, other
than this once. Thereafter I will do with you precisely as I
think fit.' She lifted Anya's breasts in turn upon the half
gloved hand and softly pinched the nipples between silken
fingertips before continuing, 'The detail as yet is undecided.' She looking steadily at Anya while she resumed
the removal of the glove. 'Tell me you agree to this.' The
glove came free, to reveal a delicate hand with pale long
fingers and a single ruby ring. 'Well?'

'My lady, I . . .' Anya's head was shaking. She wanted
pleasure but she knew she could not bear the pain.

'Ah. Just tell me you agree.' Anya felt hypnotized by
those eyes, and now the lady pressed her cool bare palm
against Anya's belly.

'I . . . I subject my body to your pleasure.' Now Anya
was very frightened by what she had said. She did not know
what she had agreed to.

'Taskmistress – unfasten her. I will punish her. Bring me
my box.'

'Yes, Countess.' The Taskmistress bowed.

Anya felt the waves of gooseflesh cascading down

between her thighs as the box was brought. It was a large black slim wooden case, its top embellished with gold leaf and inlaid with rubies and pearls. The Taskmistress held it while the Countess slipped the catches and lifted up the lid. Clipped against the red velvet lining were leather straps, whips and thin sticks wrapped tightly round with strips of leather. All the items were black. The largest was as long as the lady's hand, the smallest no larger than her little finger. The straps ranged from broad to narrow, from thick to very thin. Some of the whips had several strands; in one case they were knotted. Seeing that caused Anya's heart to miss a beat. Each instrument of cruelty had an ornate ebony handle jewelled with pearl and ruby and gold filigree. The lady's finger grazed across them, lifting and readjusting them, caressing them lovingly.

'Which would you choose, my darling?'

Anya jumped. The Countess smiled. 'An inappropriate question. Yes? For it depends upon the application – at present unspecified. It depends upon the mood – of the punisher and of the punished. Can you sense my mood, do you think?' The lady touched Anya's breasts again, taking a nipple between the fingers of her gloved hand before switching to her cool, naked fingers, not squeezing, but holding the nipple and allowing it to firm against her touch. 'How well can I judge yours? How well can you? What punishment would this body prefer, and where should it begin? And the key question . . .' the lady looked closely into Anya's face and laid her fingers upon Anya's naked belly, below her chain, making that belly quake as if the hand had been inside it, 'how long should it last, my dear? Should it never end?' The hand cupped coolly round Anya's burning sex, and Anya wanted so much to close her thighs around the hand. The lady did not move her hand, but bent forward and kissed Anya. Her lips felt cool and dry. Her tongue brushed the fine down on Anya's upper lip. The lady made her bow her legs outwards. 'This,' she said – her little finger and her thumb lay along the creases at the top of Anya's thighs, as the palm held her sex a captive – 'this belongs to me, until I tire of it.' Anya's belly shook. The Taskmistress smiled for the first time.

The Countess's hand lifted away and returned to the case. Her fingers came to rest upon a strap with a blade slightly longer than her middle finger. She lifted it in her gloved hand. The strap was shaped like a tongue, expanding upwards from the width of two fingers to the width of three or four. The leather had a springy firmness. It was as thick as Anya's flesh leaves when they were relaxed, but now of course, they were not relaxed. She could feel her flesh expanding, pumping with her pulse. She felt excited and afraid; the waves of fear kept coming, washing up her body as the lady pulled and flexed the strap, then carefully unfastened the sleeve of her gown, rolled it back and smacked the strap down hard against the inside of her forearm. Anya flinched but the lady did not move; a warm pink apparition of the strap began to ripen across the lady's milk-white skin.

'Taskmistress, brace her.' As Ildren stood in front of her, Anya was made to bend forwards and clasp her arms about Ildren's waist. Her ear pressed against the velvet robe just above the hip bone. Ildren moved Anya's hair aside and gripped her firmly underneath the arms. The Countess stood behind her. 'This pleasure shall be taken by degrees,' she declared.

She had a warder bring across a broad low wooden block for Anya to stand upon, to raise her hips to a more convenient height. She wanted to be able to see, and if needs be to touch, the downcurve of Anya's belly between her open thighs. 'Move your ankles apart. Turn your feet more inwards. Push out. We must expose that inner thigh . . .' It made shivers run up the tender skin. Anya waited for the crack of leather to deliver her from the razor edge of apprehension. 'Tighten.' She felt the lady's cool, ungloved hand press flat against her left thigh, then lift again, working up, pressing coolness to her heat, up onto her buttock, 'Push out, my precious,' pressing it to the side, opening it, making Anya catch her breath, for she thought the lady would touch her in her split, but she did not. She pressed the hand to the other side, lifting Anya open once again, then touching coolness down the right side of the inner thigh. 'Hold her tightly, Taskmistress.'

The first lash made her close her eyes from shock, but then she opened them again. Across the room, a male slave was being penetrated while he stood with legs apart and hands gripped around a bar just above floor level. A lady used a large cockstem on him. She was having some difficulty on account of the size of the cockstem and the tightness of the man. She paused to spread his cheeks and to work his cock a little.

The second slap came; the shock was less. Her skin began to prickle. After the third, the slaps stung methodically up Anya's inner thigh, following the line the hand had earlier taken, to the very top. Her buttocks were separated and the slaps directed to the facing surfaces of the cheeks, but the sensitive pushed-out mouth was carefully avoided. The Countess took her time. The smacking was not hard, so as to fill Anya's flesh with pain, and yet it was cruel, for with the salve that Ildren had applied, it stimulated her desire. It made her want to be touched in those very sensitive places, but the lady would not touch her. All she could do was watch the male slave opposite murmur while the wooden cockstem was bedded in him to the hilt and a band of thin silk was wrapped round and round his flesh to make it a cocoon.

The Countess slapped steadily down Anya's right side until her skin tingled. Soft hot and cold prickles chased each other up her thighs and across the inner faces of the cheeks. The strapping was now repeated; the prickling was redoubled. Between her legs, her flesh was burning though it had not suffered any contact with the strap. 'Stand up. Keep your ankles wide apart. Now you may kiss your Taskmistress,' the Countess announced from behind her, and the cool bare fingers now touched her again, held her hot cheeks apart. As Ildren kissed her shoulders, lifted her elbows and kissed her salted underarms, then kissed her on the lips, resting her tongue within her mouth for Anya to suck upon and taste Ildren's spiciness salted with her own fragrance, the lady's fingers gently probed her hot tight bottom mouth, searching out the entrance, and permitting Anya's body to suck the coolly worming fingertip. When Ildren's kiss released her, Anya heard a moan and, turning to the side, saw the male slave spurting in uncontrolled spasms through his silken sheath and over his tormentress's hands. Anya could not prevent her body tightening hard around the fingertip inside her. 'Hmm . . .' the Countess murmured, 'it seems our precious one prefers to witness pleasure even as she takes it . . . and who are we to deny her that delight?'

The instruction was now given that Anya be suspended from the ceiling, at a place where she could view the activities at the wheel, upon which two male slaves were disported. A harness was fitted over her shoulders. It had leather bands which looped beneath each breast and buckled tightly round them, and cuffs at the back for her wrists. The harness was connected by ropes to pulleys in the ceiling. Broad leather cuffs with thongs attached were fastened above her knees. As she was lifted, the harness took her weight without discomfort. Then her knees were drawn up tightly to each side and secured by the thongs to the harness, so as Anya hung, her weight caused her to roll slightly forwards; she was therefore trussed in such a way that the lowest point of her body was her sex, with the swollen flesh lips standing proud beneath the split heart of her bottom. She was visible to all and accessible to any touch.

The Countess was pleased by this arrangement. 'So supple, so delicious, and so convenient for the application of the punishment where it is most required,' she remarked as she stood behind her, running a fingertip beneath, lightly touching, sending cold shivers through those hot and yearning lips. The Taskmistress agreed:

'Indeed. Shall my lady choose another instrument?'

'In due course, Taskmistress, in due course.' The Countess too, had been diverted by the wheel. She moved beside Anya, occasionally allowing her fingers to drift into the crease of Anya's bottom and softly test its mouth. And always, the fingers would return to pull the flesh leaves downwards, sometimes squeezing them and rubbing gently, yet throughout, trying to draw them further away from her body, making them distend to satin smoothness, testing their heat with the cool back of her bare hand, then manipulating them once again to make them stand out to polished hardness. She did not look at Anya at all while this pleasuring progressed. She seemed engrossed in the scene before her.

The wheel resembled a mill wheel, with the slaves lashed down opposite each other and bound to pegs on the perimeter where the buckets would normally be. The slave who was right way up was being stimulated by a girl who sucked upon his cockstem, but the slave who was inverted was being punished by a lady with a strap. The lady pressed one hand flat, low down against his belly while she smacked the undersurface of his upturned cock repeatedly in short sharp slaps. Then she milked him a little, then slapped him once again. When the first moan was heard – which happened to come from the slave being smacked – the wheel was rotated half a turn, bringing the other slave into line for punishment. 'The wheel exemplifies the delicate balance of pain and pleasure,' the Countess observed. Then, as one of the slaves at last succumbed to that dubious delight, she carefully separated Anya's flesh and gently nipped her nubbin once for each and every spasm. The lady who worked the slave had ceased the slapping altogether; she merely held the base of his stem between a finger and thumb to direct the flow away from her robe and very lightly squeezed the tip while he squirted through her fingers to the floor. While a new slave was being selected to replace the one that had failed, the Countess now requested that her box be brought back.

Having stimulated Anya with those scenes of wanton torture, having kneaded her flesh until her sex lips formed two dark and polished lobes projecting downwards from her mound, now covered with a fine red sward, and having worked her to the dripping point of desire with the unrelenting squeezing, pulling and drawing down, until her flesh lips slipped against each other and round the oily pip of her rigid nubbin, the Countess stood in front of her as she selected a further instrument of cruelty.

'We will punish this purse of your desire,' she explained.

'Shh, my darling.' She lifted Anya's chin and looked at her while she brushed the backs of her fingers from side to side across the lowest and most burning part of Anya's tortured body. 'We will do this simply for our pleasure and diversion.' Anya opened her mouth again to protest; her throat felt tight and dry. 'There is no need for you to answer, for we have your prior agreement.' Anya's blood ran cold. 'We shall chastise this pouch – for its lewdness in swelling up so hard. Now, we must choose an appropriate champion of this very worthy cause. Let us see. Hmmm . . .'

The Countess's gloved fingers had come to rest upon a long thin evil-looking rod, a switch, sheathed tightly in black leather. She held it up and swung it sharply. It cut the air with a vicious, high-pitched swish. She smiled when Anya flinched. 'Ah . . . Do not fear, my darling. Our champion shall be applied but very lightly – for the present.' The Countess put down the rod and stroked Anya's cheek again, this time with her gloved hand. Her little finger wiped away the teardrop that had begun to form. 'Delicious tears . . .' she crooned. 'But this body shall adjust, my dear. In time it will come to welcome the attentions of the lash.' Anya shook her head, but the Countess was not deterred. 'Yes, be assured of it. You will look back on these moments with quiet pleasure. And your flesh, this sweet flesh, shall be satiated by this means.'

'No!' Anya could feel the tears beginning to well again. She was thinking about the cruel treatment of the women on the Horse. And now the Countess would do the same to her. She was powerless to prevent it.

'But you have already agreed, my darling.'

'No!' The tears began to roll in earnest.

'We shall see . . .' The Countess's eyes narrowed as if she were a cat about to pounce; they frightened Anya more than any verbal threats.

The Countess began by stroking Anya's body with the switch, working it up and down each breast until the nipples formed hard black bubbles. Then she collared them tightly at the base with small leather loops with gold slip rings attached, until her nipples felt like they might burst. The switch was then swept down her belly and up her inner thighs to the very ticklish place at the top, before being drawn firmly across her dangling flesh leaves. The pressure and release there forced a ripple of delight through her lower belly. She closed her eyes. The Countess made her open them and look at her while she swept the rod across the other way. Anya's tears had stopped.

'You like this pleasure?' the lady asked her gently.

'I . . .' Anya felt the gloved hand brush against her; the soft silk whispered seductively over her hard smooth swollen skin. 'Yes, my lady.' The gloved fingers took hold of her leaves and pulled, then separated them and Anya felt the cool air bathe her inner moistness. She could feel her nubbin push out. She gasped when the rod was pressed against it, very lightly.

'Then tell me you will take the pain I will inflict upon this luscious place,' the lady said simply.

Anya's belly squirmed. She knew she could not stand it. Why did this lady have to punish her, and in so cruel a fashion?

'My lady, please,' she mumbled. The eyes gazed calmly at her; the gloved finger gently sealed her flesh leaves, then held them squeezed about her nubbin, palpating them softly in time with Anya's heartbeat. The lady waited. To Anya, all the pressure, all the weight of wanting, seemed concentrated in that one point, her centre of desire. She needed her deliverance; she needed it very soon. The stimulation was cruel. Her flesh was bursting for fulfilment. She wanted the lady to bring her on, to rub her flesh leaves harder round her bud, to take away this burden, to make the pleasure burst right through her belly. The fingertips kept touching, but too gently, not enough to push her on, making the wanting painful.

'Please?' she asked again.

'Please what?'

'I beg of you – deliver me from this burden.'

'In the manner of my choosing?'

Anya had no choice. She was on the knife edge of cruelty

– the cruelty of denial. At that moment, she believed that anything would be better than this tortured wanting. She knew those eyes would tolerate no disobedience. She nodded weakly. Then the wave of fear came over her again, choking her, almost drowning her.

The lady slipped the rod through the chain at Anya's belly while she prepared her with two hands, one gloved, one bare, first pressed flat on each side of her flesh leaves, then drawn smoothly down, leaving the plump black fins standing straight out from the mound. She took up the rod. Anya turned her head away. The waves of fear kept coming until she heard the swish.

The shock of pain on that tender flesh was all-consuming. It shot up through her body and burst behind her eyes. She thought she had been branded. It was worse than anything she had dreamt possible. It caught the gasp within her throat and choked it off completely. She bit her lip but it did not help. Her flesh felt as if it had been flayed from her body, as if the skin on one side had been stretched until it split while a thousand fiery needles pricked into it.

'Open your eyes, my precious.' The Countess had an expression of wicked satisfaction, but she was breathing rapidly; she was excited by what she was doing, excited by this cruelty and the pain she was causing. 'Now this time, look at me. And do not flinch.' Anya bit her lip harder. The lady's eyes descended, then Anya saw the quick blur of the lady's forearm and then the burning stretching and the fiery prickles struck and spread over the other side. This time she did cry out, but the lady did not desist until she had whipped the switch very quickly across again from side to side. Then she stood back and folded her arms while Anya's pain ascended to a whimpering crescendo before it gradually subsided to a warmth and then to ice-cold prickles.

The Countess advanced again and stroked Anya's upper thighs, tickled in the creases, pressed her bare hand flat to Anya's belly, bestowing these little signals of tenderness as if trying to atone for the cruel pain and anguish she had just delivered. But none of this brought Anya any pleasure whatsoever. She could not understand this lady, could not understand why she wanted to mingle pain with pleasure, cruelty and tenderness so intimately. How could the lady imagine that Anya would ever welcome it or derive any satisfaction from it? It was simply hateful. But perhaps the lady did not care. Perhaps this was how she took her perverse pleasure – in the pain she administered to others.

Now the pain had lulled; at intervals, a shower of freezing stings would burst upon her flesh as if icy water had been sprayed upon her gently throbbing leaves. The yearning need within her nubbin was more intense than ever. The Countess had taken great care not to strike it with the rod, so each wicked lash upon her sex lips had transmitted as a softened pressure which only served to stimulate the deeply bedded bud.

But just when the pain had ebbed to warmth, the Countess struck again – two quick lashes upon each side of Anya's dangling purse. Again she cried out, for the pain had not lessened one bit this second time. It felt even worse. The Countess smiled, then moved out of sight, behind Anya. Now, as the hot stings and the stretching feeling turned to a pressured warmth, the Countess's bare fingers touched her in between her outspread bottom cheeks, padding up and down the groove, investigating the inturned mouth, pressing against it, feeling its shape, testing every wrinkle, then probing. 'Spread, my darling,' she whispered, then her cool middle finger probed within, sliding firmly against the intermittent tightness it induced, until it was stopped by the collar of the thick ruby ring. The lady, however, would not sanction even this refusal and forced the finger up against the tightness until Anya's flesh had distended sufficiently for the ring to push inside. Only then, with her hand pressed flat to Anya's bottom and this middle finger sheathed inside, did she reach beneath and quickly swish the rod from side to side, not quite so hard this time, but catching Anya's flesh lips at their very edges and thereby driving a much more concentrated pressure-pain upwards through her sex lips, forcing her bottom to contract hard around the finger and aggravating further yet the itching need within her pulsing nubbin.

The Countess slipped the rod through the chain, this time at Anya's back, so her gloved hand was free now to reach beneath her and tease apart the savagely punished flesh lips, draw back the hood and thus expose the nubbin, not for her touch, but so that Anya could be made to look down at the mirror which the Taskmistress now held angled between Anya's thighs at the level of her sex. She could see the grey-gloved fingers spreading her sex, and the black leaves, not burst or bleeding as she had imagined they might be, yet puffed up, throbbing, and now moistened with her seepage. She could see the slowly pulsing hardened nubflesh in between, and underneath, the Countess's slender finger disappearing into her body. She watched and felt the finger being slowly withdrawn and the ruby ring reappearing before her flesh lips were carefully pressed together once again. Then she felt the rod being removed from her chain. The Countess came round to the front again. Anya shut her eyes and tried to brace herself for the cut of the evil switch. Her belly shook; her flesh was creeping. She wanted it to be over. But she did not hear any swish, and when the contact finally came, it was not the shocking stinging. Instead the rod was pressed against her line of split, gently at first and then more definitely, until her leaves slipped open and the leather touched her bud. And for once her gasp was pleasure; the rod was drawn back and forth a fraction, in a gentle sawing action, then was very slowly rotated up against her nubbin till she moaned and tried to push. The Countess held it very still against her till she stopped moving; only then did she begin to turn it almost imperceptibly the other way until Anya could take no more and bucked and felt her pre-pleasure coming on. The lady deftly pulled the rod away and snapped the tip of it sharply on the offending nubbin, making Anya jump with shock.

'Not yet, my darling,' said the Countess firmly, 'not for a long while yet, I fear, for there is much for you to savour . . .' Before returning the rod to the box, she cleaned the moisture from it by wiping it upon Anya's belly.

'Have her taken down, Taskmistress. Spread her on the

bars and put her to the drip.' She lifted Anya's chin. 'Do not look so worried, my child. Do not look so hunted. Since this body as yet does not fully appreciate the merits of pain, we shall see how it takes to pleasure.'

But the device to which Anya was secured was not designed for pleasure at all, unless for the wicked pleasure of the masters and mistresses. It was an instrument of torture. There were two parallel bars, each at waist height, and about two feet apart. Anya was made to lie face down upon them; her wrists and ankles were then secured to the wood. Her body, being unsupported, formed a downward curve between the bars. Her ankles had been fastened in such a way that her knees remained tightly bent and her buttocks were kept widely separated. The Countess stood beside her, stroking her hair. The Taskmistress spread her flesh leaves back, then placed in position beside her a wooden support from which was suspended a large skin gourd of olive oil. The nozzle of the gourd was position an inch above the base of Anya's spine.

'I think a slow drip is in order, Taskmistress.'

'Very well, my lady.'

The oil felt warm. The first drop hit her skin and then spread quickly over the fine hairs. It did not really tickle; neither did it feel uncomfortable. She hardly felt the second drop. The Countess patiently stroked her hair. After the third drop, the oil began to seep into the groove as a fine warm film which wet across the mouth of her bottom, then spread underneath to merge with the body oil that bathed her open sex. It wasn't until the band from the base of her spine to the tip of her nubbin was fully wet that the tickling began. She felt the well of her bottom filling, then overflowing, then her sex felt very wet. The oil welled around her nub and gathered to a droplet which seemed to suck her nubbin as it dripped. And once the rhythm was established, the lady had her blindfolded, that she might concentrate more fully, before she left her to ponder her predicament. All that Anya was aware of was the rhythm – the drip upon the tip of her backbone and the reciprocal sucking droplet at her nubbin. The feeling was bitter-sweet;

it was too soft – not like the feeling lips or fingertips might give – and too infrequent. It tantalized her. It was not pleasurable. It felt as if the skin upon the tip of her spine had worn thin, as if the nerves had multiplied and were connected from that tip, through her bottom, up into her belly and down inside her sex to meet her nubbin. It was as if these tendrils sucked the oil in at her backbone and squeezed it drop by drop from the tip of her nubbin. She tried to contract to squeeze it harder; she could not close her legs; she could not alter the pace of the slow drip and the feather-light sucking.

Anya could not tell how long the torment had continued. She had half dozed and dreamed soft fingertips were smearing butter round her bud, but then she felt a movement on the bars and heard murmurs. Suddenly, the blindfold was removed. She squinted as the bright light hurt her eyes. Before her, astride the bars and balanced upright was a young bondgirl with light brown hair. The Countess stood behind the girl; the Taskmistress stood behind Anya and between her thighs. The drip was increased.

Anya's head was lifted and then she was forced to watch the bondslave deliberately being pleasured to completion. The Countess's bare hand introduced itself from behind; two fingers pushed up into the girl's sex while the gloved hand spread the lips and worked the pinkened bud; already it was hard. As the working advanced slowly but certainly towards its goal, Anya felt the Taskmistress's fingers pressing between the cheeks of her bottom, oiling themselves upon the drips, rubbing oil into the inner faces of her buttocks and then she heard the girl's first pleasured whimper; the pink flesh tightened round the fingers pushed inside. The gloved fingers pressed firmly, just above the hood, to delay the progress of the pleasure. As she watched the bud's tight pulsing ease and the silk commence to stroke it once more, lightly at the tip, she felt Ildren's oily fingers open her and smoothly push into her bottom, sending those deep tickles up inside her, making her want to tighten though she knew she must not; she knew that she must remain relaxed if those overpoweringly sweet brushing sensations were to be maintained. But when at last the fingers had reached to the knuckles, and the tips began to drift around inside and touch her inner flesh in random little kisses, and the bondgirl thrust and grunted like an animal as the Countess's bare fingers tried to hold her open while the silken tips restrained and nipped her nubbin till she came, Anya could not help but tighten to the extent that the Taskmistress's fingers, despite their oily state, had much difficulty withdrawing. The bondslave was now slumped back against the Countess, who wiped her fingers dry upon the girl's tresses as she spoke.

'How has she fared, Taskmistress?'

Ildren stroked Anya's thigh very tenderly. 'Very well, Countess. A little tight perhaps, but I'm sure that can be forgiven . . .'

'I will be the judge of that!' the Countess snapped. Anya felt Ildren's grip suddenly tense about her thigh. 'Forgiveness cannot be bestowed lightly, Taskmistress. That much, you should know. Forgiveness must be earned – by self restraint and by the lash.'

[12]

The Countess Blushes

Anya was devastated. Those words – the mention of the lash – were like an icy hand that stopped her heart. Why was the Countess so cruel to her? Why her, of all the slaves? The bondgirl had been pleasured. Even the slaves upon the wheel had been allowed release. Why was it always Anya who was punished and denied any deliverance? Why was she being tortured? It was cruel and hateful. The Countess was evil; she was worse than the Taskmistress. It was as if Anya was being punished for someone else's transgression – probably the Countess's own.

Anya gave a start; the Countess had taken her by the hair and was slowly twisting it until her head had turned to face her.

'Have the warders attend to her; have them teach her some restraint. Instruct them that her flesh must know no rest, but that under no circumstances must her wantonness suffer lustful satisfaction. And – this is most important – she must not be smacked, or punished with the strap or rod, unless by my own hand. Is that clear, Taskmistress?'

'Yes, Countess.' The Taskmistress sounded subdued.

And so, Anya was given to the warders, and the pattern for the rest of the day was set. Throughout the morning, she was kept spread-eagled against the wall. Each time a warder passed, she would be stimulated in some way: her breasts might be stroked, her flesh leaves kneaded, or her bottom tickled. On one occasion, her legs were lifted while a tusk coated in a thick clear liquid was pushed between her buttocks; it made her feel very hot and itchy, even when the tusk was taken out. On another occasion, her nub was held between the padded pincers while her nipple restraints were tightened and her breasts were sucked. Twice she was taken down from the wall, the first time to be sat astride the beam and feathered in between the legs, the second time to be made to spread her legs and touch her toes whilst the female warder used the knotted cord upon her, wetting it then drawing it repeatedly back and forth across her nubbin. It was whilst she was in this position that the Countess, after a considerable absence, happened to pass and became concerned, on the basis of the sounds being uttered, that her slave might be deriving too much pleasure from this therapy. She therefore selected from her box the smallest strap of all, a light narrow one and, holding Anya's offending flesh wide open, she smacked the inner surface of the flesh leaves, concentrating on the edges, and then she smacked the nubbin, which immediately turned numb. However, when the numbness waned to warmth and finally to pulsing heat, Anya realised that, far from assuaging her plight, the punishment had made the wanting even more pronounced and when she was allowed to stand up, she had the urgent need to press her thighs together. The Countess therefore directed that she be fastened this time facing the wall, with legs bent, drawn up and fastened out to the sides. She was left in that position, her breasts and belly pressed against the stone, for most of the afternoon, being taken down only to be provided with a bowl of dried fruit and a spicy drink which made her drowsy. 'Let her rest,' the Countess had said, but once again she was fastened to the wall, although this time her legs were permitted to touch the floor. She fell asleep, but did not dream.

She awoke with a start and gasped with the shocking cold. She thought at first she had been thrown into the cistern. The freezing water trickled down her back. The warder held a bucket. 'There, my lady, she is ready now,' he said.

'Thank you,' said the Countess. 'I hope you are refreshed, my dear. You will need your strength this night,' she added ominously. She dried Anya's back and bottom with a towel, but kept squeezing and stroking her buttocks nervously. Anya knew what was coming; the palpations were getting more intense. 'Bring me my box,' the Countess said at last. And now she sounded breathless.

As Anya dangled, the warders were called upon to bend her legs and push them as far as possible up the wall, whereupon the lady spread Anya's sex and pressed against it a folded cloth which was dripping with cold water, 'to temper that ardour, my dear,' while she slapped between her bottom cheeks with a strap which, being specially designed for the purpose, was spoon shaped, with a narrow stem crowned by a circle of soft leather. The short slaps were thereby delivered precisely into the spot where the Countess – admittedly on impulse – judged the slapping to be required. Yet with each smack delivered to the mouth of Anya's bottom, the lady demonstrated a grain of tenderness by gently squeezing the cloth against the open sex to cool its burning heat.

When the Countess had tired of this diversion, she had Anya taken down; she whispered some instruction to one of the warders, who looked thoughtful at first and then nodded.

'Yes, my lady, I think I know the one,' she said.

'And we shall need some privacy.'

'I understand.'

Anya was led into a small adjoining room. The warders positioned a table in the centre. A chair was brought for the Countess but she did not use it to sit upon. Her box was placed upon it. 'On the table, precious one,' she said. Anya obeyed. She did not know what was expected of her, so she knelt on all fours. 'Very good,' the lady said. 'You are well trained, but here,' and she pressed Anya's shoulders further down so her breasts were flat against the surface. She made her turn to lie across the width of the table. 'Good.' She eased Anya's knees wider apart. Anya closed her eyes and waited for the lash to fall, but it did not come. Then she heard the door open. 'Ah. Bring him here. Yes, very good.' It was a male slave. The warder had him tightly constricted with a collar round the stem and bag. She drew him along by a cord. The veins stood out from the surface of his flesh.

'He has been worked to the brink repeatedly,' said the

warder, 'but we have always stopped him short.'

'Hmmm.' The Countess looked from the man to Anya. 'Then you have something in common, my darlings. I wonder which of you will yield first? I hope it isn't you, my dear.' She laid her hand on Anya's hip. Anya's heart beat faster. The cockstem twitched. 'Warder – remove the lead, but leave the collar on him.'

The Countess took off her gloves, turned the slave to face her, and examined him closely. Anya noticed that the Countess's cheeks began to colour as she did this; her fingers seemed very nervous, as if she were afraid. Suddenly, she made him turn and lie forwards across the table, next to Anya, with his legs apart and his cockstem forming an uneasy upturned curve against the table top; then she pressed her thumb into the collar while she smacked the cockstem with the tongue shaped leather strap. When he stood up, his stem seemed harder than ever.

The Countess dismissed the warders, after she had appropriated from them a strap much broader than the ones in her own collection. Then she turned to Anya. 'I wish to see you take him in your mouth, my dear,' she said. Her voice had been unsteady as she said this; her cheeks had turned a deeper colour. 'You shall take him very fully . . . very deeply.'

The slave was brought closer to the table; his cockstem bobbed in front of Anya's face. The plum looked angry, red and swollen; it looked as if it had been coated in seepage and then had dried. Anya could smell his scent very strongly. She had smelled that scent before, of course, on the Prince. Although she liked the smell of maleness, she did not want to take it this way, in degradation for the two of them.

'Pout your lips, my dear.' The Countess took hold of Anya's hair to guide her. She took the male slave by the collar, edging him forwards, but then very swiftly bent her own head and took the plum into her mouth. It had happened so quickly that Anya was unsure if she had seen correctly; it was as if the Countess had not been able to control herself, as if she had wanted to do it but then the shame had taken over. Her cheeks were deep red with embarrassment. Yet she was prepared to force someone else to do it. She was using Anya to do the very things she herself felt guilty about, and then was punishing Anya to alleviate that guilt. Anya felt sure of this. The Countess was very strange, and very frightening.

Anya was made to lick the male slave's sex and stroke her tongue underneath it while the Countess watched. Then she had to push her tongue into the tip while the Countess slid the cockskin up and down. The Countess next pushed the stem into Anya's mouth. It tasted very salty despite the fact that it had already been sucked. Anya had to take it in as far as she was able, until it reached the back of her throat and made her want to gag. She had to close her lips around the stem and hold him very still in suction, breathing only through her nose, while the Countess stretched the skin back, tightened the collar and closed her hand about the exposed length of stem. With Anya maintaining this hold, the lady released him so she could step behind Anya, hold open her thighs then cup her sex in her bare hand, trapping the flesh lips in between her middle fingers while, with the tongue-shaped strap, she systematically slapped the inner thighs and at the same time pressed her thumb within the groove, against the hidden mouth. Each jerk that Anya gave allowed the thumb to slip more deeply in.

The Countess then became unsatisfied with Anya's posture. She wanted to see the cockstem clearly as it entered Anya's mouth, so she withdrew her thumb and had Anya turn first upon her side and then upon her back, without releasing the plum throughout this bodily rotation. She instructed Anya to try to take the stem more deeply, and temporarily assisted, at first by pushing the male slave from behind and then by slapping him hard across the buttocks with the broad strap borrowed from the warders and rearranging his bag so it rested on the bridge of Anya's nose and not upon her nostrils, thus enabling her to breathe once more. Then she returned to attend to Anya.

She had Anya bend her knees and press her feet down on the table, arching her back until it lifted and the Countess could comfortably reach an arm into the space beneath her.

The Countess then made her fold her arms below her back, to maintain the outcurve of her belly, then lift her feet and press them together above her. While Anya maintained this open-thighed, tight-bunched posture, with her breasts pushed out and her lips sucked tight about the thick stem in her mouth, the lady began to slap her with her bare hand, not viciously, but certainly relentlessly, slapping her belly, slapping her inner thighs, and the cheeks of her uplifted bottom close against the groove. She wet two fingers and slapped the creases at the tops of her thighs, the mound, the bridge between her sex and bottom, the bottom mouth itself, the closed lips and the hood. She spread the lips and slapped there too. Finally, using the tip of the middle finger, whipping it sharply down, the slaps were concentrated on the nubbin. The purpose of the slapping was not simply to allow the Countess to experience the tactile pleasure of slavish sensuality and drink the ripening wave of delicious body heat through her open mouth, but to make her slave buck, and grunt through her nose, and suck her lips more tightly about the male slave's fleshy plum, thereby gradually bringing him on.

Anya could taste the saltiness very strongly now, and then she could feel him start to move and moan and try to thrust down hard into her throat.

'Stop!' the Countess commanded. 'Pull out.' She then spun Anya round, so the cockstem wavered now above her quaking belly, and pressed the feet together more firmly upon that belly. 'Now, roll your belly. Push as if this cockstem were inside you; squeeze as if your flesh were milking him,' she directed Anya as she moved behind the male slave and fitted the glove to her right hand, which disappeared between his buttocks as the left hand took his collar. The silken fingers entered. 'Spread, my darling,' she said to him. 'I want to squeeze you dry.' It seemed these words, combined with the actions of her gloved fingers and the pulling of the collar tightly back, were sufficient, for he immediately thrust as if propelled forwards by his passion, and though both slaves' eyes were closed tight against this mutual degradation, Anya felt the warm thick miltings splash across her ankles and her toes, then onto her belly, into the tight spread crease of her thigh, across her open flesh lips and then more weakly down across her buttock. When she opened her eyes, the slave was gone; the warders were ushering him out. The Countess peeled off her glove and dropped it to the floor.

She massaged the stickiness into Anya – into her creases, upon the inner surfaces of her sex lips, into her groove and up around her nubbin, manipulating this carefully yet definitely, watching Anya's face, until Anya's belly tensed and she nearly came. Then the lady took a very thin strip of linen bandage from her pocket, attached it to the back of Anya's chain and pulled it up, fitting it in the groove, along the line of split of Anya's sex, across the nubbin, confining this within the narrow linen band. She fastened the end to the chain at Anya's belly. Finally she scooped up the large gobbet of milt that lay diagonally on that belly and worked it into the linen to wet it and re-tighten it until it moulded perfectly to the nubbin underneath. She sealed the sex lips round the arrangement and had the slave taken out and secured to the wall with her legs outspread. Before the lady left Anya for the night, she slapped her mound and sex lips with a narrow leather strap, then clipped the lips together with a clamp, saying, as a parting comfort, 'Tomorrow, I will have this flesh pierced and woven with the most exquisite filigree and jewels.'

When, later that night, the Taskmistress came to check upon the slave, her heart almost burst right through her breast to see her sweet love in such a state of torment and rebuff. She pressed cool kisses upon her hot body; she untethered her soft thick nipples and lifted them upon her tongue; she fitted her hand to the tight curved belly, allowed her fingertips to venture into the creases, to touch the smooth moist flesh, and then she made this promise – freely given – as she removed the cruel clip and gently peeled the sticky linen from the sweet delicious place. She caressed that moist place lovingly. 'Do not fear, my love,' she whispered. 'No one shall hurt you on the morrow. Your Taskmistress will not allow it. Your Taskmistress will take care of you and shield you from all harm.' And as the Taskmistress drank the tears that had trickled down beside the perfect nose and spread above the softly sensual lips, the slave was reassured; her worst fear was allayed; she welcomed those gentle lips – so contrasted with all the cruelty she had of late partaken – and, even as she remained pinned against the wall, she permitted the tongue to delve within her mouth, and the tender fingertips, by means of gentle coaxing in between her thighs, softly to express her pleasure, which nevertheless came in deep drawn drowning gasps against the seeking tongue which lifted up her own.

In the early hours, in the seclusion of her sitting room, the Taskmistress, uneasy, nervous, like a bride upon the evening of her wedding, took the still moist linen, dipped it in the jar of honey and very carefully, very lovingly and very, very nervously moulded it about the great carved cockstem that crowned the framework in the corner of the room, and when she kissed that honeyed stem, the wave of pleasure brought her to her knees. She knew that tomorrow, exactly one hundred and forty-four days after that fateful day when temper and impatience (and an intractable slave, to boot) had been allowed to overrule her usual level-headed guile, her plan would be back on course. She had not rushed it this time, she had taken it very slowly, and now she would reap the rewards of that patience.

The slave would be made Princess, but by then Ildren would control the Princess and Lidir would be hers. Ildren would sleep content that night.

[13]

Rabbits

Anya's dream was terrifying. In that dream, her body was racked with fever; she was bucking, pushing, resisting as Axine held her down upon the table – Axine, who was supposed to be her friend – while the Countess spread Anya's legs and slapped her belly into base submission, then took the vicious needle and cruelly pierced her flesh three times and fitted the nubbin ring. And at that point the dream turned into an even greater nightmare as the Prince walked in to witness Anya being pleasured by that means. 'This is what your Princess requires, Sire,' the wicked woman had said. 'This is how she prefers to while away the time when Your Highness is away.' But much as Anya tried to fight and kick against those lies, she could not escape Axine's grip. She could only shed salt tears of cruel frustration as the Prince turned pale and faded from her vision; all she could see was Axine above her, shaking her, then gagging her with a hand across her mouth as Anya tried to bite the hand that stopped her calling for her Prince.

'Shh! Shhhh!' Axine whispered harshly, and quickly glanced over her shoulder. 'The warders will hear you.'

Axine was real. Anya had been dreaming. She was still fastened to the wall.

'Listen, Anya: are you awake?' Axine asked, shaking her again. 'You understand?' Anya nodded, but she did not fully understand. Axine searched her eyes. 'They will be back any minute. It's morning. We haven't much time.' She was unfastening Anya when there was a movement at the far end of the room, followed by a low moan. Axine crouched down. Like Anya, she was nude apart from her chains. Her body looked smooth and agile. 'Pretend you're asleep,' she whispered, then darted away along the foot of the wall and out of sight.

The warder came into view, slowly working his way down the room. Anya felt very vulnerable for though her hands were now free, her feet were still tied. She wrapped the thongs round her hands again and half-closed her eyes. The man hesitated when he reached the next girl but one to Anya and began to play with her. Anya could hear her protesting weakly; then she heard the gentle slaps interspersed with the deep breaths as the girl's pleasure was advanced. The footfalls progressed closer. She shut her eyes tight and held her breath. He had stopped directly in front of her. She could hear the whistle of his breathing; she could feel it on her face. She almost jumped when his apron touched her knees. Then his breathing momentarily stopped.

'What?' His voice was overlain with disbelief and Anya knew she was discovered. A fraction later, his rough hand took her wrist and turned it; she jerked away and opened her eyes. His face was wrinkled up in puzzlement. She knew she must act fast. Her fist formed into a hard ball, but then an unearthly creaking groan behind the warder saved him. 'What in the – ?' he began again and, turning, let go of her. The wheel was slowly rotating, though nobody was there. The warder seemed to forget about Anya, scratched his head and set off, then thought better of it, taking up the stick from around his waist and holding it menacingly as he advanced towards the wheel. Anya was too slow. She too had been hypnotised by the seemingly ghostly intervention and she let him get almost to the wheel before she remembered she needed to get untied.

'Quick!' Axine was over by the door. Now Anya bent, forgetting she was standing flat against the hard unmoving wall, and fell forwards to her knees. The ropes bit into her ankles. She twisted round and began pulling at the first knot, which didn't want to yield. 'Hurry!' Finally she got it free, but the warder had heard the commotion and now she had only a second or two. Her back was towards him. The knot wouldn't free. Her fingers clawed it frantically. 'Anya – look out!' She ducked and jerked her foot, pulling till her ankle wrenched, but all to no avail. The warder was upon her; the stick was raised. She turned and curled up with her arms about her head, crying 'No!', trying to make her body into a ball. She screamed. The warder fell on top of her; his full weight knocked the breath from her body; he rolled sideways onto the floor.

The attack was over; the warder was unconscious. Axine stood above him rubbing her right fist against her left palm as if it were hurting very badly. She flexed her fingers and rubbed again. Anya was horrified.

'Axine! What have you done?'

'He was going to hit you with the stick. He deserved it.' But even Axine didn't sound quite sure. She was trying to keep her breathing steady, but not succeeding. Anya didn't reply. She lifted her hand and pressed it lightly to Axine's ankle, to reassure her; then she looked away. She was wondering what she would have done in Axine's place.

Her fingers began working at the knot again. It suddenly came loose. She got up quickly, but now Axine had fallen to her knees and was listening to the warder's breathing. Her hand lay upon his cheek in a strangely contradictory gesture, considering what she had done to him. As soon as he began to stir, Axine jumped up, took Anya by the hand and they were off, through the door and down the maze of sandy corridors, past the sleeping bondslaves chained to the wall and down into the area of the bathhouse and the place where Anya had taken breakfast. Anya suddenly grabbed Axine and pulled her back, putting a finger to her lips.

Thelda's drab, stooped form jerked slowly across about twenty feet in front of them, carrying a heavy bucket of water. Anya waited a few seconds before continuing. The lithe, smooth bodies of the young women passed silently in the time it took Thelda to put the bucket down. When she turned, the corridor was empty.

'But how are we going to get past the gate?' Anya whispered after they had achieved a safe distance.

'Don't worry. Marella will see to that. She got me into here.'

'She knows?'

'I had to tell her. She is on your side, Anya.' So, Marella had not forgotten her after all. Anya was relieved.

Nevertheless, Anya crept very warily past the final row of cells before the entrance hall. The cell she had been put into was occupied again, by two young sleeping bondslaves, each secured by a chain about her ankle to a corner of the bed. Everywhere seemed so quiet. Anya couldn't understand why they had met no warders. The one they had stunned would be awake by now and was sure to have raised the alarm.

Axine stopped short of the archway, held Anya back, and edged along the wall. She peeped round the column and motioned to Anya to do the same, but Anya felt as if her legs had turned to stone; she had to force herself to take a look. In the hallway sat the turnkey, unmoving and apparently asleep. Marella was there beyond the bars, pacing up and down. She held a bundle against her breast. Anya wanted to catch her eye but with the turnkey so close by, she didn't dare. She backed round the column.

'How will we get out?' she whispered.

Axine gave a wry smile. 'I'll just walk out. It's you that's the problem.' Anya knitted her brow. Axine laughed; she took her by the hand, back past the cells, to an alcove. On the floor, tucked round the corner in the half light was a heaped up cloth. Axine pulled the cloth away to reveal a tray with a small loaf broken in two, some pieces of cheese and a large mug of beer. 'This is how I got in here,' she said. 'I'm delivering this tray – overseen by Marella – on the Taskmistress's instruction. Almost anyone with a tray can get into the dungeons.' Anya smiled. 'If you're hungry,' said Axine, 'you'd better get it now. There's going to be an accident.'

Despite her nerves, Anya finished most of the food. Her friend leaned against the wall with her arms folded and watched her. 'You hide at the end of the corridor, behind the column,' she explained. 'When I drop this tray, the turnkey will come running . . .' Anya couldn't imagine the large bulk of the turnkey managing that, but she didn't interrupt. The beer was warm and sweet, the way she liked it. 'Then you slip past and get the key off the wall, and there you are.' Axine's slim smooth forearm snaked up in a flourish.

'But how will I know which key, Axine? There are so many bunches.'

'Easy. We watched what he did when he let me in. It's the second bunch from the right, and,' she headed off Anya's question, 'it's the largest key on the bunch. Well, one of the large ones anyway. You may have to try one or two.' Anya didn't like the sound of this. She could picture something going wrong. Axine was much more confident. 'There'll be time. Don't worry. And when you're out, remember to re-lock; take the keys out of the lock and throw them back to the wall. Then when he comes to let me out, he'll think they just fell on the floor. Marella will hide you. He won't know a thing.'

'Whose plan was this, Axine?'

'Don't worry. You worry too much.'

Anya stood behind the column, trying to mould her body to the wall, trying to make herself invisible. But she couldn't see how anyone coming round the corner could possibly miss her. Axine stood about twenty yards away, balancing the tray above her head. Anya glanced round the column. The turnkey still appeared to be asleep, and although she had been afraid it wouldn't be there, she could see the bunch of keys she needed. Perhaps the plan was all right after all. She gave the signal to Axine. Even Anya wasn't prepared for the crash that followed as Axine slammed the trayful hard against the wall, sending the metal plates and mug bounding into the gutter. The echoes clattered down the passageway. Anya shut her eyes and listened for the footsteps. Nothing happened. Now she didn't know what to do. If she risked looking round the corner, she knew the turnkey would have finally decided to creep across and would be staring her in the face. If she didn't look he would still be fast asleep. Axine was picking up the plates and now had her eye on the metal bars of the nearest cell. Anya could hear the slaves beginning to stir.

She had just decided to risk a look when, she smelled him – the sweet smell of sugarplums – and she froze as the turnkey floated round the corner, not two feet away, muttering to himself, then throwing up his hands.

'Sh! Shhhh!' he shrilled as Axine dropped the tray a second time, fell to her knees and began to sob. Anya counted up to five, then shot round the corner. Marella was waiting at the gate. 'Quick, my darling!' she cried. 'Get the keys. Over by the table.' Anya was already there. 'It's the third bunch from the right,' Marella shouted, just as Anya was reaching for the second. 'What?' she said, and at that point, the plan failed. She took hold of both sets, then changed her mind. 'The *third*, my pet!' Now she lifted that one, hesitated, heard Axine's voice approaching, then grabbed both sets, which promptly intertwined. As she tried to untangle them, they dropped upon the floor. They separated, but now she didn't know which was which, not that it mattered, except that she had intended to try the second bunch first and all of this was taking so much longer than expected.

'Oh! Hurry, my dear,' and now she was starting to panic. All the keys looked equally large. She would have to try them all – when she could get the first one in the lock. It didn't fit; she was fumbling now; the second key got stuck. Her hands had gone very sweaty. She looked over her shoulder. The turnkey had appeared, floating backwards, arguing with Axine, who had him by the arm. In a last desperate bid, Anya tried to wrench the key round until her hand shook and she thought her finger ends would burst. It was no good. She heard the shout; now she had been seen; he was trying to run towards her with Axine attached to his ankle. Marella had that horrified look; her voice was incoherent.

'Marella – we'll have to try something else.' Marella looked askance, but Anya's mind was working. The panic attack was passing: the turnkey had tripped and Axine had climbed on top. Anya was thinking about the back stairs to the kitchen, and there must be other exits, too. Now the turnkey was up and Axine was down and Anya had to act. She squeezed Marella's hand tightly one last time. 'Marella . . .' she whispered. She couldn't say it. 'I know,' Marella said, and took her hand and kissed her turquoise ring. It made Anya want to cry. 'Wait! Take this.' It was the bundle. Marella had to flatten it in order to squeeze it through the bars.

Anya rushed across and hit the turnkey with it, tripped him, then dangled the second set of keys before his face. 'I'm afraid I've broken your lock,' she said, hurling the keys out through the bars. Marella started laughing. The women set off at a run into the dungeons, leaving the turnkey trying to get his keys back from Marella.

They didn't get very far before Anya made them slow down. She didn't think it a good idea to rush blindly on when they might easily run into someone. They crept cautiously into the place where the stone cisterns were; there was no sign of Thelda. Anya still couldn't understand why there were no warders about.

'Axine – we're sure to be stopped before we get to the kitchen. And how will we get through without a key?'

'Why did you throw that bunch away back there? One of those might have fitted.'

Anya fell silent; she hadn't thought of that. She hadn't much faith in keys anyway, and she had something else in mind.

'Axine – are there rabbits in the dungeons?'

Axine's expression told her, even before she answered. 'Rabbits?' She looked behind her, to each side, then stared at Anya strangely. 'Rabbits live in fields, Anya.'

'I know that.' Even so, she blushed. 'But – do you ever get them in the dungeons?' she persisted.

Axine thought about it. 'Only in the stew.'

'I've seen one – a live one.'

'Are you sure it wasn't a rat?'

Anya blushed again. 'I know what a rabbit looks like.'

'What? No. I mean where,' Axine was poking fun at her. 'Where did you see this rabbit?'

'In there.' Anya pointed to the door of the room where she had breakfasted that day.

Axine shrugged. 'So?'

'Don't you see? There must be a way out.' She headed for

212

the door. She was worried it might be locked; she wanted to check that before the discussion went any further, but Axine wouldn't let up. 'Anya, we're not rabbits.'

'No – it was a big hole; I saw it.' At the exact moment she took hold of the latch and pushed, two warders appeared at the bend in the corridor.

'Quick!' said Axine. 'They're here.'

'Oh no! It won't move; it's locked.' Anya put her shoulder to it then started kicking it in a frenzy. She could feel the panics coming on. Axine pushed her aside. 'It's no good,' Anya said. She was getting ready to run; the warders had seen them and were obviously suspicious now. But the door opened as soon as Axine lifted the latch fully, and they fell into the room.

The room was occupied. The warder taking breakfast at the table was already standing, but now he jumped back in alarm. Anya's heart sank.

Axine, however, seemed to take this new shock in her stride. 'Quick!' she called to him. 'Come quickly!'

'What? What is it? His hand reached automatically for his strap.

'It's . . .' But then Axine couldn't think what it was.

Anya came to the rescue. 'It's Thelda – she's fallen in the cistern!'

The warder rushed out past them, and Axine slammed the door. 'Help me pull the table over. I doubt if the lock will hold them . . .'

The banging started even before they'd got the chairs in place. Axine looked around the room. 'Where's your tunnel?' But she suddenly changed her tune when she saw where Anya wanted to take her. Her confidence drained away.

'What are you frightened of?' asked Anya as she dislodged the stone and pushed her feet through the hole. It was a tight fit; she couldn't feel anything below her. She would have to risk it. She dropped and collapsed onto a muddy floor. Axine's face was peering down at her. 'Throw the bundle,' Anya shouted. 'Now jump!'

Axine put her feet over the edge, then changed her mind.

'I can't. We might never get out.' But the crashing at the door was getting louder. Anya decided for her – she took her by the ankles and pulled with all her weight. Axine screamed and they landed in a heap.

It was only after Anya's eyes had adjusted to the dark that she realised that was all there was down there – blackness. She could feel the waves of gooseflesh pulsing over her skin, and it wasn't only from the cold. They had only advanced a few paces when the dim light above them seemed to fade away; if they faced away from it, the darkness was complete. Axine gripped her arm as if to break it.

'Anya – I can't see anything. I'm frightened.'

Anya kept testing the floor with her foot; the ground felt like cold damp earth; it seemed to fall away in front and to the side. She turned back and tried again. Behind them was a solid wall of stone, smooth and wet and waterworn, but in every other direction, the floor sloped away steeply, and the blackness was so dense it felt as if a velvet hood had been fastened over her head. It was thick, oppressive and, despite the cold air, suffocating. The only reassuring thing was the sound of running water. Then suddenly, Axine cried out, tugging so sharply at Anya's arm that she was pulled down to her knees. Before Anya could grab her properly, the hand slipped away altogether. Now Anya screamed; Axine called out once more and slipped into the blackness. Anya's limbs turned to ice. She listened; she couldn't hear anything – no sound of falling, no more cries, nothing; only the running water. She was terrified; she tried to shout but her throat was paralysed by the fear. She knelt there, clawing the dirt up in her fingers, not knowing what to do.

'There's a light down here . . .' The echo sounded at first as if it came from above.

'Axine?'

'Come down . . . but be careful. I nearly went into the stream.'

Anya laughed and wiped away the tears. She slid down on her bottom. She could see the water faintly, even before the slope levelled out, then to the right, downstream, a pale green ghostly light, with Axine silhouetted against it. 'There, what did I tell you?' said Anya. But her friend was already on her way. Anya chased after her, stumbling on the rocks in the half light and splashing through the shallow stream. As the light strengthened, it also got deeper green. She was sure it must be the forest beyond the exit from the cave.

Axine reached the cave mouth at a run; she gasped, swayed and nearly tripped. Anya crept up more warily, then slowly sank to her knees in awe, for it was neither cavern nor countryside. It was a huge declivity in the rock, which dropped away at their feet. It looked large enough to contain the castle courtyard and, like the courtyard, it was walled in on all sides by rocks. High above was the sky, but the walls were overhanging. It was a like a giant chamber which had long ago collapsed, strewing debris to the floor, to which the stream fell to join a torrent entering from the left before weaving through the rocks and disappearing over by the far wall with a terrible roar. But the most remarkable thing about the chasm was the shaft of weakened sunlight picked out by the spray and striking down to the right, illuminating the mossy slopes in shades of brilliant green. Anya had never seen greens like this before; they appeared almost to glow against the drab grey-brown of the rocks and soil.

'Beat you to the sun-trap!' shouted Axine.

'Wait! Be careful. Mind the rocks – they're slippery.'

But Axine was off, clambering down the rocky slope. Once again, she was setting the pace and Anya had to chase behind. But Anya was worried; there was something odd about this place, something she couldn't explain. It didn't feel quite right, somehow, and it wasn't just that the rocks were slippery – slimy almost.

Now Axine was jumping up and down, waving her arms to the sunlight. 'Come on, Anya.' She lay down upon the moss. How could she do it? It made Anya's flesh go creepy.

'It's wet, Axine.'

'It won't hurt you.'

'It looks slimy: you'll be covered in green slime.'

'Well, it'll wash off. Stop worrying.'

Anya sat upon the driest rock she could find. 'I don't like it here, Axine.'

'Why not? It's warm.' Axine laughed. 'The sun will bring your freckles out.' Then suddenly she sat up, wide-eyed. 'Look! A rabbit!' It ran up the slope. Now Anya noticed that near the top, where the ground was better lit and drier and the moss was replaced by grass, there were many rabbit holes, and several rabbits scampering about. 'There – what did I tell you?' she said once again.

'Hmm,' her friend replied, lying back on the moss and closing her eyes.

Anya relaxed a little but she was still uncomfortable. She wouldn't put the bundle down. There was a faint peculiar smell, like rotting cabbage. She would rather have been away from this place. 'Let's go from h . . .' she stopped short.

A thin twig lay twisted upwards from the moss about a foot beyond Axine. It was bleached white; it looked exactly like a finger-bone. When she moved her head to look at it again, the sunlight flashed against it – metallic yellow. The shock was like a hammer blow; what she had seen was gold. It was a gold ring. Twigs did not wear rings. She screamed, jumped and then felt something round her ankle. Axine sat up and looked in horror at the long thin glistening living thing which whipped about as Anya frantically kicked the air in a hopeless effort to dislodge it.

Anya kicked it against the rock. The creature lacerated and began leaking clear liquid mixed with blood; she knew it was her own blood, for the head was suckered to her and wouldn't let go. She shut her eyes and shuddered as she took hold of it tightly in the middle and pulled as hard as she could; she felt it stretch; her fingers slipped, then suddenly it snapped. The half she held sprang back like a length of gut, wrapping round her arm before falling on the floor. She was nearly sick – her arm was smeared with pale pink glutinous mess. Now Axine was screaming as the other half writhed about, still attached to Anya's ankle. She had to force herself to grip the smooth wet rubbery head between her thumb

216

and finger and squeeze with all her might. The head split, the thing then dropped off to the ground, leaving a bloody mark upon her ankle. Anya quickly washed it at the water's edge, but the blood welled out again through a myriad tiny pinpricks.

'Uuughh!' Axine was shaking uncontrollably. Anya wasn't much better. 'Ugh . . . What was it, Anya?'

Anya suddenly remembered that her friend had been lying down, and her expression must have communicated to Axine. 'Oh no! No!' Axine began to whimper. Anya took her arm gently but firmly, in case Axine should panic and run, and lifted her up. 'Oh! Uuugh, Anya, I can feel them . . .' Anya didn't look behind her friend yet; she led her to the river. There were three of them, one between Axine's shoulders, a long one attached to her lower back, trailing down her buttocks and a small one at the back of her thigh. It made Anya's flesh creep to have to take hold of the cold slimy things – like pale pink thick glass tubes with a central thread of blood, Axine's blood. But when she squeezed the heads hard enough, the worms came away almost in one piece and she flung them in the water.

They could see them now, squirming through the wet moss where Axine had lain. Anya pointed out the skeleton. Axine found another, then a third – a skull with a nest of worms inside it. Now the women were afraid to put a foot down.

'What does it mean, Axine – all these bones?'

'It means you were right. We'd better get out of here – quick.'

'What was that?' Anya thought she'd seen something from the corner of her eye, over towards the far wall where the river disappeared. It had seemed a blur, it had moved so quickly.

'I can't see anything.' But when it moved again, they froze; their mouths fell open.

It was a wild animal, but it ran like a man, crouching, looking furtively about. It had clothing – a skin of sorts – and long and matted hair. It was digging bare-handed in the mossy bank. And then it unearthed something. The women watched with mounting horror as they heard the crack of sinew and it lifted up a large bone with flesh hanging from it, then squatted and began to eat. Ater a minute or two, it buried the remains again before glancing round then scuttling up the rock face above the river and vanishing into a cave. Anya felt very sick again. Neither of the women spoke for a long while.

'What are we going to do, Axine?'

Axine looked around her, at the overhanging walls to their right, the raging torrent to the left, and behind them, the way they'd come, then finally at the single rocky path ahead which led below the entrance to the ghoul's cave and above the precipice where the river disappeared.

'There are some rabbit holes at the top of the bank,' she announced unhelpfully.

[14]

A Friend in Deed

It was a long time – time during which their gaze remained fixed upon the cave, watching for any movement but detecting none – before the women summoned up the courage to leave; Anya slung the bundle round her shoulders and Axine led the way. Alongside the precipice, the rocks were wet from spray and the footholds few and narrow. The knew how vulnerable they were, with the chasm and the torrent way below them and the terrifying threat of the cave getting closer. If the beast should come out now . . . Anya picked up a rock, but carrying it only made it harder to clamber up the face.

Axine was very brave; Anya knew that she herself could never have gone first.

It was as they had feared; the only way was directly past the cave mouth. Her friend was almost there now. Anya's legs had turned very weak and her mouth felt dry; and she felt light-headed. She tried to concentrate on moving forwards, for if she stopped, she would never start again. She kept looking up at the cave, imagining she had heard something, and then that would make her stumble; Axine pushed on ahead as Anya fell further behind. But she had to check; she was so afraid the beast would rush out when she was not looking. And if it did, she would deliver herself from the terror – she would fling herself into the chasm first, before she let it take her; she would rather drown or be dashed upon the rocks. That thought revived the memory of that fateful night when she had been a hairs-breadth from death, and of the terrible feeling when she had been pushed backwards over the castle walls. She closed her eyes for a second and when she opened them, the ground began to sway.

'Anya!' Axine hissed. She was standing at the cave mouth, peering inside. How could she do it? It sent shivers up Anya's spine. 'I can't see anything here, Anya. Come on, quickly.' Anya put her finger to her lips; her friend was making too much noise, but she wouldn't shut up. It was almost as if she wanted to draw the creature out. 'It looks empty, but it's very dark . . .'

'Shh!'

'Come and have a look.' In the end Anya had to hurry simply to stop Axine from talking, and then in the rush, just as she reached the entrance, she tripped. Everything was going wrong; she had to drop the rock to save herself from falling. The noise it made was hair-raising. She cringed as it clattered down the face, each rebound dislodging a shower of smaller stones and resounding louder than the last. She could not move a muscle until all the echoes had died away. Only then did she dare to take a breath.

By then it was too late; it happened very quickly.

Axine screamed, held her hand up, slipped and grabbed a tree root and Anya felt a terrific slam across her shoulders; her knees went from under her and as she fell forwards, her bundle plummeted down into the torrent; she thought a rock had fallen from above and hit her. Then she was on her back, being dragged by her hair into the cave. Her neck was breaking. All she could see was the cave roof swaying wildly as the stabbing pains shot down her back and her body was jerked along the floor.

She must have passed out for a few seconds. When she opened her eyes it was a nightmare come to life. The creature knelt above her – knelt on her body – pinned her arms down at the elbows, kicked her thighs apart and pinned them with his knees. The eyes did not look human; they were the eyes of an animal at the kill. His hair hung down in knotted filth; his stench was overpowering. It was not the smell of unwashed body, but the stench of rotting flesh rolling across her face as his mouth opened to reveal a disjointed row of cracked green teeth. Now he began to grunt and Anya bucked and screamed and spat as she realised what was about to happen. The hard hot hairy flesh rod was thrust against her belly. But she tensed her flesh to stone. Her body would never let it happen; he would have to kill her and cut her open first.

The creature threw back his head and howled like a wolf; Anya retched as thick saliva bubbled out and dripped upon her face. She pressed her feet against the floor, heaving so hard she managed to lift him bodily, but he fell back again then dug his knees even harder into her upper thighs, making her scream with pain. Now his teeth were bared, his face descended; she turned her head away and felt the powerful jaws closing on her cheekbone. She was screaming continuously now, clawing at the arms that pinned her, hopelessly trying to reach the face, and then she heard and felt the sickening crack of bone – her cheekbone, she was sure. The jaws released her; the monster fell off her, stunned. Axine stood above them. Anya's hand went to her face but the skin had not been broken. Axine still held the stone that she had dashed against his skull.

Then the howl made Anya's blood freeze; the monster had come round. 'Get out! Run!' Axine threw the stone at him, picked up a stick and began to hit him, trying to keep him at bay as he dodged back and forth, snarling and snapping like a wounded animal. Anya ran to the entrance, hesitated, then began climbing down. Axine was backing up behind and above her. Then there was a cry; the creature had hold of the stick and was pulling Axine back.

'Let go!' Anya shouted.

'I daren't.'

Anya climbed up at a run, took hold of Axine's waist and pulled as hard as she was able. The tug of war edged slowly towards the entrance, the creature snapping and spitting and the women shouting to each other to let go and run. But neither one would leave the other to fight the beast alone. The blood was trickling down his forehead. Suddenly, his knees folded as if he had been struck from behind and he collapsed upon the floor, releasing his hold on the stick. The women went flying backwards; the stick went sailing through the air. Anya let go of Axine's waist, stumbled back down the first few rocky steps, her arms up in the air

221

but then, for some reason which she did not understand, her eyes simply kept following the stick back as it curved very slowly through the air. The stick never seemed to get any further away; she was mesmerised by that stick, which soared up past a waterfall flowing up into the air and vanished in the plunge pool up above, a split second before Anya's body sliced into a world of ice-cold bubbles and freezing water forcing up her nose and down her throat to quell her silent scream. And in that cold dark acquiescence, her final recollection was of a giant bird which kept swooping down, trying to spear her on its talons and lift her body back into the air.

When Anya opened her eyes, she could still hear the water, but she was face down on gravel. She felt dreadfully sick. She began to choke. A hand was slapping her back. When it stopped, she felt herself being lifted and turned over.

'Axine . . .' Anya coughed and wiped the water from her nose.

Axine was framed by forest trees; the water drops were gathered on her shoulders and her breasts. 'You made it, Anya,' she said, looking at her steadily, then slowly sitting back and sighing as if a great weight had lifted from her shoulders. 'You finally made it.' Then her head bowed down; when it lifted, Axine was smiling, but Anya saw that her eyes were sparkling with tears. Anya threw her arms around her, pulled her to her breast and kissed her very fully on the lips.

'You saved me,' Anya said very softly. 'I was drowning and you risked your life to save me.'

Axine went very shy. 'I had to get away in any case,' she said weakly. Her head went down again. But Anya knew Axine had done it to save her. She had saved her from the ghoul, and she had dived into the torrent to rescue her.

'And you're lucky.' Looking up, Axine began to laugh now, through the tears, though she didn't tell her friend how lucky she really was. 'See – your baggage made it, too,' she said, pulling the soaking bundle across. 'It was floating in this pool.'

They opened it out. It contained a thin but densely woven blanket, now saturated, some clothing – not quite so wet – a necklace, a small stoppered wine bottle which had leaked, and some squashed food. The bread was soggy, but they ate it nevertheless; the strips of smoked meat were very good and the carrot cake was delicious. Then they set the clothes on the rocks to dry and finally lay down at the top of the gravel bank, where it was sandy, to soak up the sun themselves.

Anya felt she could relax here. She couldn't forget what had happened, but her mind could put aside the horror. She liked the forest. The forest didn't frighten her in the way that place back there had, with its smell of putrefaction; the forest smelt fresh and clean and fragrant. The forest was her friend. Axine was her friend too.

She turned and looked at her. Axine had very delicate features, with soft dense eyebrows and very short black hair, cut in such a way as to emphasize her ears. They were small and perfectly formed, and her hairline was shaved back to leave a swath of smooth bare skin around them; it made Anya want to touch the smoothness of that skin. Axine's skin was not freckled as Anya's was, but neither was it milky white. It was pale gold, smooth and uniform, except for a single mole upon her neck, behind her ear. But what Anya found most attractive in Axine was the delicate precision of every feature of her face, so small and smooth and finely drawn it made you want to touch it, to make your tongue into a fine point and trace the curves of Axine's ears, to stroke the soft dense eyebrows and to lay the underside of the tip within the fold of her upper lip.

Axine shifted, revealing her small breasts, which had almost disappeared as she lay upon her back, and the graceful curve of her body – the slim waist against the definite outswell of her hips which served to mark her as a woman – for Axine, in appropriate attire, could surely have passed for a boy.

'Let me try this necklace on you,' Anya said. It suited Axine. It was a small but strong gold chain carrying a black metallic-looking stone cut into a flat square shape, and it was unusual in that the stone was bound within two gold bands which ran cornerwise around it and intersected in the middle of both sides in a cross; the pendant was attached not from one of the corner points but from the middle. Axine tucked in her chin, lifted the jewel and examined it.

'This is yours, Anya.' She spoke in a serious tone.

'But that means I can give to you, doesn't it?' She wanted to give her friend this present.

'No – you will need this. Do you know what it is?'

Anya shook her head.

'It is a lodestone. It tells you which way you must go.'

Anya took it in her fingers. 'How?' Her friend took it off, held it up and pointed out the lodemark on one of the corners, then twisted the stone round; it slowly twisted back again.

'This mark always faces north; the south is the opposite way.' Anya checked and, sure enough, the lodestone pointed away from the sun. 'The sun moves, Anya. This is better than the sun; and it works even when you cannot see the sun.'

'It works underground?' asked Anya.

Axine was not sure.

'How does it work?'

'Magic.' Axine was sure this time.

'Magic . . .' Anya's eyes widened as she held it reverently. And when Axine fastened it carefully round her neck, Anya could feel it; the waves of magic were running through her body, making the fine hairs on her skin tingle, making her heartbeat surge.

'Come with me, Axine, on the journey?'

Her friend smiled and placed her hand on Anya's, which was still closed about the magic stone. She did not answer for a while, preferring instead to stroke a finger through the downy hair which stood erect on Anya's goose-pimpled arm. 'My life is here, Anya; I belong in the castle,' she said at last. 'Your destiny lies elsewhere; you must find your Prince.'

Anya knew that what Axine said was true. 'But you will be punished . . .'

Axine lifted her head and looked towards the trees. 'That

is not so unusual – for a slave,' she added quietly. Anya reached across to stroke her cheek. Her friend looked at her again. 'I doubt if they will treat me harshly.' She smiled. 'Besides – it was worth it.' And now she grinned. 'But I think I might pick a different route back . . .'

Anya frowned at first, then she too grinned. The two of them became very quiet. Anya touched the lodestone pendant nervously; Axine dug her fingers in the sand and let it trickle through.

Then Anya stood up. She began to remove the gold chain fastened at her waist, and then her wrist chain. The ankle chain was missing; it must have been taken by the torrent. Axine watched her anxiously.

'Will you return these for me?' She handed Axine the chains.

Axine was reluctant. 'They will not welcome them.'

'Nor did I . . . I did not ask for them.' Then Anya whispered, almost to herself, 'And chains do not become me . . .' She held up her head; the sunlight caught her hair in bursts of fiery red. Her eyes sparkled; her lip began to tremble. She would never forget her friend, how she had given her love and support so selflessly and how she had saved her life – twice over, she had saved her. Axine would always hold a special place within her heart.

'Axine? Stay with me, a little while at least?'

They gathered up the things and climbed the hillside to a sunwarmed hollow, backed by pines and facing out above the endless tree-tops. They spread the blanket on the soft dry bed of fallen needles. Then it seemed all the tension of that day, the wild excitement and the dreadful fear, was transformed into an overpowering physical longing, and yet that longing was so intense it prevented Anya from moving. They faced each other. Once again, Axine had to take the lead.

But Axine, too, felt the tension. She looked at this woman – this guileless woman who had such wild, impossible dreams. She had grown to love her as a sister but now, these last few days, this woman had captured her heart and an hour ago had stopped her heart completely, by taking that fatal backward step from the overhang. Axine had had to fight her just to try to stop her from drowning; and after all that, she thought she had failed; it was as if everything had come to nothing. She believed that limp and unbreathing body was dead, with all her impossible dreams turned to dust, leaving behind not one but now two hearts devastated. She wanted to express these powerful emotions in her own way, without her having to say them; she wanted to touch her as a lover, flesh to flesh, to satiate their bodies and to spend this one short time enfolded by her lover's arms. This was all she wanted.

She stepped up to Anya, threw back her shoulders, so her small breasts lifted and the tiny nipples pointed out in defiance; she lifted her chin and edged her feet apart. With the muscles of her thighs and belly taut, her legs formed a vee. 'Kiss me,' she said. She would not move until Anya did this. Their lips touched lightly, without any other part of them coming into contact and a shiver ran through Anya's body from her hair roots to her toes. She felt Axine's fingertips upon her belly, upon the soft short hair, gently but unswervingly progressing down towards that single spot, touching her flesh leaves tremulously, then sliding back the hood so deliciously slowly that Anya thought her legs would buckle from underneath her. And that was the way Axine preferred to kiss her, keeping the flesh hood sleeved back all the while, making her purpose clear, looking at Anya with cool assurance, brushing the tip of her tongue against her lover's lip before she kissed her fully, touching her hard little pip. Throughout that kiss of liquid tongues entwined, soft shimmers ran through Anya's body. She could feel the coolness sweep across her cheek as Axine's controlled tense breaths issued through her nose, she could smell the warm scent of Axine's skin, and she could feel Axine's fingertips against her lower belly. As the kiss deepened, Axine pushed forward – maintaining Anya's nubbin in that pushed-out state – and their nipples touched; Axine's stiff small pips circled round her soft brown buds, coaxing them up to firmness.

And now it seemed Axine wanted her lover to touch her

openly and wantonly, for she stood back, then turned to face away from Anya, placing her hands behind her head and moving her feet wider yet apart, then bending from the waist, arching down until her bottom pushed out in twin firm mounds with the sunlit skin shaded from pale and almost metallic gold to smooth matt violet in the parting. Between her legs, the dense black bush was trimmed back from the small tight lips. But Anya was afraid to move; Axine had to ask her. 'Touch me,' she whispered. 'I want to feel your fingertips touching me. Touch me – there.' The knot of deeper violet tightened and the small lips tensed and lifted.

Anya's fingertips shook; they were nervous with the fear of the forbidden; they explored her lover fitfully, trailing across the small of her back, then down the smooth round buttocks, venturing in the groove only a little way, half touching before retreating, yet returning to touch the violet mouth more definitely. In broad daylight, on that hillside, with her lover bent down and sighing with soft pleasure, Anya's fingertips were touching her lover's bottom, testing it apprehensively like a soft kitten's paw might touch an unknown thing, inducing subdued contractions by the nervousness of those touches, then straying beneath, easing away the few stray curls impressed across the nubbin, not daring yet to touch it fully.

Axine stood up and faced her. Anya's blood was hot with lust from all the touching. Axine knew this very well. She placed her hands lightly about Anya's neck, but before she kissed her again, she raised her own right leg, sliding it up Anya's body, on and up and round until her foot pressed into Anya's back, low down above the buttocks. Then, balanced with her own right buttock lifted open to expose herself to her lover's touch, she took hold of Anya's hand, brought it round and placed it firmly underneath as a living saddle to support her sex and to squeeze it in rhythm with the deep kisses whilst the middle finger, stretching back within the groove, pressed its pad against the secret mouth. Axine wished her lover to hold her in this fashion when she kissed her, for that feeling of being open, with the skin contact along her line of parting and the sweet round pressure there, the defencelessness – for should that finger choose to slip into her bottom, she could never prevent it – the threat each time her lover sucked upon her tongue and the finger moved almost imperceptibly against her, petting her velvet skin, rendering her body rigid, it made her belly sink with pleasure. It was the same feeling that came whenever the Taskmistress made her bend and display her body before some new lord or lady; as they discussed her, perhaps as they approached, the delicious sensation would sink inside, over and over, and she would be wet before the lord or lady even touched her.

So now she wanted her lover to experience this pleasure too. She stood behind her, spread her lover's thighs and the cheeks of her lover's bottom and touched her in that way, without shame, allowing her fingers to investigate her lover, to press lightly against the hot tight mouth before she slid her middle finger underneath, on and up past the slippery split of lips to bed beneath the hood and to push against the nubbin. Then, holding her lover upright thus, palm between thighs, the moist lips clinging to her finger as it touched the liquid tip, and her arm around, encompassing her lover's breasts, with her lover's head turned round to meet her, she kissed her once again.

Axine next made Anya kneel and sit back on her heels, with her thighs spread wide apart so Axine could kneel beside her, across one thigh, separating her own wet flesh upon the hard curved muscle while she kissed her – her lips and neck and nipples – playing with the liquid folds of Anya's open flesh, edging her lover's body onwards, moving herself against the thigh until a wet slick had developed there and Anya's flesh began to pulse in rapid bursts of forepleasure.

Axine wet her fingertips in her lover's mouth, held back the hood and very carefully tapped the sticky tip till the rapid bursts came again, when she took hold of it to stay its pulsing, pushing the middle finger of her other hand first into her own wet flesh then up her lover's bottom. And when the finger reached the second joint, her lover's body tried to break the finger amid half-murmurs of nonassent.

Axine therefore allowed her lover to turn onto her side, though with the finger still inside her, while she stroked her back, then stroked her belly, then made her lift her leg while she caressed the thickened tip at first then rubbed it up again to bursting, pushing two fingers into her at the front as deeply as she could until the imminence of pleasure ebbed away, after which all three fingers were withdrawn and Anya was turned upon her back.

As Anya lay upon the blanket, Axine knelt astride her waist, kissed her on the eyebrows, on the nose, then sucked her lower lip. Axine knelt up higher. She spread her own flesh. When Anya's eyes drifted to the side, towards the trees, Axine took her head very gently and turned it back again then, with her hands framed about Anya's face, bent forward, searching her eyes. She pushed out her tongue, waiting for Anya to take it between her lips and suck upon it. She wanted her lover to look at her, to watch her, to do these things to her. She leaned further, resting her hands upon the ground above Anya's head and proffering her small firm breasts for Anya to suck and lick and nip her teeth upon. Anya took hold of the wing-muscles extending from Axine's underarms to her breasts and squeezed them. She pressèd her hands to Axine's ribcage, underneath her breasts, against her slimly sculpted body, while she sucked her breasts again. This time, as Axine knelt up, Anya watched her fingertips crossing the boundary of the tight-trimmed triangle of black and separating the lips to expose the small distended bud and stroke it. A shiver ran through Anya's body as the fingertip was lifted up and offered to her lips, for that gesture triggered a memory of that first night at the castle, the night she had been made to share Lord Aldrid's bed with Axine and her training in obedience had begun, with pleasure being forced upon her without promise or prospect of release. Yet now, as then, she complied: her tongue pushed out nervously, licking the fingertip foretaste of Axine's honeydew, depositing a drop of spittle there to re-moisten Axine's tip.

Axine worked herself until her eyelids became heavy, yet she would not have them close; she would look upon her lover while she gave herself pleasure, and she would stay her fingertip at times to bend and kiss her lover's lips or to have her lover recharge the fingertip until the touching became so insistent and the belly so tense, with the body arched forwards of its own accord and the fingertip out of sight, that Axine was forced to stop and wrench her torso upright, straining on the very edge of pleasure. 'Hold me. Press your hands against me,' she murmured and Anya held her palms up, supported by her elbows on the ground, while Axine lifted her belly onto them. Only then did she close her eyes. She went very still and tense; gradually her breathing smoothed to normal and she lifted. Anye lowered her hands, pressing them against Axine's thighs. She used her thumbs to open her, pushing them inside, holding her wetness open, then sliding them up and out against the slippery nubbin.

Axine sank back away from Anya's hands and slowly opened her eyes. Anya could feel the heat of Axine's moistness where her belly touched against her. She knew this loving would be long-drawn-out. The pressure of wanting slowly swelled. It was a feeling Anya had experienced many times; it was as feeling she usually hated, but now the feeling was good, for it was a prolongation of desire and pleasure but not denial. It was done in love, not hate and torment. She could wait: experiencing pleasure, bestowing pleasure, watching, feeling pleasure taken by a lover, were all part of Anya's lovemaking, part of her joy, and she knew deliverance would come this time. It would never be denied.

Axine had lifted up and spread her sex once more. She moved up to the level of Anya's chin and waited, holding her body open. Anya's heart was in her throat as Axine worked two fingers into herself, drew them out and held them up. Then Anya could not stop herself; she licked them shamelessly, arching up her tongue for more while Axine lowered and drew her flesh tip slowly up its undersurface until Anya could feel the hard hot ball of Axine's nubbin sliding up the groove. Her lover's scent enveloped her. She opened her again, licking her greedily, tasting Axine's moistness, licking the small hard lips, licking the thumbs that held her open, slipping up inside to bathe her tongue in Axine's heat then slicking that wetness up across the hood repeatedly to soften it, to draw it back, to make the nubbin stand out till it could not be retracted. She forced the sex lips wider to render that bud more prominent while she nipped and sucked upon its rigid slipping tip; she wanted to advance it to the point of pleasure where her lover was enslaved. She carefully took away her thumbs but maintained a sweet and inescapable tongue-tip pressure there, against the tension, the shivers, the little cries and protests, allowing the warmth of Axine's oil to trickle down her tongue, until the point was reached where her lover was able to breathe in yet could not now breathe out. Only when that crucial point had been achieved did she reach beneath to spread apart the cheeks.

Again, Axine experienced the feeling, the deep, defenceless pleasure of submission; but this time, it was total. Her body was now delivered to her lover; Axine had no control over how her lover chose to use her. It was the same sensation that would overwhelm her when a master and a mistress, having selected her together, having decided they would share her body, and having played with her body throughout the night, with fingers, flesh and tongues, would chance upon that blissful permutation in which Axine would be pinned, face down, upon her master, his weight of flesh inside her, her thighs locked open by his legs, spreading her buttocks wide. Axine would be unable to breathe; she would be drowning, while the lady took her time. She would feel the weight behind her on the bed; she would feel the brush of the lady's sleeves against the skin hairs of her thighs, and she would feel the lady's fluttering fingers spread her inner cheeks. And then it would come – the cool breath on her velvet. She would die with pleasure when that tongue-tip touched her skittishness . . .

And as Anya's finger touched, then stroked, then pressed against the pulsing velvet ring, then lifted, waited, stroked and pressed again, Axine did not move; she did not breathe, but a fine mist moistened the creases at the tops of her thighs as her pleasure was delivered upon the tongue-tip, a pleasure triggered by the fingertip control, the hesitant touching, the lightness of the brushing and the nervous finger-kissing of the trembling velvet mouth. And though Axine's whole body shuddered, she did not collapse, and neither did she die of it; it simply served to make her crave such pleasure all the more.

Axine dismounted from Anya's tongue, reached behind her back and separated Anya's flesh lips. She held her open with one hand and touched her with the other, painting Anya's wetness round the edges of her leaves, working by feel, guided by the expression on her lover's face. Reaching underneath, she touched the entrance to her bottom. When the tender opening tightened, Axine locked her lover's thighs wide open with her feet – in the same way Axine would be locked open when the lords and ladies played with her – and she touched her there again, touching more lightly than any butterfly could, not stopping till her lover moaned. Now she slid down Anya's body and laid her head against her belly whilst she stretched the cheeks more tightly yet and she rubbed the entrance with a moistened finger until the belly shook. She slid further down; Anya felt the point of Axine's tongue along the creases of each thigh, before the tongue and upper lip formed a suction cup which fitted to her nubbin, sucking her only in that place, drawing it outwards from the shelter of the hood, milking it between the wet-tubed tongue-tip and the lip. When Anya's belly tightened hard, the sucking was suspended but the pressure was maintained as a tight flesh band of lip and tongue around the bursting nubbin. When her belly relaxed, the sucking began again, slowly at first, then steadily and then more strongly, with the point of the tongue beneath the nubbin, probing at its root, pressing till the tightness came again – a higher plane of tightness and of desperate wanting this time – and the flesh band still imprisoned her. Now the fingertip stroking began, the very gentle butterfly whispers, the uncertain touching round her tight and secret mouth. As the sucking took up again, Anya's body slowly leaked until it wet the fingertip.

Axine let it happen; she let her lover trickle. Then she turned her over on her belly, quickly, with her legs spread very wide, and with her tongue she drew a thin clear line of nectar up and deposited it in the cup. And now she would progress her lover's pleasure by the same means those lords and ladies had used upon herself, by the method that she knew could bring such deep and drowning feelings of submission. So first, she eased apart her lover's buttocks while she held her in that state of outspread tightness; she was waiting for that first contraction. Anya's breathing changed; the contraction came; the small cup overflowed. Axine reached beneath and spread the softened flesh lips back to expose the nubbin – though not to touch it – while the tip of her tongue kissed that other mouth, drinking up the nectar, licking, tickling, making it contract repeatedly, kissing each contraction as it came, then pressing in the centre, so as each tightening waned to relaxation, the stiff tongue slipped more deeply until it was bedded to the root. And now the control was perfect; Axine could advance the pleasure at the pace she chose. And she chose to make her lover drown with pleasure taken in this intimate way.

Once the penetration was complete and her lover was defenceless she began to tease and play with her lover's sex, just as their ladyships would do to Axine when they played the 'winter game,' when the freezing wind whistled round the castle walls but, within the bedroom, the flames burned bright in the fireplace that Axine was held in front of, supported by two houseguards, her legs doubled up and her body held open. The air would be heavy with the scent of warm mulled wine, and Axine's body would know no rest from the delicious torture. Their ladyships would lick her and penetrate her sex and bottom with their tongues, but mainly, they would play with her; they would take turns to massage her lips and nubbin till she dripped upon the floor, and they would discuss the progress of Axine's pleasure – the softness of her sex lips, the degree to which her bud distended, the way her flesh contracted round their fingers, her muskiness of taste – and the various means by which they might prolong that pleasure, or if such were to be permitted, the manner of her deliverance. And when, on those occasions, a lady would stand before Axine – still held outspread by the guards – and, laying a hand upon her inner thigh, would whisper, 'Shall we play the winter game?' Axine's throat would be blocked completely by the surge of wanton pleasure. The instruction would be given, the accessories brought, the pot set by the fire, and then the aroma of warming spicy honey would drift into the air. Their ladyships would assume the respective mantles of Ice-lady and Fire; then Ice and Fire would take turns to win that slave's deliverance. Axine could never tell in advance when, or by which means, such deliverance would come – whether by the slow licking of the warm thin honey from her sex lips; by the oiled cockstem, dusted with spice, that would be pushed into her fleshpot while the fire-lady massaged her nubbin with a hot and honeyed finger; or by the icicle, fresh picked from the battlements, that would film in melt water as its tip of freezing pleasure, fitted between the cheeks of her bottom, was slipped slowly up inside her while the ice-lady sucked her nubbin with a mouth that was filled with snow.

Axine therefore loved the winter; she loved the long nights by the fire, and the sweet, exquisite torture of the winter game. And she loved the way that afterwards, in the bed, the ladies would use her to bring them pleasure by the method they had taught her, the way she was using now upon her lover.

With her tongue still bedded firmly in that living tube of flesh, she pressed her thumbs to the creases at the top of Anya's thighs and, pressing a fingertip to each side of Anya's nub, massaged it firmly, slowly, as if it were a tiny cockstem which those fingers were drawing off. The finger at one side would be kept very still while the other finger worked the nub against that steady pad of pressure; then the roles would be reversed, but always, one finger was kept still while the other massaged the tip of flesh against it. The rubbing drew out the nubflesh; it made it hard, like a tiny bone; the massage progressed slowly, beyond the level where her lover begged for mercy, to the higher state where

234

the pleasure was so intense – yet still controlled by Axine's measured fingertip pressure about the throbbing nubbin, and the tight distension of the flesh tube by her tongue – that her lover almost passed out with desire.

She wanted to stop her lover's heart with pleasure in the same way Axine's heart had been stopped that day with fear.

And when Axine finally judged her lover had paid the price, she turned her on her back again, spread her lover's thighs and lay between them. She spread her lover's liquid leaves and pressed her own smaller, firmer flesh lips in between, then sealed her lover's round her own and held them with her fingers. As she moved her hips, her nubbin brushed and kissed and stroked against her lover's hardened bud, and when their wetness was quite mixed, she smeared that wet upon her hand and raised it to their lips. Two tongues licked that wetness side by side, then pressed against each other, pressing slowly, kissing very gently.

As Axine's small hips moved against her in tight insistent circles, while Axine's fingers held her flesh lips open now to keep the nubflesh poking out, the pleasure was pulled out from Anya's body as if it were a tangible thing, as if it were a plaited rope of silken twine, splayed out within and bedded to her womb. And that thin rope, wet with thickened seepage, was now stretched taut and very thin and Axine was controlling it, pulling it, not roughly so it would snap and leave Anya's pleasure incomplete, but, aware of her lover's needs throughout, making it draw deeply, uprooting every fibre cleanly, slipping the silken threads out in a bunch of tight delight through the tip of Anya's nubbin, making the waves of satisfaction merge to soft and velvet blackness, a blackness in which Anya closed her arms and legs about her lover's body, her mouth about her lover's lips and her melting flesh about her lover's fingers and that was all that mattered – nothing else.

Axine drew the blanket round them and they lay, cocooned together on that warm spring afternoon.

*　　*　　*

When Anya's eyes opened, Axine's head lay upon her breast; the afternoon was waning. She knew that time was short now, if Axine were to get back before dark.

'Axine – stay with me tonight?'

It was as if those words had broken the spell.

Axine sat up and stared across the treetops to where the sun was beginning to soften above the sea of clouds. She did not move for a long while; she did not speak; then she turned and straightened out the blanket. She glanced at Anya before lifting the bundle of clothes, folding it carefully, then placing it neatly beside her friend. Axine hesitated, looking once more at the weakening sun, then slid slowly forwards until her belly came to rest upon the bundle. She stretched her arms out flat upon the ground.

'Persuade me,' Axine murmured, drawing one leg up beside her. 'Show no mercy. Torture me with pleasure; torture me through the night . . .'

And as the first chill of evening descended to cool those moistened fingertips as they entered Axine's body from behind, two dreams were stirred, visions which caressed each mind with pleasure: one dream the south, the sun, a strong hand on a belly; the other dream a crackling fire, a fresh snowfall, and night-pleasures of the winter.